TIMBAL GULCH TRAIL

TIMBAL GULCH TRAIL

MAX BRAND ™

Thorndike Press • Chivers Press
Thorndike, Maine USA   Bath, Avon, England

This Large Print edition is published by Thorndike Press, USA
and by Chivers Press, England.

Published in 1995 in the U.S. by arrangement with the
Golden West Literary Agency.

Published in 1995 in the U.K. by arrangement with the
author's estate.

U.S. Hardcover 0-7862-0480-X (Western Series Edition)
U.K. Hardcover 0-7451-2586-7 (Chivers Large Print)

The text of this Large Print edition is unabridged.
Other aspects of the book may vary from the original edition.

Set in 16 pt. News Plantin by Minnie B. Raven.

Printed in Great Britain on permanent paper.

British Library Cataloguing in Publication Data available

Library of Congress Cataloging in Publication Data

Brand, Max, 1892–1944.
    Timbal Gulch trail / Max Brand.
        p.   cm.
    ISBN 0-7862-0480-X (lg. print : hc)
    1. Large type books. I. Title.
    [PS3511.A87T58 1995]
    813'.52—dc20   95-13693

19.95

TIMBAL GULCH
TRAIL

I. THE DEATH SIGNAL

All the dark length of the rear veranda of the Palace was spotted with the glow of pipes or the pulsing red points of cigarettes.

Walter Devon looked with pleasure upon this trembling pattern of lights, for he knew that only dwellers in the wilderness enjoy a smoke in the dark — hunters and trappers, say, whose only rest comes after nightfall, or cowpunchers who toast their noses on winter nights.

There was no hunting in West London, he knew, except for gold, and there was no trapping except of greenhorns and tenderfeet and fools in general, whose pelts were lifted painlessly every day; but whatever their occupation at the moment, these were men of the desert, of the mountains.

There was another breed inside, already swarming back to the gaming tables, or lining the bar; sometimes the veranda floor trembled with their shouts; but up and down the veranda there was never an alteration in the tone of the deep, quiet voices, speaking guardedly as though of secrets.

Now and again one of the smokers finished and went inside, and as the door opened, the droning voice of a croupier floated out.

Walter Devon listened, and sighing with content, he drew in a longer breath flavored with the fragrance of many tobaccos and the pure sweetness of the pines. He was in no hurry to go back to work, with his hands resting on the green felt; he had not even picked his game for the night!

So he dwelt with aimless pleasure upon the glow of pipes and the glimpses they gave him of mustaches, and of young straight noses, and of noses thin and crooked with age; or again he considered what the cigarettes showed him when, for an instant, they made a pair of eyes look out from the night.

These lights were capable of movements, the pipes stirring slowly, the cigarettes jerking rapidly up and down as the smokers gesticulated. By sheer chance, since he had turned his attention to the subject, he saw — or thought he saw — a cigarette at the far end of the veranda wigwag, in dots and dashes clearly made, a question mark!

Walter Devon smiled at such a coincidence of gesture and unconscious ideas, and he continued to look dreamily at the distant smoker when, quickly and neatly, he saw that gleaming little point of light spell out: *"Four!"*

Once could be accident; the second time could not. Devon knew that the smoker was signaling the length of the veranda to some other man. And yet it seemed very strange that signals should be necessary when ten steps would take the signaler to the other end of the porch!

Devon left his chair and went to the side of the veranda. Over the railing he glanced down the steep sides of the gulch, covered by the ragged shadows of the pines, and in the bottom the stars found the water in an open pool showing a tarnished face of silver. Opposite the Palace, Timbal Mountain stepped grandly up the sky.

"Kind of like ridin' on the observation platform, eh?" said one who lounged nearby, against the railing.

It was, Devon agreed, turning a little toward the speaker. In this manner he faced away from the signaler whom he first had spotted, and immediately, at the farther end of the porch, he saw the duller glow of a pipe spell in the air the same question mark which he had noticed before!

The heart of Devon stirred in him. There were times when he told himself that he roamed the world seeking his fortune, whether it should be found in war, or cards, or a lucky

9

marriage; but he knew in his heart that all he wanted was the excitement of adventure.

In the thirty-odd years of his life while he had grown lean and hard with many labors, no gold had stuck to his fingers except a few thousand dollars to make him feel comfortable in a poker game of any size; but though he had no money, he had found again and again the electric spark which leaped now in his brain as he observed this little mystery on the veranda of the Palace.

It would not be altogether safe, perhaps, to attempt to observe both of these signalers, though unless he watched the two of them he was not apt to make much from their strange and silent conversation. It was not safe, because the two men themselves dared not leave their chairs and speak together! They must be under observation of the closest kind, and they spoke by this code only in the faith that the observers would not understand what they said.

What were they saying, who were they, and who was keeping them under watch? These were small questions, perhaps, and had little to do with Walter Devon, but at least the solution would fill him with pleasure.

In the meantime, he had to arrange some method of keeping his eye upon the first signaler as well as the second, but this was done by taking a little pocket mirror into the palm of his hand. The signals of Number One streaked in dim red flashes across the small surface; Number Two he was facing while he talked to the man at the railing.

"Like an observation platform," he agreed, "except that the mountains don't close up behind us."

"They ain't likely to close up," said the stranger. "They're more likely to spread apart, what with the gougin' and washin' and blastin' they're doin' on the side of old Timbal."

Across the face of the mirror streaked the signal: *"One way only!"*

Before him there was no answering movement of the lighted pipe, as Devon answered his new companion: "It was not like this when I was last here."

"You know the lay of the land in the old days?"

"Yes."

"So do I. Twenty year back I forked a mule and rode down Timbal's face. He didn't wear a name, then. I come to the river. It didn't wear no name, neither."

"Speaking of names, how did the town pick up this one?"

"Why, that's a yarn," said the other in his deep, soft voice, so guarded that it barely reached the ear of Devon. "Old Les Burchard come along here — but that was ten years ago!"

"It's fifteen since I was here before."

"Well, Burchard come along with eight mules haulin' at his wagon. He was aimin' at Farralone, and he'd took this here valley for a shortcut. Les had a barrel of white-faced poison in his wagon; when he got to Farralone he aimed to mix it up with tan bark and prune juice and call it whisky, but he thought that he'd better sample it on the way to see it wasn't gettin' bad.

"He took a taste, but he was kind of doubtful. He tasted agin, and still he wasn't plumb clear about it. He didn't finish tastin' until his wagon come along to this place, and by that time he'd tasted himself nearly blind and run the right fore wheel of his wagon off of the bluff. It pretty near turned the outfit over and smashed the wheel to bits on a rock. Les sat down and looked things over. He could pack part of his truck along on the mules, of course, but he didn't have no proper pack-saddles, and so Les Burchard says to himself that if he can't get to a town, a town'll have to get to him!"

The narrator paused, chuckling softly, and now a match flared as Number Two lighted his pipe. Devon clearly saw a young, hand-

12

some face, and a good, square-tipped jaw such as a fighter is apt to wear. It pleased him, that face, and he registered it clearly, feature by feature, in his memory.

For there are ways and ways of looking at a human face, and the poorest way of all is to depend upon a mere ensemble effect; the best is to dwell on details which cannot be altered by fictitious scars that pucker the skin, or changes of expression, or a growth of beard. The silhouette of the nose will alter very little. The angle of the nose bridge and the forehead is another thing, and the height and spread of the cheek bones, and the ear, above all, if the memory be very photographic indeed!

It was so with Devon, and he told himself that he would know this man to the very end of time!

His companion was continuing the story softly:

"Right there, Les Burchard he spread out his stuff, and he built himself a log shack, and he stowed things away, and he waited for a town to come and catch him!

"Back yonder behind Timbal was a man run some cows on the hills. By name of Devon, he was. Les went over and sold him a couple of his mules, and then he went back and waited a while more. He had a gun; and the valley had game; and he lived prime for a couple

13

of months on venison and that white-faced poison of his.

"When he was feelin' pretty groggy one mornin', he got up and found the valley soaked and blind with a fog. Burchard had been a sailor, and that fog reminded him of London harbor up the Thames. So he stuck out a sign that afternoon, and on the sign was 'London.' He'd found a name for his new town, you understand?

"But after a while it seemed to Burchard that London wasn't quite enough, because folks might get it mixed up with that other old town that most people have heard about now and then. So the next day he wrote 'West' in front of London, and that's how this joint come to be known as West London."

Number Two's pipe suddenly moved in wigwag:

"What way?"

And the rapid cigarette point, blown upon until it glowed orange-red, made answer in the mirror:

"Death!"

The narrator went on:

"Les Burchard had not been in the valley long before that greaser that Devon kicked off of his place picked up the chunk of ore in the valley and guessed what he'd got. He hit town a week later, and th' next mornin'

14

Les woke up and heard single-jacks chattering away at the rocks; and ten days later there was five thousand men laborin' in the gulch. Les, he ladled out eggshells of his white death at a dollar a taste. He sold the timber of his wagon for two thousand dollars in gold. His mules, they brung in a coupla hundred apiece, and the leather of the harness was pretty near worth its weight in gold. Les, he made enough money out of that lay to pretty near retire on, but of course he didn't. One day, when the valley was all filled with gents, Les, he was full of something better than sunshine, the last of his barrel, and he mooched off down the gulch and says to himself that he'll try his luck at diggin' gold."

Number Two, who had made a pause as though the last word startled him, as well it might, now signaled: *"When?"*

"Tonight," answered the cigarette smoker.

"Where?"

"Purley's at eleven."

"Old Les Burchard," said the narrator, "was so full of redeye that he didn't know where he was. But he had along a pick and shovel that was the last of his wagonload of stuff. When he got down into the valley he seen where a flat face of rock had been blasted out and hollowed away pretty deep, where some gents had sunk a shaft, or started to, but the

15

vein had pinched out on 'em. Old Les, he says: 'Here's a hole part way dug already. It's sure saved me a lot of work.'

"He stepped in there and he started pickin' away, and some of the boys in the other holes around, they come and laughed to see him bending the point of his pick ag'in' a solid wall of rock where there wasn't any sign of color. They laughed, and waited for him to work himself sober and see what a fool he'd been. But pretty soon he hauls off and says: 'One last lick for luck!' and he soaks in the short end of his pick and breaks out a chunk, and the inside of that chunk was fair burnished and shining with pure wire gold! It sure dazzled the eyes of the boys, and it made Les Burchard so rich that he didn't know what to do with his coin.

"However, storekeepin' and such always was his line, and so, in spite of his money, he come up here where his wagon had broke down, and he built this here Palace, and I gotta say that he found a good set of dealers to put behind his tables, but the best of all is the cook that he found. That Chinaman can certainly talk with a fryin' pan!"

Walter Devon heard and murmured interest, but his heart was otherwise, for "Purley's" was the name of the boarding house where he lived!

II. THE ZERO HOUR

There were no more signals; presently the whole body of people on the veranda began to move back into the gaming house, and they went in such confusion that he, drifting with the rest, lost sight of signaler Number One. Number Two he spotted bucking faro with a rich stock of chips, and Devon put some coins on roulette at the nearest table.

Number Two was a half-breed, he decided, for there was the smoke in the eyes and the highness of cheek bones; he played like an Indian, also, with perfect indifference, no matter how much he lost, no matter how much he won. Faro and roulette were to Devon the drunkard's games. They required nothing but luck, and nobody but a fool really could expect to beat them.

When he felt that he had observed the stranger long enough, Devon left shortly after ten and went to Mrs. Purley's house. It was the largest boarding house in West London. Mr. Purley had established it as a saloon and gambling place, but the roulette wheels failed to make money fast enough, so he made a little home improvement in them so that he could collect faster. Unfortunately, a curious cowpuncher took one of the machines apart one day, and afterward he shot Mr. Purley twice through the head.

The big saloon stood vacant; Mr. Purley's debts slightly exceeded his credits; and the saloon was about to be taken over by the first bidder, when Mrs. Purley arrived from the East.

She kicked the auction and the auctioneer into the street, closed the house again, scrubbed it from top to bottom, split the big rooms into little ones with canvas partitions, hung up hammocks for beds, and straightaway opened to an enormous business. She herself stood behind the bar, and twice she was known to have felled turbulent bullies with a stout beer bottle and then to have dragged them into the street.

To this house went Walter Devon, and found Mrs. Purley herself in the "library." Thrice a day it served as a dining room; the rest of the time it was open to loungers, but this evening there was not a soul in it other than the landlady.

"You have a quiet house, Mrs. Purley," Devon remarked in appreciation.

"It *is* quiet," said she. "It's quiet from top

to bottom. There ain't a note of music in it, not even the poppin' of a few bottles of beer; there is no sound of drunks turnin' out their pockets full of gold. All these big-hearted Western miners do for me is to flop on their bunks and snore from midnight to mornin'. I would rather be an organ grinder on Third Avenue than Queen of the May in a dead town like this joint!"

"It's a token of their respect for you, Mrs. Purley," her lodger commented. "They don't —"

"It's a token of the heads that I've cracked," said the gentle lady, "which ain't a thing to the ones that I'm goin' to bust. But I dunno how it is. The boys around this neck of the woods don't seem to know how to absorb their bottles and go to sleep without goin' through a screechin' stage like a pack of howlin' hyenas. I ain't gunna have it. These cheap sports, the minute they got a jolt of whisky inside of them, they gotta sprain their larynxes tellin' the world about it. I ain't gunna furnish a free hall for that kind of song and dance. The next yahoo that opens his trap on high C, I'm gunna bust him for a home run."

She dropped her formidable fist upon the long table, and it quaked throughout its length.

"Have a drink with me," invited Devon.

19

"I don't mind if I do," said Mrs. Purley, "if I can pry that ham of a bartender out of his sleep."

"Maybe he works long hours."

"Him? He don't do nothing except wash up his place before the boys go to work."

"That's about daybreak?" suggested Devon.

"What of it? Then all he's gotta do is to stand behind his nice cool bar all day long and serve out drinks. I give him a hand myself when the crush starts. Would I ask an easier job than runnin' that bar all by myself? I wouldn't, but the boys don't feel like drinkin' too free when there's a lady around. It sort of cramps their style, I've always noticed. I mean except a real gentleman like you, Mr. Devon, which is a pleasure to have you around, I gotta say!"

The bartender was, in fact, soundly snoring. Mrs. Purley roused him with a whack of her broad hand, and he placed foaming glasses of beer before them.

"There ain't so much in it for the house," Mrs. Purley explained, "and the turnover of beer ain't so quick, but it's more genteel, that's what I mean to say. Here's lookin' in your eye, Mr. Devon, and may she always be good to you! Say, Bill, sweep the cobwebs out of your eye, will you, and look like you hoped to see us agin!"

She said to Devon: "You ain't gunna dip into this minin' game, are you?"

"I've never dug deeper than the spots on a pack of cards," he explained.

"That's the only business," sighed Mrs. Purley. "Look what an ass Jim was when he had everything goin' good; he had to switch off and doctor the luck he was havin'. The world with a fence around it wasn't good enough for Jim, but he had to have it set in platinum, the big sap."

A chair scraped in the "library." Glancing through the door, Devon saw the handsome face of Number Two, as he settled down to the table with a newspaper spread before him.

"Who is that?" Devon asked.

"That's Grierson," said Mrs. Purley.

"A fine-looking fellow!" said Devon.

"Him? For a picture he is! I tell you what kind he is; in the Bowery it's so thick with them that they squash under foot. What's the name of them white flowers that turn yellow and rotten when you handle 'em? He's a white camellia, he is. And under the pit of his arm he's got a thorn that'll repeat six times. Look at those long fingers! He never did no honest stroke, I'll tell a man! Pretty kids like him is what has brought down the price of murder in Manhattan to fifty bucks a throw; and a

21

dray horse costs as much as a bank president. So long, Mr. Devon; it's been a real pleasure to have this little chat with you. If anybody disturbs you in my house, you let me know and I'll spread 'em out as thin as gold leaf. *Good* night!"

Mrs. Purley disappeared with a long stride. Devon, strolling into the library, found for himself another paper not more than a month old, and tried to bring himself to a state of interest in the "news." He glanced at his watch. It was a quarter before eleven, and if all went as scheduled, Mr. Murderer Grierson should be at work in this house within fifteen minutes. Quietly Devon promised himself that he would not be far away when the crisis came!

"Gotta match?" asked Grierson.

He passed the box across the table. Grierson thanked him from around a cigarette; plainly he wanted to talk.

He said: "Is that a straight game of faro they got at the Palace?"

"I've never bucked it," Devon replied.

"Take it from me, and don't," snarled handsome young Grierson. "It's the limit, the raw deal that they give you there!"

"Ah?"

"Sure. I never seen nothin' like it. One of these days some hard-boiled bird is gunna cop the box and look at the inside of it. I come pretty near doin' it myself, but, aw, what's the good?"

"To show up a crooked game? A great deal of good, I should say."

"Should you?" yawned Grierson. "Aw, I dunno. You take the way a guy's money floats away, it don't make so much difference. Most usually the ponies gets my wad, and I dunno that faro has anything on the ponies. Whacha think?"

Devon merely nodded as the other man rattled on. It was only five minutes before the hour. Perhaps he could keep the killer engaged for the extra moments.

In the distance a clock began to chime with an impatient rapidity, and Grierson's talk died away as he listened. Yet he made no offer to move from his chair, but looked with a curious intensity into Devon's face.

And suddenly the latter understood. *The killing was truly determined for eleven o'clock, and he, for mysterious reasons, was to be the victim!*

23

III. A CONFESSION

That hurrying toll of the clock had reached nine when Devon ventured a hasty glance over his shoulder which told him, he thought, that a shadowy form moved past the open screen door behind him.

He looked back toward young Grierson, ready for trouble, and trouble was there. The shoulder of that worthy young man was hunched and his right hand flung back for the draw when Devon fired.

The draw was a matter which never bothered him greatly, for the simple reason that, in such affairs as this, he never pulled a weapon. He carried in his coat pocket a single shot pistol with a snub nose, so that it was easily accommodated and made no bulge at all — or at least nothing to speak of. But it fired a forty-five caliber slug with enough force to knock a man down at close range, and that was, after all, what a full-sized Colt accomplished.

It took a great deal of practice to handle the weapon with any accuracy, but such en-

24

counters as need surprise attacks are usually almost body to body. So he dropped his hand into his pocket, pulled the trigger, and stepped back a little, to await the fall of young Grierson with a bullet hole torn through his stomach.

But Grierson did not fall. The pocket of Walter Devon filled with hot fumes, and suddenly he realized that the shot he fired was a blank!

Grierson, with an oath, had snatched at his own gun, and his face wrinkled with disgust as the gun hung. He jerked again and there was a loud tearing of cloth, while Devon saw the big revolver swing clear.

He had three choices. He could race for the door, plunge under the table, or drive straight at the gunman. Devon took the third choice, because both of the others invited a bullet in the back; and a natural left hook which had helped him through his school days lodged accurately on the side of Grierson's chin.

It had an effect almost as potent as a large caliber bullet. As the knees of Grierson buckled and his eyes turned blank, Devon received the gun from the numbed fingers of the killer with one hand, and with the other he eased the youngster into a chair.

Over the head of Grierson he stared at the screen door, but no form stirred there. He glanced down and spun the cylinder of

25

the Colt. There was no doubt about the reality of the bullets which filled that gun; there was no doubt, either, as to the reality of the murder plot which had been formed against him, or the cunning of the rascals who had picked the charge from his gun before he engaged.

The voice of Mrs. Purley was heard in the distance. She came bulging suddenly through a doorway, thrusting a pair of sleepy, yawning men before her.

"If you call yourselves men, you hulking calves," said Mrs. Purley, "step out and do something. There's murder around here — I heard a gun — hey, what? Mr. Devon, or I'm a liar!"

Devon stood behind the chair of Grierson and passed the Colt into his pocket. It was very much more bulky, but his grip was comfortably on its handle, and he pressed the muzzle against the back of the man's neck.

"I was talking to Grierson," he explained, "and while I was talking, I tried to demonstrate a little gun of mine. The trigger has a very light pull; I'm sorry for the noise!"

"Is that all?" the widow inquired. "Young man, you look as if you'd had a hole poked through your gizzard. Are you all right?"

"Me?" Grierson said faintly. "Sure, I'm all right."

"Go back to bed," Mrs. Purley ordered her

two champions, and they sleepily obeyed. She confronted Devon, arms akimbo, saying:

"I dunno what the game is, Mr. Devon, but there ain't any shootin' allowed in this house. You mind what I say. I like you fine, but there's nothing like a couple of killin's to give a place a bad name!"

And with this mild admonition, she disappeared.

Grierson slowly rose from the chair and found the muzzle of his own gun lodged in the pit of his stomach; he raised his hands with a groan.

"What's the main idea?" said Grierson. "I got no more poison aboard. But where did you get that hook? I thought I'd ducked it when it jumped down and nicked me. Ain't I seen you work in the ring, Slim?"

Devon "fanned" his man with care. There was, in fact, no other sign of a weapon than a slingshot secured to the wrist of Grierson with an elastic band, so that it could be shaken down into the tips of his fingers at the first emergency. He took the slingshot as well, though Grierson protested.

"What's a little thing like that in this alley?" Grierson asked sadly.

"It's better with me," said Devon. "I don't like to make you feel lonesome, Grierson, but I think this will just fit into my pocket."

And he took the other into the farthest corner of the room, where neither door nor window looked in upon them. There he sat him down and stood Grierson before him, his shoulders against the wall.

"Grierson," he began, "I never saw you before tonight."

"No," said Grierson, "I don't suppose you did."

"Somebody put you onto this job?"

The boy was silent, looking at the floor, his handsome face sullen and dejected.

"There are two ways of handling this job," Devon continued. "One is to turn you over to the sheriff. That would land you in a jail where the walls are not very thick. The other way is to march you downtown and make a little speech in any saloon, telling them just what has been done to me up here."

"Try it," said Grierson defiantly. "There ain't a thing you can prove!"

"Powder burns on the inside of my pocket, and yet no hole punched through the cloth. I'd call that sufficient proof that my gun had had its teeth pulled before you came here to murder me, my friend. People in this part of the world don't mind a gunfight, now and then, as long as it's fair. But they hate dirty murder. I know exactly how they feel, because I'm a Westerner myself. And if I tell them what I have to say, they'll believe me, young fellow, and they'll take you out and hang you to a high tree."

During this quiet talk, Grierson gradually had been losing color. Now he fumbled at the back of a chair and finally slumped into it. He kept passing his fingers over the bruised place on his jaw, looking more and more blankly.

"I dunno how it happened," said Grierson finally, more to himself than to his companion. "The old gun sort of hitched onto my trousers. My God, it never done that before!"

Then his fury blazed, wide-awake.

"You'd be clean in hell, by now, if you hadn't had all the luck!"

"I believe you," said Devon. "Now, Grierson, I'm sorry about this. It's a sad thing that your luck ran out on you, and your trousers were torn, and all of that; but there's only one thing I want out of you, and that's the name of the man who hired you for this piece of work."

"Nobody hired me," Grierson snarled.

"Is that final?"

"It is, and you be damned!"

"Stand up, then," said Devon, "and walk ahead of me; I'm going to take you downtown, my friend, and tell some of the boys exactly what you've done."

"I'm not gunna move," Grierson declared

29

with a sort of childish stubbornness.

But Devon smiled, and suddenly the boy leaped to his feet.

"My God," said he. "You'd murder me and never care!"

"It isn't murder to brush your kind out of the way," he was assured by Devon. "It's simply an act of public spirit — like seeing that the streets are clean, Grierson! Mind you, you have my word for it. If you'll tell me the truth, you're free!"

Grierson raised his hand, slowly — for fear the gesture might be misinterpreted — and loosened his collar. Once more he stared upon the floor, and there is no better way for a man to lose his nerve.

"Whatchawant?" he asked huskily.

"The name of the man who handled my gun, in the first place."

"I dunno," said Grierson. "He's got twenty workin' for him that could do that trick right under your eyes, and you'd never know — not even a smart guy like you!" the killer finished, some of his usual sneer returning.

"I'll even drop that," said Devon. "But who hired you?"

Grierson blinked.

"He'd find me if I fly like a snipe and dodge all the way around the world!" he communed with himself.

"It's better to fly like a snipe," Devon retorted, "than to hang by the neck. What do you think?"

Grierson moistened his lips. His shifting eyes flashed upon his captor.

"They'd do it," said he. "My God, I seen them take out a Mexican last week and string him up. They — they didn't think nothin' of murderin' a guy like that! It was soup for them!"

He shrugged his shoulders; then he shuddered.

"Look here," he exclaimed suddenly, "you think that you wanta know. You don't want to know at all. If you know, you'll know that *you're* in the soup, a lot worse than I'll ever be!"

"I've taken chances all my life," said Devon, "and this will be only one more."

Grierson closed his eyes, set his teeth, and exploded:

"Take it, then! It's the big guy — it's the main squeeze himself!"

"What main squeeze?"

"Why, who do I mean but the main squeeze of this joint? It's the old fat guy himself!"

He was hardly more than whispering this, his eyes bulging.

"I'm still in the dark," said Devon.

The other made a gesture of the most intense

31

disgust. Then he drew nearer, crouched and tense. As he spoke his face was as that of one who shouted against a great wind, but only a faint whisper came to Devon.

"Burchard!"

IV. A GAMBLER SHOWS HIS HAND

"Burchard? The man who owns the gambling house — the Palace? Is that the fellow you mean?"

Grierson glared on each side of him as though tigers were stalking him.

"Put it in the papers, why don't you?" he snarled. "Hell, is it gunna do anything but get you bumped off all the quicker if you go shoutin' it all over town?"

"Burchard? Burchard?" said Devon. "By Heavens, it's not possible. I've never laid eyes on him in my life."

"That's a lie," answered the gunman fiercely. "He wanted to buy your land, and you wouldn't sell!"

"I wouldn't sell? To Burchard? He never approached me for it. No one but Williams —"

"Why, Clancy Williams is always nothin' but Burchard's goat!" the other assured him.

"Williams? Does he belong to Burchard?"

"I've said my piece, and I ain't gunna say another word," was the reply. "If it don't suit

33

you — why, break your word, and take me down the line!"

"Very well," said Devon. "You've told me what I asked to know. Good night, Grierson! I'll keep this on deposit — until tomorrow, say!"

He smiled genially and touched the revolver, while Grierson stood up and walked slowly from the room, pausing once or twice with tightly gripped hands, as though on the verge of whirling about and throwing himself at his conqueror. Then, with a shrug, he jerked open the door and was gone.

Devon went up to his bed, locked his door, placed upon his window sill a row of little tin tacks, point up, and then turned in and slept like a sailor, dreamlessly and deep.

In the morning he had an appointment to meet Clancy Williams at the "Two Angels" at ten o'clock, but between the end of his breakfast and that hour he had time on his hands. He employed it by strapping a spring holster under the pit of his left arm; into that holster he fitted a long-nosed Colt and then walked into the woods, for practice — a very odd practice, which consisted of sudden snap shots to right and left, at blazes on trees, and at stumps and stones. He scored his share of misses, his share of hits.

"I'm slow as a fat old dog," said Walter Devon, "and I'm walking through a fog!"

Before he went back to town, he paused on the edge of the woods. Even at this hour the nearer face of Timbal Mountain was tangled with threads of blue mist, but the lower summits on either side let the full light of the morning into the valley.

West London seemed to him like a dream that might blow away with the morning mist from the face of Mount Timbal. For his memory of the valley as it had been before this long street sprawled on the hill, was very clear.

And again, for the thousandth time, he asked himself what could make Burchard so desperately eager to get his land that even a small delay about the purchase had determined the saloon owner and miner on murder. However, since he could not conceive a possible answer, he resolutely put the thing behind him and went down to the Two Angels.

In the bar he found Clancy Williams, long and lean, with a downward look and wolfish grin. He walked up and said, without preliminary:

"I understand that you buy for Burchard, Williams. Is that correct?"

Mr. Williams parted his lips to answer, and then seemed to change his mind. He stared at Devon, agape. Then:

"No matter who I buy for, I offered you a price, and I have the money here for you.

Is that good enough?"

"And I've drawn up the papers here and have them all ready to sign the deed and all, Williams."

"Well," said Williams, pacified, "that's better. Sounded like you were trying to make a point of trouble. I'm glad you didn't. Glad for your sake, young man. It's the last time in your life that you'll have fifteen thousand offered for such land as that!"

"A fine, handsome tract, though," Devon commented. "Nearly a thousand acres of beautiful grazing land, Williams!"

"Beautiful?" Williams retorted sourly. "It burns the backs off the cows in the summer, and freezes their horns off in the winter."

"Aye," said Devon; "but when West London spreads out there around the shoulder of Mount Timbal, you'll be selling building lots at —"

"Mr. Devon," Williams asked coldly, "are you joshing me, by any chance? D'you realize you could lay down Chicago between here and your land?"

"However," said Devon, "I don't think fifteen thousand is a great deal for it."

"I don't suppose you do," Williams replied in his dry manner; "but it's all that you'll get out of me for it. You can take it or leave it, young man, and good luck to you!"

"Well," said Devon, "I'll tell you frankly that everything is arranged."

He took the papers from an inside coat pocket and spread them on the bar.

"It's all in perfect order," said he, "and a signature will make it right."

"Very well, then," Williams agreed, "let's have the signature and finish it up. I've other work on my hands today!"

"This work won't take you long," said Devon gently.

He gathered up the papers and ripped them lengthwise, and then across. After this he threw them into a corner.

"What sort of a bluff is this?" asked Williams, his temper rising rapidly. "What sort of a deal are you trying? Do you think you can buck up the price on me by any of those stage tricks and dodges? Not by a damned sight, young fellow!"

"Go back to your employer," said Devon, "and tell him what I've done."

All heads were raised in that crowded barroom by this time and wide eyes stared at them. It was what Devon desired and he failed to lower his voice.

"I'll tell him that he wanted me to do business with a fool!" Clancy Williams howled, balling his huge fists.

Devon smiled upon him, and suddenly

Clancy Williams began to blink his eyes and claw backward along the bar, as though he had seen a snake.

"Tell Burchard," said Devon, "that I'm going to call on him in person before the day is much older, and tell him, besides, that if I should disappear suddenly, the town of West London will have a great many questions to ask him about my disappearance! Do you understand?"

Clancy Williams gave him one last, wolfish, sidelong glance, and then glided through the side door of the saloon, and was gone. If there were any victory achieved, it was on the side of Devon, but he was not so sure. It depended on how this odd game should be played, and so far he was not at all sure of the fall of the cards.

V. A TIP FROM THE SHERIFF

One thing Devon greatly regretted, and that was the attention which he had been obliged to attract in this affairs, for in his business nothing was so profitable as obscurity, and nothing reduced his profits more and increased his hazards to a greater degree than to be pointed out as a celebrity.

However, this was rather a different matter. And he had two potent reasons for wishing to call the public attention upon him. The one was that it would guard his back, so to speak; the second was that even a man as powerful as Burchard night be stopped if he knew that public attention had been called down upon him.

After the leaving of Clancy Williams, there was more than one wistful eye fixed upon him, but Devon did not talk to them, for he understood that the less he said the more confidence the people would have in him. He set up a round of drinks, and left at once with his own scarcely tasted.

His next visit took him to the office of the sheriff.

Sheriff Naxon had as an office a little shack removed to a small distance from the street. There his wife kept house for him, and there his two gangling sons were growing up, lank and lean as their father, with the same sad faces and pale, uncertain eyes.

Sheriff Naxon, on this day, sat upon the rail of his little corral and observed a horse inside it. When he spied Devon, he nodded with the Westerner's casual courtesy.

Said the sheriff: "Would you look over that hoss, stranger?"

Devon rested his elbows on the top rail. It was a pot-bellied horse that he was asked to criticize, a lump-headed, thin-necked creature.

"He has legs," said Devon non-committally.

"Four of 'em," agreed the sad-faced sheriff. "But what kind, would you say?"

"I can't tell the bone," Devon responded; "there's too much hair on 'em."

"Aye," said the sheriff. "That's what I say myself. What would you say about a lot of hair on the legs of a hoss?"

"I don't know. Warm in winter, I suppose."

"Aye, I suppose it is."

The sheriff resumed his thoughtful whittling at a stick of soft white pine. "That hoss there," he said, "is one of the outbeatin'est hosses that ever you seen."

"Is he?"

"He is. But what I can't make out, is he really a hoss?"

"I don't think he's a mule," Devon remarked, ready to smile. "Not by his ears."

"But he's got a mouse-colored muzzle, like a mule," said the sheriff, "and they *has* been short-eared mules, for all of that!"

"I suppose there have been."

"Which if you was to see him in the hills, you'd think he was a goat."

"He's sure-footed, is he?"

"He ain't nothin' but sure-footed. If I was to ride him on that picket fence, he might bust the pickets, but he'd never fall down!"

"Ah!" said Devon politely.

"Walkin' a ledge on the side of a cliff is his idea of a cheerful ride," the sheriff continued, "and slidin' down a cliff a hundred yards deep is the only thing that gets his ears at all forward."

"Aye, but those are grand qualities."

"They are."

"He can run, I suppose? Every mustang can."

"He can't run much," said the sheriff. "He ain't got much speed, but when he gets into his best clip he can hold it all day long. He thinks he's a dog-gone buzzard floatin' in the air, and if you ride him upstairs or down, it don't make no difference. Not to Monty!"

41

"Are you selling him?" asked Devon.

The sheriff looked at the visitor earnestly.

"Would you be wantin' a hoss?"

"Not that kind," Devon responded. "I mean," he corrected himself, "I already have a horse that will do me fairly well. But are you selling that one?"

The sheriff sighed and closed his eyes.

"Three times," said he, "I've worked myself up to the point of sellin' that hoss, and three times I have lost my nerve, because they ain't anybody I hate that bad."

"And what's wrong with him?"

"Kinks," said the sheriff. "He is full of kinks. You couldn't iron 'em out straight any more'n you could iron the curl out of a darky's hair, I'm gunna swear."

"He takes a little to pitching in the morning, I suppose," said Devon, "but then, a lot of good ponies have to be warmed up."

"It ain't the time that matters to him," the sheriff explained. "Any time, mostly, will suit him pretty good. But it's the place that matters the most with him. If he's on a ledge where he can't put down more'n two feet at a time, that's the ledge he picks out for a cakewalk. And if you get him on the top of a bank with a sixty-mile-a-minute toboggan comin' ahead of you, that's the place where he shines at sunfishin'. Because he thinks that he's a bird, and when he comes to one of them places, he shows you how plumb nacheral he feels walkin' the air."

The sheriff sighed and shook his head with bitterness.

"I have growed gray since I owned this hoss," he said.

"How long have you had him?" Devon asked.

"Nigh onto twelve year."

Devon swallowed a smile.

"And he never gets used to you — or you to him?"

"We don't fit," said Naxon dismally. "We don't get on together. We ain't got the same tastes. It ain't that he's ever let me down, and they ain't a crook in the world that can get loose when Monty has pointed his nose at the tail of that crook's hoss. That other hoss has gotta come back, and I don't care what his breedin' might be. Spanish flier or English thoroughbred, that hoss has gotta come back to Monty before the end of the day, because upstairs and downstairs, he flies it just the same. But him and me, we ain't suited. We ain't — what they say in the divorce courts, which I forget the word. And that's why I'm always askin' would maybe somebody want to buy this old hoss?"

"Some horse thief or rustler would, of

course," Devon replied. "They need that kind to get them over the country."

"I would aim to find that there rustler or hoss thief," the sheriff said mournfully. "I wouldn't sell this hoss to him. I would make him a present of Monty and I wouldn't never wish him in jail, because the sufferin' that he would do on the back of Monty would sure be enough! Might you of come over to jest take a picture of him, maybe?" asked the gentle Naxon.

"I came over about something else," Devon confessed. "I came over to tell you that I think Burchard is trying to get my scalp, Sheriff."

He waited for this bomb to take effect, but the sheriff only nodded and smiled as though he had been expecting such a remark — as though he had long suspected such things of the founder of West London.

"The point is," Devon added, "if anything happens, I'd like to have it known that Burchard is the man to call upon."

"Sure," said the sheriff, "I've knowed him for a long time, and he never would mind me droppin' in to have a chat with him."

"I've never laid eyes on him," Devon admitted. "Is he the sort of fellow who *would* be out to kill, Sheriff? Can you tell me that?"

"Why, sir," said the sheriff, "I jest nacherally can't. The fact is, I could pick out a yegg, or a pickpocket, or a second-story gent, or a hoss thief, even, because I've got sort of a run of patterns of 'em in my mind's eye. But murderers are like baseball players. They come fat and thin, tall and short, young and old. You can't tell by his looks which gent's likely to steal the bases, and you can't tell by his looks which man is gunna do a murder. So that's a thing I can't help you out on, partner."

"But you know Burchard?"

"Him? Oh, yes! Burchard is by way of bein' my best friend."

"Good God!" breathed Devon.

"Don't mind me," said the lean, sad sheriff. "Because I ain't nothin' to be considered. I'm only a public servant, hired and paid regular, so my feelin's don't come into any account, thank you!"

"I'm going down to see Burchard now."

"Have you got guns on you?"

"Yes."

"That's right," said Naxon, "because you might need 'em. If you was to drop Burchard you'd still be likely to have a long way to shoot yourself out of trouble, he's got so many handy gents all around him."

VI. IN THE LION'S DEN

The interview with the sheriff was sufficient to convince Devon that the sheriff was a "character," and also, probably, an honest man, but his experience in the world had been such that he kept his trust in his own pocket until there was only the slightest chance that it was misplaced abroad.

However, the surety with which he had received the information about Burchard from Grierson was now dimmed more than a little. The sheriff had called him his best friend, and if the sheriff were honest, that presupposed a good deal for the keeper of the gaming house.

He went straight to the Palace to have an interview on his own account. Burchard was having breakfast, although it was nearly eleven in the morning. He was done up like a child in a great bib, tucked not only under his chin, but also into the armpits of his vest.

Burchard was like a baby in more than the bib. He was a man of sixty, and his hair had fallen so that on his rosy poll there was only a blond fuzz like that which appears on the head of an infant. His body was as rotund as the body of a baby, and his legs seemed as short, as bowed, as useless; his wrists were mere dimples between the fat of his hands and the fat of his forearms.

Above all, the resemblance was in his face, which was not seamed by a single line, and was so rosy red that it looked as though the very touch of the air were irritating to this delicate epidermis; at every emotion from laughter to mere thought, his fat cheeks almost shut his eyes from sight, and then it was hard to say whether he was about to weep or to smile, exactly as the eyes of a baby alter.

Burchard had just finished a platter load of chops and went on to several great venison steaks which were carried in steaming by a Chinese waiter, who also uncovered a large wooden board on which was a heap of steaming oven muffins, light as foam and crusted with the most delicate brown.

In ordered attack, the founder of West London advanced into the heart of these viands, and though he never stopped eating, he looked up with a merry smile at Devon, as though inviting him to laugh at such a prodigious appetite, and perhaps envy such copious means of satisfying it.

He said to Devon:

"Sit down, stranger. It's a little early for

47

dinner, maybe, for you — but if you can help me out with these venison steaks, I'd be happy to have you sit here and work alongside of me."

Devon thanked him and explained he already had breakfasted, and would not have lunch for some time.

"Aye, aye," said Burchard, "there's the trouble with the way most folks live. They gotta have a time set aside for everything. A time to go to bed, and a time to get up; a time to work, and a time to eat. Why, it ain't nacheral any way you look at it."

"How should you do?" asked Devon, curious and amused.

The fat man split a hot muffin with his knife, larded it with yellow butter, and established between layers a rich slice of venison dripping with juice. It made a sandwich so thick that the jaws of Devon ached beholding it. Burchard poised this morsel and smiled; his eyes disappeared; there was only a smiling mask of the joy of life.

"The time to sleep is when you're tired; the time to play is when you feel dull; work when you have to; and when you're hungry, eat. I've ate six times in a day; and I've had one meal in two. I've smoked ten cigars one after another, and gone a week without tastin' tobacco. And that's why I'm young, partner

— so young and tender that the flies like me!"

He laughed. His laughter was curiously soft and restrained, as though he did not wish to shake too violently that large bulk of his. Then his mouth expanded with easy flexibility, and the great sandwich was shorn in twain without effort — without effort the eater masticated this enormous mouthful, then poured home half a pint of coffee.

"I don't want to bother you," said Devon, "but if I can interrupt your lunch for five minutes —"

"Don't you do it," Burchard protested. "Don't you interrupt this what you call a lunch. You can talk to me as much as you please, and I'll hear you fine. Eating opens my ears and opens my brains better. I sort of can understand more, partner. So you say right along with what you gotta say, but don't you interrupt my meal!"

Said Devon: "Clancy Williams works for you?"

"Times is he does, times is he don't," the fat man replied, proceeding with his attack on the muffins and venison. "What work might you mean?"

"He was buying my ranch for you — my name is Devon."

"Oh, you're Devon! You're old Jack Devon's son, are you? Now ain't it a funny

49

thing? I recognized something about you when you come in. I says to myself that I'd seen you before. But him that I'd seen was old Jack Devon, dead and gone these years. Hey! But time slides! Yes, Williams was askin' to get the place for me. Here in West London, I got a bit of property, here and there. But there ain't hardly room for a fat man to spread his elbows in this here town, with it buildin' up so fast. I hankered after a place back in the hills. Old Jack Devon and me used to fry trout over the same fire; so I know all about that place of yours, son!"

Devon nodded.

"The fact is, I've been informed that you wanted that land so badly that when I delayed a while in getting the papers ready, you were willing to have me put out of the way."

"Bumped off, you mean? Rubbed out?" asked the fat man, proceeding without interruption with his meal.

"Aye. Exactly that."

Burchard clucked in disapproval of such a thought.

"Where would you pick up that idea?" he asked.

"It was pointed out to me," said Devon, "with a man-sized Colt, which is a pointer that most people take a careful account of."

"Don't they, though!" agreed Burchard in

the most impersonal manner. "I've seen sixteen men in one barroom with their hands pushed up over their heads, and every one of them sixteen would of swore that the gent behind the Colt was lookin' straight at him!"

He laughed gently.

"And so, to come back to this little affair of mine?" said Devon more firmly.

"Yes, yes, to come back to you, why should I be wantin' to murder you for the sake of your land, son? I don't do murder. I don't have to. If it come to gun plays, there's too much of me to make a handy target."

"That ends it, then," Devon announced. "I didn't want to press any point, but on the other hand, I don't want to hold any erroneous ideas against you."

"Exactly right," said the fat man, "I always want a hoss that does his buckin' in the mornin' and runs straight the rest of the day. Now that you've come and talked to me, why, it's as though we'd had a good introduction — from your father, say! Now, there's a man that would of laughed if he'd heard such things said about Les Burchard. You might tell me who put such an idea into your head?"

"I can't tell you that."

"And why not?"

"Because if he lied, as I hope he did," said Devon, "a bit of time will show me the truth

51

about what he said. And if he was *not* lying, he'll be murdered for having told."

"Well, well," murmured the fat man, "that's as true as true! But now, who would of thought it out as logical as all of that? Was you raised for the law, maybe?"

And he looked with kindly admiration upon the youth.

Devon stood up and shook his head.

"I was raised for medicine."

"A good trade, a mighty good trade!" said Burchard. "I only been to a doctor once, when my stomach got a mite out of order. What would you think he told me? To eat nothin' for five days! I done it, and it worked. What's more, I've fasted pretty near that long a good many times since, for the sakes of the first meal that comes my way afterwards! You gotta go, son? You wouldn't even have a cup of coffee?"

"I have to go," said Devon. "I think we're friends, Burchard?"

"Aye, and your father's friend before you, son."

The hand of the gambler was lost in the soft grip of Burchard, and yet there was strength beneath the thick flesh and in the moist touch.

"Good-by, Burchard."

"So long, doctor."

"Not doctor. I took a crossroads, and wound up dealing cards."

Burchard laughed again until his sides quivered.

"Good luck to your cards, then, except in my house."

"Thanks. And before I go, I must say that I'll be looking about a bit. If I find anything in what I heard against you, I'll come back and tell you to your face. Is that right?"

"Of course it's right. If you want to put a brand on me, do it in daylight."

He waved his pink hand, and Devon went out from the room. In the outer hall he was aware of two sour-faced Mexicans, one with a scarred face; they sat apart from one another, apart from the world in a mutual bitterness, and for some reason Devon was sure that they were placed here at the beck and call of Burchard.

It made a rather pointed footnote to his conversation with the fat man, and he went out into the blinding white of the sunlight more thoughtful than he had been before.

He went to the livery stable, then, and hired a strong bay gelding for the rest of the day. He was fairly well convinced that Grierson had lied to him, and yet it was difficult for him to leave this unpromising trail. If Grierson had lied, he had done so under peculiarly difficult circumstances, for a pointed revolver is a notable summoner of truth!

So Devon rode out to cut for sign.

VII. DEVON SPRINGS A SURPRISE

Devon rode out of the town on the first valley trail, which dropped with quick turns and sharp angles toward the bottom of the gulch, and into what was now a well of sweltering heat, for the sun was well above the top of even Mount Timbal, and its floods of light were reflected from the walls of polished rock on either side of the gulch. Farther up, beneath the Palace, the slopes were well wooded, but at this point there was nothing to break the furious force of the sun, and the heat was stifling.

Through the thin mountain air, voices shouting, hammer strokes falling on drill heads, floated upward thin as a dream to the rider. Looking down, he could see the color of the river change. Toward the head of the valley it was crystal clear; beneath him it was growing muddy.

Devon came down into the heart of the gorge. Men and their voices and the noise of their work loomed greater here; but above them the mountains rose more gigantic still.

He climbed the farther slope, letting the gelding zigzag on the trail, and rapidly the confusion of sounds grew fainter until it was no more than the buzzing of bees.

From the farther ridge he looked back again at the busy gorge, and at the town of West London. Suddenly it was as though he were a boy again, as though he never had left these mountains, but riding out on a morning, he found a great specter of civilization spread out before him.

Then he took the downward slope that led off toward the hills of the ranch.

It was a sheltered stretch between the loftier mountains which had been worn down at this point by a stream that no longer flowed with water. Only when the snows melted, water stood in the old draw, which was now black with willows.

Those spring waters, reënforced by the occasional summer showers, had to supply the ranch for the hot part of the year, and for this purpose sections of the draw were cleared of brush, dammed, and the waters collected in tanks to stand stagnant there for month after weary month.

Devon looked down on them with a slight feeling of disgust as he saw their edges, green with dried slime. It was the tanks which had driven him away in his youth. The mountains were well enough; the solitude could be endured; but the horror of that stale, standing water had gone to his heart and forced him away against his grim old father's protests.

He saw the ranch house presently standing in a dell — a naked little shack, with a squat barn, and a few stretches of corral behind it. The trees which might have sheltered and shaded it had been felled to a considerable distance. The unsightly stumps remained.

As he came up, he saw the place as it always had been — the stretch of earth before the door, stamped bare and hard by the hoofs of horses. Against the face of the log cabin leaned a few stretchers on which the hides of coyotes and bobcats were drying.

Now he heard, from the deep distance, a sound like the booming of cannon. In the mines, he could guess, they were firing their shots. It was noon, and the first shift had finished its work.

The long, hollow echoes died faintly in the air as he dismounted and tethered the horse; then he stepped into the doorway and saw Harry and Jim. Through fifty thousand square miles they were known by no other names.

In the grand old days of buffalo and Indians, Jim and Harry had been companions of Jack Devon. The three had hunted, trapped, and traded together. They had fought Indians, taken scalps, ridden through danger of guns and trader whisky, prospected, mined together. When Jack Devon settled on this ranch, it was considered only natural that Harry and Jim should come when they chose and go when they chose.

They used to come down out of the mountains bringing presents of good pelts, or ammunition and guns, to Jack Devon. Or if they came empty-handed, it was no matter. When they arrived, they put their horses into the barn if the weather were bitter winter, or into the pasture if it were mild, and trooped into the house carrying saddles and bridles, which they hung up in the rear wash room. They greeted the family with a brief "howdy," even if they had been away for half a year, and then they sat down and lighted their pipes.

Devon's mother always grumbled when the pair arrived. They might remain for a day, or for the entire winter, but so long as they were there, they could be counted upon never to lift a hand in chopping wood or caring for horses, or in doing any task about the house. They gave Jack Devon some help with his cows, that was all.

"They think I'm a squaw!" Mrs. Devon used to mutter.

But once she told him how an outlaw had ridden that way and come into the house with a leveled rifle, and how Harry had thrown the man out, bodily, and then bent the rifle over his knee, and hurled it after the broken criminal.

After Mrs. Devon passed away, they came still more often. Old age was stiffening them; their traps gave smaller yields; and since the death of his father they had remained on the place, taking care of the dwindling herd. The bulk had, before this, been sold to supply the butcher shops of West London.

Now, from the doorway, Devon surveyed them with a twinkle in his eye. Jim, tall, slender, handsome with his long white hair and snowy imperial, was as ever dignified and erect — only slower in his movements, which once had been catlike for speed.

Harry was half a foot shorter than in his prime; his back bent forward from the waist and his great shoulders hung in a heavy stoop. But still there was said to be the strength of two men in his huge old hands.

It was he who worked at the stove, scattering ashes into the air; Jim, with slow dignity, laid out the table, spreading a ragged red cloth. Both of them worked, regardless of the form in the doorway; so much had age filmed their eyes.

A whiff of flying ashes entered the nose of Jim and he sneezed; the tin cups rattled perilously in his hand.

"If you was in a camp, Harry," said Jim, "the noise you make would scare the game ten mile off. If you was in a boiler factory, the dust you raise would get you fired."

"This ain't an Injun council," declared Harry, "and speeches ain't asked for. Stir up some pone and shut up."

"The pone is stirred and baked," said Jim.

He brought it forth from the cupboard. Heat and age had dried it and warped its stony substance.

"If that's pone," Harry remarked, "you could build a house with some more like it."

"If it's a mite dry," said Jim, "it's better for your stummick. Besides, you got some teeth left, and if you exercise your jaw you won't have to talk so much."

"Hello!" Devon called out.

They turned on him with a start. Instinctively Harry gripped the poker with a force that made the heavy iron bar quiver, and the clawlike hand of Jim snapped down to his gun. Then they saw the face of the visitor and broad smiles instantly appeared.

VIII. CONFLICTING VIEWPOINTS

The pair gave Devon a most cheerful welcome. They had seen little of him, and he was far from them in ideas and generation; but he was the son of Jack Devon, and therefore he could do no wrong!

They sat him down in the best chair; they proffered chewing and pipe tobacco; and when he would not have it, they set a third place at the table and the preparations for lunch went on more rapidly.

They laid out broiled rabbit, so tender that the flesh fell away from the bones; mustard greens gathered on an upland meadow; new-baked corn pone, and wild honey of an exquisite fragrance to eat with it; coffee of a rare brew; and small, sweet melons that grew near the verge of one of the tanks and had been fenced in from the cattle.

These old men, when they chose, had the gracious manners of kindly nobles; they could have put at ease a king or a red Indian; and when they lighted their pipes after the lunch, the old days, glorious with distance in a sort of sunset light, were brought up into that naked little shack.

Then Jim went out to bring in more wood to heat the dish water.

"Jim looks as straight as ever," Devon remarked.

"So does a reed," said Harry, shaking his head. "So does a reed what has lost its pith and is turnin' brown in the fall of the year."

"Why, what do you mean, Harry?"

"I'm feared for Jim," was the reply. "Now's he can't go rampin' and ragin' over the hills like he used to a few year back, they's come a change over him. Seems like he's feelin' his age more'n he should, and I'll tell you the reason why!"

"I'd like to know."

"It's the lack of education, Walt. Dog-gone my hide if it ain't! Books ain't a pile of use when you're livin' on the trail, packin' in the deer meat on your own shoulders of a mornin'. But when you're housed up a lot, especial of a long winter, then is where education comes in pretty handy. Take me now — if the winter begins to pinch, I enjoy a dog-gone lot of readin'."

"What do you read, Harry?"

"I save up the papers mighty careful. I got a whole box full of 'em, over yonder! And in the winter evenings, when I get through

62

cleanin' hides or fleshin' 'em, or whatever there is to do, I turn in and put away a couple of hours and get sleepy. But you take Jim, he ain't got no resource like that. He's got no good way of puttin' in his time, and it tells on him. He can only make horsehair bridles, and ropes, and things like that. And when he gets tired of it, he's gotta try to tell me the same old yarns that I've listened to time and time agin!"

Jim returned, the water was put on to heat; and then a great bawling began in the corral.

"It's that fool of a jinny," said Harry. "Tryin' to climb into the corral and talk to your hoss. Wait till I lay a length of rail alongside of its fool ribs!"

And away he rushed, bent far over with age, shuffling up the dust.

Old Jim shook his head as he looked after his partner. He said in his deep and gentle voice, into which a slight tremor was just beginning to enter:

"Maybe you've noticed what's happened to pore old Harry?"

"What?" asked Devon.

"The change in him, I mean?"

"I can't see a bit. He's the same old Harry, it seems to me!"

Jim nodded thoughtfully.

"It's not seein' him close, or follerin' him

63

from day to day. You wouldn't notice no change. But me, I notice it! Look at the way he jumped up, just now, and tore out there after a fool of a jinny? Why, I seen the day that a whole dog-gone Cheyenne charge wouldn't of made Harry get up and spoil his after-eatin' pipe. But be's changed. He ain't got no hold on himself!"

"And what's the cause of it, Jim?"

Jim stepped closer and lowered his voice until it was almost inaudible.

"It's the failin' of his teeth. He's still got two that meet, but one of them is beginnin' to wobble, and then I dunno what's gunna happen to pore old Harry. It'll mean watchin' over him like a baby, and mincin' up his food — him that could bite the leg off a buffalo when I knowed him first! Yes, sir, Walt, I can see the time comin', and a mighty miserable time I'm gunna have of it with Harry when his old age sets in!"

Jim saw something through the rear door that startled him, and running to it, he shouted suddenly:

"Harry, you dog-gone old bow-legged, hobble-footed ijit! Leave that jinny be, will you?"

"I'm gunna larn her some sense!" came the distant bass roar of Harry. "I'm gunna let some light into her!"

64

"Leave — that — jinny be!" yelled Jim, and started at a weak run through the door.

Presently the two came back.

"Who owns that jinny?" Jim was heard to ask.

"Dog-gone my heart if I know," said Harry. "Do you?"

"No," said Jim. "I disremember which one of the span it was that was mine; but I'm likely to remember, one of these here days, and if it turns out to be my jinny that you put your time in abusin', they's gunna be a pile of trouble between you and me, young feller!"

They came gloomily back into the house, and found Devon at work at the dish pan.

They paused with mutual exclamations of dismay.

"Look at there!" said Harry. "You gotta go gallivantin' around about a worthless jinny, and Jack Devon's son, he comes out here and he's treated like a damn Injun squaw on account of you!"

For once Jim had no answer. He seized a stained dishcloth and sadly began to dry the tins.

IX. A THUNDERBOLT FROM JIM

"Hey," muttered Harry, screening his eyes as he stared out the door, "ain't that Steve Maloney comin' over yonder?"

Jim at once stepped to the door and peered.

He said: "Pore old Harry, yore eyes are kind of saggin' and givin' way, it looks like! Can't you see, plain as your own nose, that that's Tucker Vincent's straw boss? That's Way. I can tell him five mile off by the way he slants in the saddle!"

At last the rider swept up before the shack and leaped down from his silver-horned Mexican saddle. He was a lean-faced man of the range, gaudily done up in the style of a Mexican cavalier on holiday, from the gay, short jacket to the bright conchos down the seam of his chaps. He came with jingling spurs into the house, pushing the weight of his lofty sombrero to the back of his head.

"Hello, Harry and Jim." He turned to Devon. "You're Walt Devon, ain't you?"

"Yes."

"My name is Way. I come over to see you

for Tucker Vincent."

"I don't know Tucker Vincent."

Mr. Way paused in the midst of his next word, then closed his mouth and opened his eyes.

"You don't know Tucker Vincent?" he ventured at last.

Said Harry: "Walt ain't been back here hardly a week. He don't know much about the people in Timbal Gulch." Then he explained to Devon: "Tucker Vincent hauls out a mule load of gold every day taken from the rocks. He's so rich that he dunno what to do with his coin. Way, here, is sort of a straw boss for him."

"I used to work for Vincent back on the Stinson Valley — fifty mile over yonder," said Way.

"I know the Stinson Valley."

"When Burchard made his strike, Vincent was off tryin' to trail rustlers, and he got down this way just in time for the good news. Vincent is a prospector that knows color when he sees it. And what he staked was worth stakin', I can tell you! He's made so much money that I'm to talk to you in a funny way, Devon."

The gambler nodded. Since the sun was westering, they went out before the house and sat down in the shadow. Jim, a lover of horseflesh, went over to stare disapprovingly at the spur marks on the flanks of Way's mustang, and to admire the beauty of the fierce little animal.

"What is it that Vincent's money means to me?" asked Devon. "Unless I could get him to sit down at a poker table with me," he added frankly.

Way grinned — a quick, almost evil flash of mirth.

"That depends on what I can wangle out of him for you," he said.

"Wangle out of him for what?"

"This here place."

"Hey?" exclaimed Harry.

"Yep. This here land," said Way again.

"Jim!" called Harry. "Here's Way, tryin' to buy our place!"

"Hold on," said Jim. "We wouldn't sell, Way. This here is our home."

"It is," agreed Harry, "and we ain't the kind of folks to sell the home off'n our heads!"

"*Your* home?" sneered Way with sudden malignity. "You two ain't gotta right to a blade of grass that grows on these here hills. When'd you ever take out a homestead, or when did you ever pay down a penny for it, or any parcel of it? And where's your deed to prove on it?"

Harry, having attempted to break in on this fierce speech, once or twice, now said to his companion: "Why, Jim, you come to think of it, Way is right, ain't he?"

Jim scratched his head.

"Of course, the place belongs to Walt," said he. "But we got a claim to it, just the same. It's our home, I reckon?"

"Aye!" said Harry, with dubious enthusiasm. "But how far would that go in law?"

"Not a damn inch," Way assured them.

"It's never coming to the law," said Devon. "Of course they have a right in this place!"

The two old men turned their heads slowly toward him; speech was unnecessary.

"Do I foller this drift?" asked Way slowly. "You give these old gents a claim on your place?"

"I certainly do," said Devon.

"What sort of claim?"

"An equal claim with me."

"Hold on!" Harry gasped.

"You know what you're sayin', do you?" Way inquired, almost bitterly.

"I suppose I do."

"Well," said Way, "you don't — but I'm gunna show you what it would mean!"

"Walt, Walt," protested Jim in his deep, somewhat uncertain voice, "this is a fine thing you're sayin'. But, God A'mighty, what would we lay a claim to, except to layin' our heads under the roof of the cabin, here, so long as you're pleased to have us!"

Devon rested a hand on the thin shoulder of the old man.

"If my father were alive and here," said he, "what would he say? His blood is my blood, Harry and Jim. So — no more talk!"

"There's been too much talk already, as I'm about to prove to you, Devon," said Way. "I come over here from Vincent to buy this place right off of your hands!"

"Hey, wil you listen to that?" Harry vociferated. "Vincent wants to buy this place!"

"All right," said Way. "If you got a share in it, an equal share, what sort of a price would you lay onto it? Name it!"

"Lemme see. What would you say, Jim?"

"There's nigh a thousand acres," said Jim.

"What about ten dollars an acre?" said Harry.

"Well," said Devon, "does that suit you, Jim?"

"I ain't sellin'," Jim retorted shortly, "and neither is either of you two."

Way turned on him, but checked his words. He said to Devon, instead:

"This here is a mighty fine and generous way that you're carryin' on with the two old boys. It'll get you talked of in a good way all through the range, too. But when it comes

70

to doin' the business, I suppose you can see that I can't talk to three men. I'd rather talk to one, and you got the legal right to do the talkin' "

"Very well. What's your offer?"

"They've named ten thousand."

"They have. Not I," Devon retorted. "I have a better offer."

"Did Burchard bid more than that?"

"You knew he was after it, did you?"

"Burchard is so big, now," Way said with a grin, "that every time he moves, what he does is pretty well known. We knew Burchard was after it, the same reason as Vincent!"

"I don't suppose you'll tell me that reason?"

"Why not? It ain't such a secret. Vincent has brains, so has Burchard. But chiefly, them two love to beat out each other at the same jobs. Burchard, he made the strike in Timbal Gulch, and Vincent has coined the most money out of it! It's always that way!"

"But why does Vincent want this old ranch?" asked Devon.

"Because he has an idea that West London is gunna grow and grow. And he's got all kinds of plans. This here is the closest farm land. Gunna dig deep wells here and raise truck garden vegetables for West London. This here is the closest land for the runnin' of cattle. Gunna run a lot of cows here, and fat them for the West London market. He says he'll have to spend a lot of money to make the place pay, but when it does, he says it'll be another gold mine for him!"

"And the price?" Devon inquired.

"Somebody said ten thousand," Way replied. "Burchard offered you more. How much more?"

"Five thousand more."

"Well, right off I might offer you sixteen thousand. But I won't. I'm gunna lay the cards down on the table. Vincent told me that I was to bid as high as twenty-five thousand dollars, which is his top price. I won't try to buy in for sixteen or eighteen thousand. I'll come right to the top to begin with. Suppose I say twenty-five thousand dollars? I can tell Vincent that I couldn't get it out of you for a penny less. I'm tired of seeing him get the lion's share."

"Twenty-five thousand dollars!" Harry muttered. "Why, that's a mighty pile of money."

"That's a hundred dollars a month clear income and not a lick of work done," Way said sharply. "That's how much money it is. A hundred a month forever — and twenty-five thousand dollars still left at the end of forever!"

Two minutes passed in silence.

"Well, Devon," asked Way, impatiently, "d'you think I'm doing right by you? Could anything be fairer than that? That's the top price!"

"Suppose I should want to try my own hand at this game of growing vegetables and beef?"

"Nothin' to stop you except capital," was the cheerful response. "Cost forty-fifty thousand dollars to do what Vincent wants to do with the land."

Devon half closed his eyes.

He was no business man. The speculations of the gaming table were his forte.

But he knew that wealth could be taken from the soil. What weary days of labor went into the making of such money he had seen, also; nevertheless, it was true that his place was the best farming ground near West London. Perhaps there was in this a speculation sufficiently attractive to make Burchard willing to send a murderer to brush him aside and leave only these two old men on the place — and they with no legal right to the ground!

Twenty-five thousand dollars, even divided as he proposed to divide it, would richly increase his capital. It was thrice what he ever had expected to get from these semi-bare hills.

"It *is* a good price," he said aloud.

"A good price?" said Way, his eyes sparkling with impatience. "I tell you, it's a hell of a bang-up robbery, a price like that! Tucker Vincent is a fool for once, to offer any such a thing!"

"Aye, it sort of looks that way," said Harry. "I hardly ever heard of such a whackin' heap of money. Eh, Jim?"

Old Jim stiffened a little, and removed his pipe from between his white teeth.

"We ain't gunna sell," said he.

Way shrugged his shoulders.

"The old boy is kind of batty, I guess. But what about it, Devon? D'you close?"

"Why —" began Devon.

"Don't need no papers. Shake hands on it, and it's closed!" suggested Way.

Jim strode suddenly between Devon and the other.

"Way," he said, "git off the land! We ain't gunna talk no more to you!"

X. TELLTALE FOOTPRINTS

Old Jim was a man of such exceeding mild-ness, except with Harry, that this crisp and insulting language was a thunder shock to Devon. He could not believe his ears as Jim repeated:

"I've told you once. I tell you twice. Git off the land. I don't like the looks of ye!"

"You damn old rattle bones!" cried Way, blood rushing to his face. "What you —"

"Back up!" said Jim, his lean hand on the handle of his Colt. "In all my life I never have had gents talk to me like this here. Back up, and get out, Way, or I'll let light into you!"

"Devon," cried Way, "this old fool will spoil the deal for you if you sit by and let him talk like this. I gotta lot of patience, but by God, they's a bottom to the deepest well!"

Devon, amazed, stepped up beside Jim.

"I'm sorry," he said to Way, "but we're partners of sixty-five years' standing, you see, and what Jim says will have to go, I'm afraid."

The face of Way turned purple, splotched with rage and incredulity.

"Why, God A'mighty, man! You're chuckin' ten thousand dollars of honest money over your shoulder."

"It ain't honest," said Jim. "There never was a penny of Tucker Vincent's money made honest. And that I know!"

Way turned on his heel, strode to his pony, and mounted.

"Devon!" he called.

"I'm sorry," said Devon, following him a little, "that you've found rough language here, Way. I'm mightily sorry. But Harry and Jim mean more to me than a price on this place."

"You've had your chance," Way blurted out, biting his lips with extreme passion. "What I say is — God help a fool that won't help himself!"

He jerked the pony around and rushed it furiously away.

Then Harry took the arm of his partner.

"Jim," said he, "I don't want to ask no foolish questions, but I'd like to know what's in the mind of you? You talkin' as though you owned the place! Why — my God, Jim, it's almost as though you was takin' up Walt in his offer to us!"

"I'm takin' nothin'," said Jim, growing decidedly red at the mere thought of such a thing. "But I'm talkin' for Walt's own good. You two come here, will you?"

He led the way to the hitching rack.

"Look there, Harry, if your pore old eyes can see that far!"

"Me? I ain't bat-blind like you! And even if I was, I could see the print of a bar-shoe, there."

"The kind of a shoe they'd put on a hoss, say, that had the thrush?"

"Well, maybe."

"You see that, Walt?"

"I see that, of course."

"Now, Walt, if you'll slant an eye over there —"

The eye of Devon was by no means accustomed to the sign of the trail, but this was an imprint as clear as a photograph upon a field of white. It showed the deep incision of a horse's shoe, with a bar across the heels of it, at a spot where Way had not ridden that day.

"Is that the same print?" Devon inquired.

"Son," said Jim, "it is!"

"But there might be other horses wearing the same shoes?"

"Thrush would mostly come of stable-kept hosses — like that flash mustang of Way's. They ain't many stable-kept hosses around here. But when Way wants a hoss, he wants it bad, and so he keeps up his best, and throws the grain into 'em, regardless!"

"I don't see," said Devon, "that this hoof mark is so very important. Of course, any man can ride across our range if he wants to."

"Sure he can," returned Jim, "if he wants exercise that bad and can't get enough ridin' through the dog-gone mountains."

Harry took off his battered felt hat and passed his calloused hand over his head tenderly.

"It's like this, Walt," he explained carefully. "They ain't been but one rain in a month. That rain was five days back. And it come at night. Half an hour of hard rain, and then it quit. Now you step on this ground."

Devon complied.

"Hard, ain't it?"

"As a brick!"

"Sure it is. Would a hoss make much mark on that?"

"I don't suppose so."

"Wal, it wouldn't. Not much more'n on a stone. But look at that print! It sure is plain to the eye."

"Yes. It's deep."

"That there rain come early. About nine. Jest as we was turnin' in to sleep. It rattled loud on the roof, and I went off dreamin' on the tune of it. It stopped soon, Jim said. A wind come up out of the south and dried the ground again, so's by mornin' the surface was hard. Your heels didn't pick up no earth when you walked. Well, old son, that print was made while the ground was still wet! Look how easy the toe of the shoe sloshed out of the deep hole it had made! That happened durin' the rain or mighty shortly after. And it means that this here Way was sashaying around the premises of our ranch in the dark. What for? Where was he headed? He sure didn't call at our house that night!"

XI. THE GATHERING OF THE MOB

Harry was the first to mount, and by the time the other two were in their saddles, he was jogging his horse in short circles around them. Finally his course touched the edge of the tank, then he came back up the slope to his companions, looking worried.

"What would a man come here for after dark but mud?" he asked.

"Maybe it's a kind of a healin' mud," said Jim. "It's got a bad enough smell to be mighty good for something."

"A man ain't a bear to waller in mud like a hog!" said Harry.

"There's a man," Jim said to Devon, "that's one of the most newspaper readingest gents that I ever heard tell of. But still he don't know about mud baths!"

"Who'd take a mud bath in green slime like that?" asked Harry. "Full of wigglers, too!"

"Wal, to take a took at that there tank," Jim remarked, "I'd say that was what brought Way over here!"

"To sit in the mud?" Devon grinned. "Why,

80

he's welcome to come and sit here forever, if he wants to!"

"You laugh," said Jim, "but supposin' that that's a good medical mud, why, it'd be worth as much as a mine!"

"How come?" Harry asked.

"Folks would come over here in stacks. Tucker Vincent or Les Burchard could build up a great big hotel, and charge as high as five or six dollars a day to live in it. And every mud bath they'd charge ten dollars more. They'd haul in piles of cash!"

"If Way came over, and not for a mud bath," smiled Devon, "what other reason could he have had? Both Burchard and Vincent are mining men. Couldn't it be that they're after pay dirt?"

"It's nacheral to think that way," said Jim, "but there ain't an inch of the highest mountains, even, that ain't been worked over by prospectors around here; and if one man has tramped up and down this here ranch, tappin' every outcrop of rock, I've seen a hundred. There ain't any gold in these here stones, Walt!"

"If we say that he didn't come for gold and he didn't come for — mud, perhaps. What's left?"

"Aye, that's what we'd like to know. That's what we *will* know," said Harry.

81

They rode back to the shack, where Devon left them, with a double question to consider.

Would it be possible to carry out the plan which Burchard and Vincent were reported to have conceived, of selling what cattle they had at a high price in West London, and herding in fresh droves of cheaper beef from the north to fatten on this range, and sell in turn?

But, above all, why had Way made this night excursion?

Then Devon rode off, without thinking fit to tell his partners of the attack which had been made upon him the night before. However, he had barely crossed the first row of hills when, at a sound of hoofs, he turned and saw Harry coming after him on the little jinny, whose head bobbed patiently up and down under the great burden it had to carry.

"Did I forget something, Harry?" asked Devon.

'The old man looked at him with brightened eyes.

"You did," said he. "You forgot that it would take a pile of weight off the mind of Vincent or of Burchard, both, if you was to cash in your checks!"

"Are you coming along to take care of me?"

"Maybe I look old for that," said Harry, "but I still can see things that get between me and the sun."

"But there's good old Jim, left out in the shack alone."

"That's true, but somebody has gotta take care of the ranch and watch out; and if they come to jump the house while Jim is there, they're gunna think that they've run into a cyclone. He sleeps with a sawed-off shotgun under his head." Harry chuckled. "They ain't gunna bother Jim none. He's dried up like a wild cat — there's nothin' to him much except his teeth and his claws! I'll go on with you!"

Devon knew it was useless to argue. The old men looked upon him as a child, and he understood that they must have their way, so the two jogged on side by side back to West London. They had climbed to the edge of the town when a roar came up from Timbal Gulch behind them, like the roar of the wind through crowded pine trees, and they saw many men climbing up the twisting trails to the town.

"Somebody's made a strike. West London is gunna howl tonight!" declared Harry.

They had barely put the horses up in the livery stable when the front ranks of the crowd reached the level of the town and spilled up the main street like a current of water, swirling from side to side, drawing in every idler on the way, sucking the clerks out of stores, the citizens out of their houses.

The saloons were the only dams which could hold that force, and inside of these segments of the crowd were detached and foamed and shouted. The swinging doors flapped constantly, like wings, and the word went out that one Tom Fagan had split open a veritable pouch of gold, and that behind the pouch a broad, rich vein appeared, promising wealth in unknown quantities unless it pinched out soon.

Tom Fagan himself, in the "Main Chance," was inviting the entire town to drink. He bought two barrels of whisky outright, and had them broached and placed one on each side of the main street. Two bartenders guarded each barrel, and served out the drinks free to all who passed, giving forth dippers filled with the liquid fire.

Other bartenders labored in the Main Chance itself; and every saloon in the town was filled to the doors. No one was immune from the excitement. The miners rejoiced because it was apparent that Timbal Gulch held countless possibilities still in reserve; the luckless prospectors were cheered for the same reason; the gamblers, confidence men, pickpockets, yeggs, and social parasites of all kinds grew gay with the assurance that there was still more honest blood to be drawn upon profitably.

Old Harry insisted that he and Devon should keep clear of the mob. Because, as he said, this was exactly the sort of situation in which a man shot through the back would fall almost unnoticed.

XII. LUCKY JACK'S SISTER

Devon headed straight toward his rooming house, and, as they went, he told old Harry of the attack which had been made upon him by the hired assassin. Harry pulled his thin mustache as he listened. And then he clapped his hand loudly on the handle of his Colt.

"If I was you, Walt, I'd pick up out of this and get away," he advised. "Leave me and Jim to look out after things here, and you get away, will you?"

Devon shook his head.

"The money isn't the only part worth while. The game is the thing," said he. "I'll stay and watch the play of the cards."

"Aye," returned Harry, "that's all very well when you know what sort of pack you're playing with!"

"Why," answered Devon, "they know their own minds, but they don't know what we suspect. They can't be too sure of us, you see. And if so much as the rim of a head shows with you and Jim on the job — why, good-by to one of them. Furthermore, they know that they have to go slowly — because they see that you're in town with me."

This touch of flattery pleased the old fellow immensely, and so they turned in at Mrs. Purley's house. Her bar, like all the others in West London, was now crowded. Through the doorway they looked in on the thick line of drinkers and listened for a moment to the roar of voices, as the miners sang and laughed and shouted like sailors newly come ashore.

Mrs. Purley saw Devon and rushed to him from behind the bar. Perspiration streamed down her face as she elbowed through the crowd and came to the gambler.

"It's like seein' an angel to have this flash of you," said she. "Come along. I'm gunna tell you a story that'll make you swear. Who's your grandpa? Hello, Harry. You come too. I need advice!"

Mrs. Purley gathered them into her own private office and there she crashed into a chair, limply relaxing. Dragging out a large handkerchief from the pocket of her apron which, in the fashion of a male bartender, covered her to the neck, she swabbed the perspiration from her brow, then dropped her heavy hand on her desk.

"I'm beat!" said Mrs. Purley.

She shook her head and stared hopelessly on the gambler.

"You're tired out, with the rush," said Devon.

"Am I? I tell you, they can't rush me! As fast as they line up at the bar, I can knock 'em over with this white mule that they call whisky around here. It ain't the work that's laid me out!"

"What is it?" asked Devon.

"What do you think wandered into my house this afternoon?"

"I've no idea. Some rowdy with a pair of bad guns?"

"Rowdy? Guns?" shouted Mrs. Purley. "Listen, honey. I eat that kind. I eat 'em without salt like spring onions. They ain't nothin' to me. You guess again."

"You've had bad news of some sort," said the good-humored Devon.

She mopped her forehead again.

"I'll cut it short. I can't stand even thinkin' about it," said she. "Tell Methusalem to take his glass eye off of me. It gives me the shakes!"

This reference to old Harry went unnoticed, and Mrs. Purley went on with a suppressed emotion that shook her mannish form:

"There comes a ring at the door. I hollers: 'Who's the sap that's playin' a joke at my door?' Why, I never heard that doorbell rung before. Hardly ever heard so much as a rap there, the door bein' open to ask the outside in — and the inside out, unless they suit me!

"There wasn't any answer, and the bell rings again. It made me hot. I was just doin' up accounts, and figgers always make my head ache, anyway. I got up and picked a billy off of the table where I keep it lyin' handy" — here she indicated carelessly a short-handled but formidably knobby club — "and I hid it behind me in the fold of my apron. I was gunna knock that green-headed yap into the far corner of next month, but when I come to the door, what did I see?

"I'll tell you, Mr. Devon," the narrator continued, "it was hardly out of the shell, with yella hair and baby big eyes. 'Are you Mrs. Purley?' says she. I admitted I was, and took her by the hand and steered her into the house. I asked her would she have a glass of beer and a sausage, or something. She looked at me like I had said it in French. Then she told me that she never had had a drink of any liquor.

" 'Beer ain't liquor,' I told her. 'Beer is just colored water, as you might say.' She would take a glass of water, and thank you very much. You are very kind.

"She pulled out her purse, and took out a photograph — she was on the trail of a man. Did I know him? I gave that picture one look. Did I know it? Sure I did. 'Oh, how wonderful! How beautiful!' says she. 'How lucky I am that I found you!' Now, look here, you two. This is the picture she showed me. You know it, Mr. Devon?"

Mrs. Purley held out a photograph of a keen looking, handsome youth. But Devon had to shake his head.

"Try grandpa on it," said she.

Old Harry responded instantly: "That's Lucky Jack, or I'm a liar!"

"Who's Lucky Jack?" asked Devon.

"I'll tell you," said Harry. "One of his bits of luck was gettin' away from the front door of my gun, when it was open in his face. That was his luck. Who is Lucky Jack? Why — you better ask younger and faster talkin' gents to describe that rattler!"

"Lucky Jack," explained Mrs. Purley, "came out here to get amusement. Ever since then he's got it. Takes about ten men and ten horses on the road night and day to keep Jack stirred up. They used to think that the tough ones out this way were hard boiled; but after Lucky Jack came on, they sent back for more starch. The first thing he done was to meet up with a couple of bad gun-slingin' guys, and he makes them chaw the lead out of their own cartridges and spit it on the bar-room floor. Then he kicks them out into the street.

"He's a handy body, is Lucky. He's got the real bouncer style. He could get a job on the Bowery any day. He didn't need any brass knuckles to help him out, and I stood by myself and seen him fight his way through a crowd in Charlie's saloon.

"That crowd was filled with knives and guns and slungshots, but Lucky went at them with his fists. It was a pretty sight. It made me wish I was a man! He took his time, and picked them one by one. Every time he hit out he punched the button, and every time he rang the bell they went down face first. He stepped on their shoulder blades and walked on. Sometimes he gave them a straight arm punch, and sometimes he hooked, and sometimes he bobbed their heads with a long range uppercut.

"Then the kid jumps on a horse and says he'll come back to talk to them another day. He rides up the street, hops off and walks into another saloon and dumps the insides of the cash register into a saddlebag. He backed through the door, shot down the sign by clipping the ropes that held it with a couple of snap shots, and then off he goes on his horse.

"They turned West London inside out, and swarmed out four stacks of heroes to find him. While they were out huntin' for him, he came back on the inside of 'em, went into the Palace in the evenin', and there he played the piano for the crowd, and livened up the dancin' a good deal by callin' for drinks for the crowd, and always on the house! There was about forty men in the Palace that night, and the kid ran it for an hour. The bouncers didn't like the looks of the big black guns that he laid on the lid of the piano; and the rest of the boys in the crowd didn't mind the free drinks.

"So he got away with *that,* and took the best horse in the livery stable and rode away again. You begin to get an idea of what Lucky is like?"

"I understand — a little," said the gambler, who had been looking at the photograph all this time.

"I ain't gone into details," Mrs. Purley announced. "I've just throwed a few of the headlines at you, as you might say! Now that you know somethin' about him, lemme tell you about the girl —"

"Might be his sweetheart, pore little thing?" asked old Harry.

"Don't start droolin' about her," Mrs. Purley said fiercely. "*I've* had an achin' heart ever since the little fool showed up here. Now don't you rub it in like an old fool! She ain't his sweetheart. She's worse! She's his sister!"

Mrs. Purley threw up her hand with a groan.

"His sister!" said old Harry, aghast.

"Shut up!" Mrs. Purley snapped. "You give me a turn, the way you talk. She's his sister. She's come all the way out from the East to see him. Because he hasn't written very many letters, and the letters he's sent are pretty shabby and short. And she's afraid that poor, darlin' William is in bad health, bein' always awful nervous, if you know what I mean! Nervous trigger fingers! It made me sick to hear her talk. And I had to sit there and grin like an ape with its head cut off! But she went on to tell me that all of their troubles were over. Because poor dear old grandpa had died and left about a million to be split two ways between her and Bill."

"His name ain't Jack?" asked Harry.

"My Gawd!" said Mrs. Purley. "Of course it ain't! He's William Maynard, with a couple of more initials in between. And his sister is Prue, the sweet little fool. But their troubles are over, she says, and she's come out here herself to break the bad news to poor dear Willie, and make the shock a little less, him always bein' frightful partial to the old goat that just passed out, as it seems.

" 'And how wonderfully lucky,' says she, 'that I've found you, because you know where I can find him!'

" 'Him?' says I. 'I don't know nothin' about him!'

" 'But you told me that you knew him very well when I showed you his photograph,' says she.

"I chawed my lip and thought a minute, and then I said that of course I knew him, but I didn't know where I could put my hand on him, but I *would* find out right away.

"Then I sat down and stewed. Who was there in this ornery town that I could trust a secret like that to? Then I seen you across the bar, and I knew you were the meat for that job. And you can have it, Mr. Devon. You go get Lucky Jack and bring him in tame and brushed up, and let this here child put a rope on him and lead him off home! Thank God, I can wash my hands of her soon!"

XIII. SLUGGER LEWIS

"How shall *I* find him?" asked Devon, a little annoyed. "I don't know anything about the fellow."

"You can ask, can't you?" snapped Mrs. Purley. "Or do I have to close up my bar and go all by myself? Ain't there a man West London that will play a decent part by a poor girl like that? But wait a minute! I'm gunna bring her in here to see you. Then you can back out if you dare!"

"Just a moment!" urged Devon. "There's nothing gained by that. There's no necessity at all, Mrs. Purley. As a matter of fact, I'll start out to —"

"You stand where you are," commanded she.

She jerked open an inner door.

"Hey, Miss Maynard!"

"Yes, Mrs. Purley."

"If you've rested enough for a minute, will you come out here and get some news?"

"*Oh*, yes!"

And Prue Maynard came to the doorway

with parted lips and shining eyes of eagerness. A faint shade of disappointment appeared in her face when she saw only old Harry and Devon.

"Oh, it ain't your brother, honey," said Mrs. Purley, "but it's the next thing to him."

She led the girl in with an arm around her. "This is Mr. Devon, your brother's partner."

Devon blinked with the shock.

"Oh," said Prue Maynard. "I didn't know Willie was in business! I thought he was only resting, poor dear. What is his business, Mr. Devon?"

Walt was dumb.

"Minin', mostly," the cheerful Mrs. Purley volunteered. "And then they do other things. They pack in a lot of stuff to the other mines. You're doin' pretty well, ain't you, Mr. Devon?"

"Yes," he said faintly.

"But can Willie stand such hard work?" asked the girl.

"Aw, it ain't such hard work," said Mrs. Purley. "You take it from me, honey, most of this hard work that men talk about ain't hard at all. They gotta talk about somethin'. They come back home and find their wife with her face raw from standin' over the stove, and her back achin' from scrubbin' floors, and her head ringing with the yappin' of the kids, and a man has gotta have somethin' to talk about. So he tells how hard he's been at it under the sun — the loafers! They lead the easy life! Eight hours with a hammer — what's that compared to eighteen with a house on your hands? How do they size up together?"

The girl looked rather blankly at Mrs. Purley, and then, seeing the sour smile of that veteran, she smiled faintly in return.

"Dear Willie is well?"

"He is," said Devon. "The last I heard of him —"

"The last you heard of him!" cried the girl. "Has it been very long?"

"He's close by — out of town," said Mrs. Purley. "Devon will fetch him in here in no time!"

"I'll go with you, of course!" Prue offered.

"You'll set still and rest your poor little feet," said Mrs. Purley. "Let Devon bring him in. He'll be rampin' when he hears that you're here, honey. You set here quiet!" She turned on Devon. "You better start for your partner."

She hustled Devon to the door and whispered in his ear.

"Be a good sport, old-timer. You gotta find him. Out there at the bar you'll find Slugger Lewis. They say he knows a good deal about Lucky Jack. Find the Slugger and ask him."

"Will he tell me, d'you think?"

"I dunno. I hope so. Make up some kind of a lie. The Slugger has had a few shots. Maybe his tongue is loosened up a little."

Devon went into the bar with Harry at his heels, and as they entered a blast of raw voices thundered the chorus of a biscuit, and that the singers intended to break that biscuit open and get at the filling, which was soft and rich!

One or two inquiries directed Devon to the Slugger.

He was a great man, with flannel sleeves rolled up over hairy forearms to his elbows, and he regarded the world from beneath habitually bent brows.

"You're Lewis?"

"I'm Slugger Lewis, if anybody asks you. Whatcha want?"

"I want to find Lucky Jack. Can you give me a tip, Slugger?"

The Slugger stared at him with profound disgust.

"It's likely, ain't it?"

"I don't know."

"Who steered you my way on this, stranger?"

Devon paused and looked earnestly at the big fellow.

"Lewis," he said, "you don't know me, and therefore I can't ask you to take my word for

98

it. I don't mean harm to Lucky Jack. I'm bringing him news that he'll consider important. Can you believe that?"

"Half an ounce of lead in the right place always is important news," the Slugger sneered. "And there's a price for it, too!"

Said Devon: "If you can show us the way, Slugger, you can ride behind us. I'm here with old Harry, my friend. He goes with me. If you stay behind you have us pretty well under your thumb. And if you steer us to Lucky Jack, he's not helpless, so far as that goes!"

The Slugger scowled more blackly than ever.

"It's a holiday," he declared.

"Can you squeeze the work into ten dollars?" said Devon.

The Slugger's brow cleared considerably.

"Why," he said, "that's reasonable talk, after all. Why not?" He stood up. "I'll have my hoss around here in a jiffy. You two be ready?"

Ready they were, as fast as they could bring their horses from the livery stable, and they rode off with the Slugger behind them, down the street of West London, and out into the broken timber lands beyond.

XIV. A BULLET BETWEEN THE EYES

The way, after the nature of forest roads, had suddenly narrowed to a bridle path, winding through the heavy timber. In this manner Devon and old Harry were a slight distance in the lead, with Slugger winding behind them.

Said old Harry: "Are you happy, Walt?"

"I'm not," was the reply.

"There's a kind of funny thing, now you speak about it," Harry commented. "Because here you are, out turnin' yourself into the partner of a yegg and bad gunman, and all for the sake of a mighty pretty girl, and yet you don't like it!"

"Harry," said Devon, "you old hypocrite, you don't like this business any better than I do!"

"Why, when you come right down to it," the old man rejoined, "I dunno that I do."

"You wouldn't have let yourself to be herded into this job?"

"Not while I had my own two feet to walk on, I wouldn't," said Harry.

"Will you tell me why?"

"It's the lady."

"The lady? Harry, Harry! The poor girl is hardly more than a child."

"A child?" Harry said with a philosophical air. "Well, I dunno that I ever seen a woman that was clean growed up. Mostly they're sort of young, in one way or another, and they manage to make a gent feel that he's their older brother. But —"

He paused, and his eyes wandered off through the branches of the trees above them.

"But what?" asked Devon. "What's wrong with her, Harry? Have you got it in for that poor girl?"

"Well, why should I?"

"I don't know, I'm sure," Devon answered sharply. "The poor youngster is to be pitied, of course."

"Why, yes," said Harry. "Of course she's to be pitied."

"She is," Devon insisted. "Out here in this wild country!"

"Kind of wonderful," said Harry, "how she ever got here, ain't it? I mean a child of fourteen or fifteen?"

Devon looked at the old man compassionately.

"She's twenty, I should say."

"Is she, now!" exclaimed Harry. "Well,

well, by the way she talked and looked, and by the way that she opened her eyes, maybe I was fooled. I wouldn't of said that she was more than fourteen."

Devon laughed.

"It's the effect of a sheltered life on a very gentle and refined nature."

"Maybe she ain't been exposed to the air, none," said Harry.

"What do you mean by that?"

"Why, simply that you take most pretty girls, and they soon got men around them, like ants around honey, and if any girl is gunna learn anythin' about men, I'd say that the pretty girl is gunna learn the quickest of all. But it's easy to be seen that she don't know nothin'!"

"The protected life," Devon remarked complacently. "I don't think I've ever seen a more beautiful creature in my life, Harry!"

"You don't mean it, Walt! Well, sir, men must have changed since I was young. Because when I was young, men was so wild and crazy that you couldn't build walls that would keep men from climbin' them in order to have the pleasure of makin' fools o' themselves about a pretty girl! But I guess men have got somethin' else to do now, and they don't bother so much about the beautiful girls."

"I don't think men change their nature very much, Harry."

"You don't think so, Walt? Now, that's surprisin', because in that case I'd say that this here mighty pretty girl would sure of had a chance at the age of twenty to know all about what fools men are."

"H-m," mused Devon. "And would you?"

"Of course I would. But she don't. That's plain."

"Well, why are you so sure?"

"Because of her ways, Walt. You take the way that she went up to you and opened her eyes at you. It made me sort of dizzy to look at her."

"Did it?" chuckled Devon.

"Yes. And the way you looked, I thought that maybe you were a mite dizzy yourself, Walt. Have a caution."

Devon flushed a trifle.

"What do you mean?"

"A man or a woman twenty years old," Harry replied, "ain't a child any longer. I would put my pelts on that, Walt! She's growed up, or she never would of got this far by herself."

"Why beat around the bush?" Devon inquired sharply. "You consider she is — dangerous — or what?"

"Yes," was the answer. "Dangerous to you,

Walt, and dangerous to me, because where you drop, I aim to drop over you!"

Harry spoke with such simplicity that Devon stared at him. There was no doubting the old man's sincerity.

"Come, come," said Devon. "As a matter of fact, there's no duplicity in her."

"I dunno," said Harry. "I ain't no student except of things the way that I've found 'em. But I recollect once bein' in trouble in San Antone, and I had to go to see a lawyer, and that gent was a settin' in a swivel chair, and while he talked to me, he turned this way, and then he turned that. And he reminded me of a weather vane that was turnin' and changin' in the wind."

"But what has that to do with today, Harry?"

"Nothin', except that ever since we left the town I been twistin' and turnin' in my saddle, and tryin' to keep an eye on the gent that's ridin' behind."

"Hello! You don't trust him, either?"

"After you seen a painter sharpenin' its claws on a tree and leavin' the bark furrowed and the white wood showin' through, would you say that that was a harmless footed beast?"

"How have you seen the claws of Slugger Lewis?" asked Devon.

"In his eyes, Walt," said the trapper. "In

his eyes, old son, where I've seen the claws of many another showin'!"

The concern of Devon grew greater and greater.

"Harry," he said, "you think we're riding into a trap?"

"Now, I wouldn't say that."

"You wouldn't?"

"No. I'd say we was already there!"

Devon stared.

"In what way?"

"Listen!" ordered the old man.

And from behind them Devon grew aware of the whistling of Slugger Lewis.

"The fellow is only whistling," said he.

"Look here," said Harry. "Does he know you?"

"I don't suppose he does."

"Mightn't he be wrong about you?"

"In what way?"

"You say that you mean no wrong to Lucky Jack."

"I've told him that."

"If you wanted the price on Lucky's head, mightn't you say the same thing?"

Devon drew a quick breath.

"Man, man," he remonstrated, "to listen to you, one would soon learn to distrust everything in nature."

"Maybe," said Harry frankly, "because in

the woods you learn to take everythin' by what it can do. You trust them animals not to poison you that ain't got poison glands, and you trust them not to claw you that ain't got the claws. And them that live on nuts you trust them not to eat you. But most of the men you meet on the hills and in the woods has claws and poison, and they eat raw meat!"

He held up one hand a little.

And from behind Devon heard the whistling of their guide turn into two quick, sharp blasts.

"Back into the trees, Walt!" snapped the old man, and suited his action to the words by swinging his jinny straight into the brush beside the trail.

Devon swung his own mount to the other side of the road, and as he did so a rifle bullet neatly divided the space between his own head and that of the trapper.

He whirled in the saddle and saw Slugger Lewis driving straight to the side of the woods, and at that flying shadow of treachery he tried a snap shot.

A long-drawn, wolfish yell of rage and pain answered him, and from before him a blast of rifles crashed upon his ears, and the sharp singing of the balls.

The bay gelding coughed and fell upon its knees, then toppled to its side and lay

106

motionless, dead.

Devon himself was thrown against the knobby roots of a tree, gathered like knees above the soil, but he retained his grip upon his gun, as a trained rider keeps his hold upon the reins. More than half dazed, sick with the shock of the fall he had received, nevertheless he was aware of three men running among the trees toward him.

Then a rifle rang out across the way, and one of those shadows bounded like a wounded cat into the air, clutching at his breast, cast out his arms and fell face downward.

Devon crawled to his knees. Two of those ominously racing shadows remained, and he fired point-blank at one of them; the man swerved to the side with a curse, and from a thick bit of brush came a burst of fire. Six rapid revolver shots clipped the air about Devon, or sank with a spat into the wood of the tree which partially sheltered him.

Then the fighting instinct which was in his blood mastered his brain, and made him leap to his feet and rush forward with his gun ready. Afterward he could remember thinking that there still were four bullets for the two men. Two apiece, and if they failed, he had his strong and well-trained hands.

Straight through the screen of brush he charged. A shadow swerved away before him, and he fired at it, once and again. A snarl of pain and rage answered him. Then only the crackling of twigs underfoot in the distance. To his left there was another sound of scampering, and still a third to his rear.

Devon turned in time to see old Harry come charging, gasping for breath and uncertain with rage. Crashing through the brush, the veteran reached his side.

The language of the old man was by no means complimentary.

"You young jackass!" said Harry. "Get down behind that tree. There ain't an emptier head in the whole range than you're packin' on your shoulders!"

"They're gone," Devon gasped.

For answer Harry caught him by the shoulder. Devon tripped. They both came crashing to a bed of pine needles.

"Don't think — don't breathe!" said Harry.

For a long moment they remained thus. But out of the forest not a sound reached their ears. Then, from the distance, and far to their left, they heard two quick blasts of whistling.

"Maybe," said Harry, "you was right after all!"

"Yes, yes, they're gone, Harry. Let's go after them as fast as we can."

Harry glared without a word.

"Leave 'em be," said he. "Follerin' in the

woods is worse than runnin' on the open plains. But come along with me, and we'll see how these folks walk with bullets sunk between their eyes."

He led the way at once to a narrow gap between two trees, and there they found a man lying face downward, unmoving, both his hands deeply buried in the leaves, his rifle beside him.

They turned him on his back. As the old frontiersman had said, a bullet had struck home squarely between the eyes.

XV. ONE WAY TO PREVENT HANGING

It was dreadful beyond words to Devon to see the body at his feet. In his adventures he had seen death a hundred times, but the peace of the woods hardly had been broken the moment before, and now there was one dead in the forest.

The thoughts of Devon still clung, as it were, to the picture of the girl which had been floating in a golden haze through his mind.

"He's dead," Devon said slowly. "Poor devil!"

"Poor? Why, he might be rich, now, compared with us," Harry responded. "Maybe his ghost is hangin' up there on the branch of the tree and kind of laughin' at us, to think that he's rid of the pack that he's had to carry around with him ever since the day that he was born! But anyways, we'll have a look at him. You know this man, Walt?"

Devon stared closely at the faintly smiling face of death. He was young, this man of the forest, with a short mustache just beginning on the upper lip, and sunburned at the tips.

There was nothing distinctive about him. He was of medium height, middle weight, and young — about twenty-five.

And, perhaps because of the beauty of the tall trees around them, and the rich gold which the westering sun let fall among the trunks, it seemed to Devon that never before had he had such a picture of the stamping out of life, the crushing of youth, the annihilation of that which cannot be destroyed.

"This here back trail," said Harry, "ain't apt to bring us to nothin' more than trouble, and so we'll see what sign are printed right on the gent himself!"

Forthwith he searched every pocket, and laid the spoil upon the ground.

The heap contained, finally, a big pocket knife with a single huge blade that worked on a spring, and unfolded, was quite large enough to have served for the skinning of a deer. There was a wallet with one dollar in it, and a much worn letter from some ignorant girl, filled with misspelled terms of worship. It had not even the name of the man at the beginning. It was only to "My deerest!"

There was a ball of strong twine among the pockets, and a little kit filled with needles, thread, buttons, and such odds and ends as men who live by themselves find necessary in the woods or on the range. They found matches, and plug tobacco wrapped in a piece of chamois.

"Why, look here," said the old trapper, "if this ain't Piper Heidsick, I'm a liar! I ain't seen a piece of that for the longest half of a year, or I'm a liar."

Straightaway his much enfeebled teeth were fixed in a corner of the cut, and with much wagging of the head and jerking of the hand, he worked off an enormous mouthful.

"It's prime," he averred, when he finally had stowed this great morsel in the center of his cheek. "I never tasted better tobacco in my life. Look at this gent again, Walt, because his tobacco sure don't taste like murder!"

Devon, much amused by this viewpoint, regarded the dead man once more, and it seemed to him, in fact, that he perceived a greater refinement in the features.

But he made no comment. It was beginning to appear to Devon that the old trapper knew vastly more than he about life, at least from certain aspects. He remained resolutely silent.

"Now, you look at his head," said Harry. "What would you say about this gent, Walt?"

"I'd say that he was once a better man than he is today, Harry."

"Because he's dead?"

"Because he tried murder."

"Murder with a gang? Mostly that's pretty

bad. But no self-respectin' man is very bad at heart, until more time has passed over his head than ever passed over the head of this here poor boy!" said the veteran.

"What was he, then?"

"A good, honest enough boy, well raised, and come of a farm, I'd say. He ain't been long in the wild," added Harry, "and he never learned murder proper."

"Will you tell me how you know all of these things?"

"I don't know any of 'em. I only guess. But he run wild through the trees at us, not sneakin' from tree to tree like the rest, and that's the sign of one that ain't been long a man hunter."

"I suppose it is," Devon nodded.

"He ain't been long in the wild, because look at the tears and the breaches in his clothes, and never no sewin' done and not patchin', though somebody had told him to fix himself up with this patchin' kit."

"Ah, I wouldn't have thought of that!"

"Maybe you wouldn't, Walt, because you've spent a lot of your time lookin' at books, and you can't read nacher and men and work much at books. They're wrote in different kinds of print!"

"But you say that he's the son of some decent farmer, Harry. Will you tell me how you know that?"

"Look at the callus over the middle of the palm of his right hand. They ain't nothin' but the butt end of a pitchfork that will make that, Walt. And look at the whiteness of his teeth! Well, son, the first thing that a boy that goes wild forgets is to take care of his teeth. The brushin' of them don't seem so important when his ma ain't gunna raise Cain with him for neglectin' of 'em! But this boy, he hadn't had time to ferget! He hadn't hardly turned sour, this here boy, when he run into a bullet that flattened him, Walt. And that's a sad thing, now you come to think about it."

"You saved him from hanging," suggested Devon.

"Ahah," said Harry, "who wants to be the executioner? Not me, old son, and not you, I'd reckon, either?"

"What shall we do with him, Harry?"

"Take him straight to the sheriff."

"What!"

"Why not?"

"Why run yourself into jail, Harry?"

"It ain't runnin' yourself into jail. We gotta lot of bad features about this here county, but we got one good one, thank God, and that's a sheriff that no State in the Union can lay over, Walt. Go fetch the jinny, like a good boy, and we'll load what's left of this here onto her back!"

So Devon, very meek and mild, now, did as he was directed, and onto the back of the jinny the body of the dead man was lifted, and firmly tied there with lengths of his own twine.

So they started out from the woods on the back trail. They found that the sun was down; the woods were turning black, and within the bluffs of Timbal Gulch the waters ran rosy gold, patched with royal purple that fell from the heights.

It was a time of peace. From the heart of the valley the lights shone white at the mouths of the mines; up the sharp slopes came the cheerful, peaceful voices of the miners, climbing back to the town at the end of their shifts of labor; and out of distant West London, as out of a dream, laughter and sweet, faint singing.

XVI. A MYSTERIOUS DISAPPEARANCE

When they reached the house of Sheriff Naxon with their grim burden, they found that the front door was open, and down the gravel path to the garden gate traveled a dim shaft of lamplight. Up this they walked, and old Harry kept the laden jinny at the side of the house, while the gambler entered to find the sheriff.

Devon expected an interior as slovenly as the outside of the place, and the garden, in keeping, in fact, with the person of the sheriff himself. He was amazed to look through the front screen door into the neatest of parlors. And in answer to his knock a dignified woman of middle age came to the door and smiled pleasantly at him. She had a quiet eye, and perfect peace was in her face.

Walt asked for the sheriff, and she stepped back to make him welcome. Presently he was standing on a round center rug made of rags, arranged in a circular pattern and gayly spotted with bright colors. The red and blue of flannel shirts, he thought, could be identified in that arrangement.

While he waited, Devon mentally listed the furniture, from the little upright piano in the corner, to the table opposite, with its books stacked carefully between two bookends. There was a Bible, a "Faerie Queene" in a binding of flowered cloth, a history of the county, and a thick-shouldered Shakespeare. These were the treasures chosen to show the face of culture in the house.

There was a little bowl of desert flowers beside the books, and a large picture album, bound in wood and iron, with a burned design in the wood.

From the dining room a spicy fragrance of good cooking passed through the house and flavored even the air of the parlor.

"Well, sir," Devon heard the sheriff drawling, "why'd you leave him in there to stand around? Alf, you go fetch him in, will you?"

There was a subdued protest from the lady of the house, and then bare feet spattered on the hall floor; at the door appeared a freckled face, and a broad grin.

"Pa wants you to come into the dining room."

"I'd rather see the sheriff here, for one minute."

"That ain't any good, what you want. Pa says he'll have you there, so you'd better come there."

At this Devon followed him into a dining room as neatly built and as trim as a cabin on a ship. The wife was rising, a little flushed by the presence of a stranger. The sheriff waved a hand at an extra chair.

"Set down, partner," said he. "Set down and tell me what I can do for you. But first, have a bite of something."

"I'm not hungry, thank you."

"You got room for a wedge of apple pie, though."

"No."

"Come, come. Dog-gone me if he ain't shy. Mary, he's shy. Go and put him to home with a piece of that pie, will you? And give him a slosh of that there coffee, with plenty of cream in it, will you?"

"Of course, I will," said she.

"Sheriff, what I've come to talk to you about —"

"No matter what you've come about, you can eat a bite first. That's it, Mary. I wished you'd cut pie for *me* on that kind of a plan. Set down, Devon. How's your pa, anyway?"

His wife gasped.

"What's the matter?" asked the sheriff.

"Don't you know, dear? Poor Mr. Devon —"

"Poor Mr. Devon? I wouldn't call a man poor that has a thousand acres."

"That's not what I mean."

"Why don't you speak out and tell me, then? The trouble with a woman is that she's always talkin' around a corner. The shortest line between two points ain't good enough for her!"

"She means that my father is dead," said Devon.

"Dead? Hold on! Jack Devon dead? Why, now that I come to think of it, so he is. Jack Devon is dead! There's a loss to the county and to the whole damn range."

"You mustn't swear so," the wife protested.

" 'Damn' ain't swearin'," said the sheriff. "It's only a kind of way of underlinin' things while talkin'. I'd as soon read a book without no punctuation in it, as to listen to a gent talk without damnin'. Young feller, you ain't set down, yet. Don't that pie look good to you?"

"Old Harry is outside with me," Devon answered, "and of course I can't —"

"You mean Jack Devon's Harry?"

"Yes."

"Why didn't he come in, then? Does he have to wait and get a special invite? Dog-gone me if ever I heard of anything half as foolish as that! Go holler to Harry to come in, Alf!"

The boy was out of his chair in a flash. But Devon stopped him.

"There's another man with him," he said,

looking straight at the sheriff for instructions.

"If they's a whole regiment outside, of course we can't get 'em all in here! No matter how I'd like to! Come along with me, Devon, will you? You stay here where you belong, Alf, and if I catch you sneakin' out of doors this time of night, I'll take your hide off and tan it for you!"

Mrs. Naxon, with an anxious look at her husband, said nothing at all, but put her arm over the shoulders of her boy and held him close; and suddenly Devon understood that expression of refinement in her face, that dignity in her bearing, because she was forced continually to endure the chance of life and death when her husband left his house on duty.

Sheriff Lew Naxon went out with Devon to the front porch.

There he said simply: "Whose job is this?"

"My job, and Harry's."

"Well," said the sheriff, "we'll have a look. You've got somebody that may need jail, eh?"

"Whatever he needs, he doesn't need jail," Devon replied curtly, and led the way down the steps and around the corner of the house.

They found old Harry there, and the motionless form strapped on the back of the jinny. Naxon regarded the body with attention. Then he took from his pocket a small square box and flicked open a shutter; a strong ray of light issued, and this the sheriff played upon the dead face of the other man.

"Who did this?" said Naxon.

"Me," said Harry.

"We did it together," said Devon.

"I stopped him," insisted Harry.

"Aye, aye," nodded Naxon. "I can see your handiwork in this here. What made you slap this boy in the face?"

"Because he and about three more jumped us in the woods."

"What come of the other three? Did you just bring in this one for a sample?"

"The other three got off. A couple of them were nicked by Walt, here. The third one was a gent by name of Slugger Lewis."

"I remember to of seen that one."

"What kind is he?"

"Never was bridle broke, to my knowin'," said the sheriff.

"Who did he work for?"

"The devil, as the minister says!"

"Is that all?"

"He does odd jobs for Les Burchard, from time to time."

"Does that finish him?"

"It about does."

"Do you know this boy?"

"By name of Jack Watts, he went."

"What was his line?"

121

"Nothin' much. Used to keep books for Burchard, for a while."

"That settles it," said Devon with decision. "I had enough cause to suspect Burchard before, but now it's certain that he wants to murder me, Harry!"

"You can't tell a hawk from a buzzard, when they're far enough off. Don't be too sure of Burchard until he takes a shot at you himself," said Harry.

"You think Burchard did this?" asked the sheriff in his gentle voice.

"I do."

"Well, well! Burchard? I'm surprised."

And in spite of his mildness it was fairly clear that he meant it.

Said Harry: "It looks like they want us. They want Walt more than me or Jim."

"Why should they want any of you?"

"They want the land, and Walt don't much want to sell it."

"Why should they want it?"

"To run cows on it, and that's a good enough reason to think that they got somethin' else in their heads."

"Well, maybe it is."

"What's gunna come of this, Sheriff?"

"Of young Jack Watts bein' killed like this?"

"Yes. We gotta have jail for it?"

"No. I turn you loose, and you come in

122

if I send for you, Harry."

"That's right. I'll do that. And Walt, here?"

"He'll come with you, when you come, I take it."

"Where'll we cart the body?"

"We'll put it down here and send for the coroner."

"I'd like to know who his friends are!"

"So's you can draw on 'em? Leave that be, Harry. You ain't shootin' squirrels now!"

Then briefly Devon told the story of what had happened to him at the Purley boarding house, and how he had gone on the trail.

"I'll step over with you and see the girl," said Naxon.

"It's no good," said Devon. "She's as innocent as the day's long."

"Sure she is," agreed the sheriff. "But I'd sure like to talk to her, anyway."

They left Jack Watts lying on the ground, because, as Naxon said, he wouldn't be apt to wander far. Then they went to the house of Mrs. Purley, and at their first inquiry they learned that beautiful Miss Maynard had gone they knew not where!

XVII. DEVON SEEKS EXCITEMENT

Mrs. Purley herself was called into the room. And when she saw the sheriff, she frowned.

"What you got up your sleeve, Naxon?" she asked him. "What're you gunna slam *me* for?"

"I ain't here to rope you in, ma'am," said the sheriff.

"That's a good thing. Every time I see you come around, it brings up into my mind a long picture of all the phony drinks that have been passed across this bar! But you know how it is, Sheriff. I'm no worse than the rest. And a woman has gotta live, the same as a man!"

The sheriff smiled broadly at her.

"A man that could get a good hoss cheap would be a fool to pay high, wouldn't he? And I can get plenty of good trouble in this here town cheap enough without botherin' you, Mrs. Purley. I've come to ask you where Miss Maynard is."

"I'm clean out of my wits about that girl," said Mrs. Purley. "She stepped out for a walk. She'll be back pretty soon, though. I gotta thank God there's a decent streak in Western men. She'll be steppin' back pretty soon. It's supper time, about!"

"You heard anything more about her?" asked the sheriff.

"About her? About her?" Mrs. Purley repeated, her voice rising. "What you mean, Naxon? What about her?"

"Why nothin' very much, except that she tried to run young Devon here under a steam roller."

"Her? Him?" gasped Mrs. Purley. "I don't believe it! If she ain't straight, there ain't any straightness in the world! God love my heart! *She* tried to run him under? My God, Sheriff, you don't mean murder?"

They left Mrs. Purley in the greatest distress of body and mind and went out into the town.

"Walkin' in the dark is a good way to think," declared the sheriff. "We'll just stroll along and try to talk it out. You take in a lighted room, your eye is always seein' something and pullin' your mind after it. Ain't that right?"

So they went slowly along the street and twisting through the alleys and the bypaths, talking in low voices. Now and again they paused while some point of importance was elaborated, and in those pauses the noise of the town rumbled in the distance, or broke

125

like a wave close at hand in shrill, tingling voices. Said the sheriff at one point:

"How you like the bawlin' of my bull calf, Harry?"

"What calf, Lew?"

"This here town of West London?"

"I never heard it called a bull calf before."

"Didn't you? But it is! Ain't a bull calf always pawin' the ground and aimin' at a fight? Ain't a bull calf always roarin' itself hoarse and raising a dust? Pettin' and bran mash ain't what makes a bull calf feel good, but a slug on the top of its head with a fence rail is all that it pays any attention to. This here is a bull calf, and what it needs is a ring fitted into its nose. But right up to now I ain't found the way of gettin' it down. Maybe I'll find that way later on — maybe later on," mused the sheriff.

As they walked and chatted, he learned the details of all that Harry and young Devon knew.

"Burchard!" said Harry. "It's that fat pig!"

"Maybe it is," agreed the sheriff, "because before this pigs has turned wild and taken to meat eatin'. But where does Tucker Vincent come into this?"

"I dunno," said Harry. "I don't manage to figger this out at all. There's Charlie Way, sure as sin mixed up in this here. And where

Charlie Way is, you can bet that Tucker Vincent has got his thin nose poked. I dunno how to work it out, unless Vincent and Burchard are both workin' together to try to get the land away from you, Devon! We gotta get somebody onto the other side of the fence!"

They reached the sheriff's house.

"We'll go see if Jack Watts is sleepin' sound," said the sheriff. They went around the corner of the house, and he added, without the slightest surprise or excitement: "There ain't any Jack Watts. He's got up and walked away."

"Aye, that's likely," said old Harry. "Him with the air let into his brains. It's likely that he's got up and walked away!"

"How do you know?" asked the sheriff. "Ain't it likely that your bullet grazed him and went off his head?"

"And grazed out agin through the back of his head? Is that what you mean, Lew?"

"The point is," said the sheriff, "there ain't any dead body. And unless you got one of those corpuses, there ain't any trial for murder."

Old Harry chuckled.

"This here law," said he, "is like a balky team of mules. Sometimes it lets the wagon roll back and break your neck. Sometimes it snakes you right over the top of the hill. But

127

who would of taken Jack Watts away?"

"Them that hired him," said the grim sheriff, "for fear lest somebody should read Jack's mind. Oh, but there'd be a pile of difference between Jack dead and Jack livin'. What a lot of interestin' talk Jack could of made for us all!"

The others agreed.

"And if," the sheriff continued, "I could get ahold of one of 'em, wouldn't it be a treat to hear what he'd have to say?"

"How would you persuade him to talk?" Devon asked curiously.

"I'd turn him over to old Harry, here, to guard. That is, if the worst come to the worst. Maybe Harry could persuade him. Harry is one of the most persuadin' men in the world, ain't you, Harry?"

The old man laughed deeply in answer, and Devon could tell that there was much more behind this comment than he understood.

They agreed to separate for that night. The sheriff stood near his house; Devon and old Harry returned to Mrs. Purley's place. Mrs. Purley herself met them, for she was striding up and down in front of her house. She was plainly half distraught, and she caught the arm of Devon as he came up.

"If," said she, "that bit of a child or a girl meant harm to you, Devon, what would of put the idea into her head?"

"Money," Devon replied bitterly. "For money they can hire the best man and the best woman in the world, it appears. I thought it was different here in the West, but apparently not!"

"East and West, they're all alike," Mrs. Purley said with great savagery. "But her! Her and the eyes of her! Oh, God, Devon, when I seen her, all at once there come an ache in me, and a sort of homesickness that never was caused by house or folks that ever I knew, but it was the yearnin' and the miserable longin', Devon, to of had a child. I never had none. I been too busy takin' care of a fool of a husband, and his fool business after him. But when I seen her, the blue of her eyes was more to me than the blue of the ocean is to a sailor. Now you come tellin' me that she's a fake. But she ain't a fake, I tell you. But murder," vociferated Mrs. Purley, whose emotion actually made her voice shake. *Murder!*"

And she ended with a groan.

"Hello, Jerry?" she called to a man who ambled past, his blue flannel shirt sleeves rolled up to the elbows.

"Hello, Mrs. Purley. Come in and have a drink with me, will you?"

"Go on and drink by yourself," said Mrs.

Purley. "I ain't drinkin' this night. Hey, Sheriff, come here."

She followed Jerry with her eyes.

"He's a bold one for you. He wants to marry me — and the boardin' house. That would be kind of him, Sheriff, wouldn't it? But I'll see him dead, first. And yet he ain't a bad sort at all! Kind of fresh, maybe. Is that right, Sheriff?"

"Kind of fresh with his tongue?"

"He'd blarney a brass image of an angel," Mrs. Purley responded, with a rather self-conscious giggle.

"He's done some blarneyin', too," said the sheriff, "with a mighty sight louder thing than a tongue."

"And how d'you mean by that?"

"With a six-shooter, ma'am, is how I mean!"

"Gun fightin', is he?" Mrs. Purley demanded fiercely. "I'd teach 'em something, if there was to be a gun pulled out in my bar. I'd make two of 'em eat their guns at the same time! I'd teach 'em manners, I would! Good night, boys. But — if you hear anything," said she, coming hastily back to Devon and taking his arm in a way that was half confidential and half appealing, "you'll let me know right off, like a good man?"

They promised her, and she went slowly

off into the house, with her head bent in worry and grief.

"She'll be a married woman agin inside of six months," said old Harry.

"How can you tell?" asked Devon.

"By the good sense that God give me, I can tell. Did you hear how she spoke to that Jerry? Well, that's the kind of man that'll marry for an easy place. That's Jerry Noonan, and he's lived long enough, wild enough, to make him willin' to settle down, I'd say. And he's the man that would master her. Even her!"

"I don't think there's a man alive who could master her, Harry."

"Her? A thousand, and ten thousand besides. There never was a woman on earth but there was ten thousand men born her masters! And there's Jerry Noonan, like a wild bull — oh, he'd master her, fast enough, the devil!"

"Is he a famous fighter?"

"He ain't famous. That's the smartness of him. He never does no talkin'. And what's the difference if a few gents are strung out along your trail, so long as you don't talk about it? It ain't gossip, and it ain't newspapers that keeps news so fresh, but it's the fool talk that falls off of the tongue of them that had ought to be still about themselves! Good night, Walt. I'm gunna go up and turn in. I'm a mite fagged, and they's a whole day tomorrow!"

They shook hands to conclude their strange experiences of this day of days, and then Harry disappeared, while Devon went into the bar to look for excitement of a new kind.

XVIII. THE HIGH SIGN

He gambled for a living; he also gambled for pleasure, and it was for sheer diversion rather than for anything else that Walter Devon was looking now.

No one had far to look for a card game in this town. He needed merely to step into the bar and run his keen eyes over the faces of the men there in order to pick out possible contestants. They would be more numerous in such places as the Palace, but he could find them here also.

One he recognized from another game which he had watched — a very rich cattleman; there was a hardheaded investor in the mines who was down instantly for another chair; and a shrewd, professional gambler from Canada made a fourth. The fifth they would get on without, or else try to find a man on the way.

Devon stepped up to these men one after another, and they accepted the invitation very gladly; then, through the weaving and changing forms of the crowd, as he marshaled his troop toward the quiet of the card rooms, he saw a face convulse, a blue-barreled Colt flash in the air.

Ordinarily he took no part in brawls — he was no seeker after fighting for its own sake — but the flash of this gun was so close to him, and the face of the wielder was so hideous with the murder that was in his brain, that Devon grappled with him suddenly and dragged down the struggling gun arm of the other.

The man fought like a demon to finish the work he had started. He tried to tip up the muzzle of his Colt and free himself with a bullet; and the crowd about them spilled suddenly back, all except him behind whose back the gun had been drawn. He, spinning about on his heel, said quietly:

"You want me, Runt, do you?"

And instantly his fist shot over the shoulder of Devon and landed like a club of iron on the face of the gunman. The latter became a limp weight in the arms of Devon, who let him slip to the floor. The same hand which had smitten the gun fighter now gripped his arm with impressive force, and Devon looked down into an ugly face with a wide jaw and glittering small eyes.

"Thanks, partner," said the other. "I'm Jerry Noonan. I'll square this with you some

134

day if I go bust on it. Leave this here sneak to me!"

Devon nodded, picked up his party, and in five minutes was cutting for the deal on green felt. It was an excellent game. For the first hour Devon lost gradually; by the end of that hour he knew the others. The rancher had a certain ability in palming; the gambler ran up a deck with one crimp in it; and the mining investor worked with a tiny morsel of pink dye, which he applied with the sharpened tip of a forefinger nail.

As soon as he knew their games, Walt matched them with his own illegal skill, with a quiet contentment. It was the sort of contest he enjoyed — wits against wits, cunning against cunning. As for the fleecing of the mere greenhorn and innocent, it was a pastime in which he never indulged.

In another half hour the Canadian gambler suddenly began to bet heavily, lost fifteen hundred dollars in two pots, and pushed back his chair.

"There's my limit," he said. "You don't mind me backing out after I've fattened the game, I suppose? Two of you are suckers. You'll find out which ones for yourself."

It required another entire hour for that decision to be made. The mine owner, after a few minutes, seemed to grow suspicious and diminished the size of his bets, but the ranchman, confident in his own trick, stayed valiantly with the game, puzzled but resolute. Six thousand dollars, all told, passed into the pocket of Devon before the two looked at each other grimly.

"I guess we're the suckers," the miner remarked.

"Son, we are!" said the cattleman. "I'm out," he added to Devon. "I've another cold thousand or two for you to see how you do it, partner."

"Thanks," said Devon. "But who can explain the luck of the cards?"

He rose; they stood at the bar and drank together; then Devon stepped out into the cool of the night. He was pleased with the town, pleased with himself, pleased with the uncertainty of the future that lay before him, and the danger that surrounded him.

Lew Naxon's "bull calf" was roaring and rumbling up and down the street, and it was not hard to analyze the sound into loud voices of argument in two nearby saloons, a laughing and shouting group in one of the houses, and far off, the barking of dogs, a horse neighing, and a broad rumble of many voices dissolving into space.

It seemed to Devon like the sound of a battle, and a battle, to be sure, it was.

Something stirred at his side. Instinctively he stepped back and put his shoulders against the wall. Out of the dark a squat, brawny form approached, with the brim of a sloppy felt hat flapping over his eyes.

"Hello, Devon. You know me?"

"Are you Noonan?"

"I'm Noonan. I wanta talk with you."

"I'm glad to listen."

"Wherever you please, then."

Devon led instantly to his room, but Noonan refused to follow. He would come in his own way, a little later.

Scarcely had Devon settled himself when there was a knock at the door, and it opened on Noonan's broad, rather grim face. He jerked a look behind him, over his shoulder, and then shut the door with a sort of thoughtful care.

In response to Devon's invitation to sit down he waved a deprecatory hand.

"I'm gunna get an idea of this layout, first," said he.

And he stepped cautiously about the room, almost as though he suspected that the floor might sink beneath his feet.

There was one door, opening onto a narrow hall. But there were two windows, for it was a corner room. The partitions were very thin; from one side they could hear every breath

137

of a snoring man.

Then Noonan approached his companion and sat down very close. He leaned over, planting a hairy fist upon his knee.

"You're Devon?"

"Yes."

"You got the Devon place over yonder in the hills?"

"Yes."

"You ain't gunna have it for long," said Noonan with the grimmest of smiles. And he nodded his conviction at Devon.

"Why not?"

"Because it's gettin' sort of restless. It's gunna ramble away from you, or you're gunna ramble away from it. Now, look here, Devon, you done me a good turn, and I'm gunna give you good advice, and I won't charge for it, neither."

"Thank you," said Devon.

"Don't laugh at me. I mean it. You been offered something for that place."

"That's true." Devon was growing more and more interested.

"You been offered what the land's worth?"

"That depends," said Devon.

"The first day you landed here, if fifteen thousand had been offered to you for that place, would you of sold?"

"Yes, I would."

"Well, then, in your mind the fifteen thousand was all that the land was worth. Since then, you got different ideas."

"Yes, perhaps I have."

"Sure you have! You turned down twenty-five thousand — or you let those old birds do it for you!"

Devon was silent.

Said Noonan, scowling suddenly: "You think you can stall them off, do you?"

Devon shrugged his shoulders.

"I take my chances."

Noonan grinned as suddenly as he had scowled.

"You take your chances. Sure you do, and damn well you take 'em — at cards. Or maybe with guns, too. But they got this deal stacked against you!"

This he said, leaning farther forward than before, and his eyes glaring with conviction, his nostrils spread and quivering.

"You take it from me," Noonan added, "that your job is to get the ready cash and beat it out of here. Will you listen to me, old-timer?"

Devon smiled straight in his face.

"You mean this well, Noonan," he admitted, "and I thank you for your meaning, but I must admit that I'm not ready to do what you want. I don't exactly understand why my land has so much value to the people who want it — Tucker Vincent, Burchard, or whoever it may be, but since they've tried murder on me, I believe that it's going to be worth while to hold on and fight the thing out."

"Murder?" said Noonan.

"Murder," said Devon.

"When — for God's sake?"

"At sunset of this same day."

Noonan winced.

"The devils!" said he. "They — they'd cut a throat for a thousand dollars. What's a life or a death to them? Oh, damn their black hearts, but I always hated the lot of 'em!"

Devon waited, saying nothing, watching; but he felt that he was near the solution of his mystery.

Noonan jumped up from his chair.

"I'll tell you what I'm gunna do," said he. "I'm gunna blow the whole crooked game to you! Where'd I be except for you? I'd be in hell, that's where! I'd be clean in hell, except for you, this night. What was I to you? Nothing!"

So, breathing hard, with a sort of desperation, he faced Devon, and Devon rose in turn.

"You know who's at the bottom of the whole deal?" asked Jerry Noonan.

"Is it Tucker Vincent, or Burchard?" Devon countered.

As he spoke the face of Noonan changed suddenly, wonderfully, and at first Devon thought that it was because of the nearness with which he had come to the truth. But then he saw that Noonan was listening, and presently he, in turn, could hear the dying fall of a whistle which trailed far off, like a night bird, singing and flying down the wind.

XIX. A CAT-AND-MOUSE GAME

Never was dog called to his master's heel more quickly than Jerry Noonan. Sullen and frightened, he listened to that whistle, and his face blanched with fear and ineffectual revolt. He could only shrug his shoulders and stammer at Devon: "I gotta find out something — I'll — be back in a minute —"

And Jerry Noonan was gone through the door, jerking it open with a shudder, and instantly fleeing as fast as he could down the hall beyond.

But Devon wanted with a great passion to learn what it was that had frightened away Noonan — what was the message conveyed in the whistle — what warning, or what command.

He stepped to the table, blew out the lamp which he had just lighted, and hurried to one of the corner windows. He opened this and leaned out. He saw before him the empty corner of the Purleys' garden, or what should have been a garden, though the ground bristled merely with a few rose shrubs more than half dead.

142

And Devon, convinced that no eye was watching him, slipped over the window sill, hung by his hands, and dropped clear of the shrubs. After that he turned the corner of the building in time to see Jerry Noonan headed rapidly away across the street, walking with head down, his shoulders swaying with his speed.

Devon followed.

It was difficult to remain in sight of Jerry Noonan, because almost at once he turned off the main street toward the confused tangle of houses and huts and corrals for stock which lay between West London and the great, dark woods. The moon was up, making the lights of the houses look dim and useless, and presently they came to the pines.

Here Noonan broke into a run, and Devon, after hesitating a moment, followed. In woodcraft he knew that he was no accomplished trailer, and he felt like one out of his depth; but still he was driven on by a relentless curiosity to learn what power had drawn Jerry Noonan away at the very moment when his confession was about to be made.

He ran in pursuit. There was no way in which he could keep Noonan constantly in sight. The black shafts of the trees wavered before him as he ran, and he was continually dodging, but before him he could hear the

143

footfalls of Noonan, and he was guided by his ear almost entirely, though now and again he had a cold slant of moonshine that showed Noonan running before him through the woods.

By one of those flickers of light he saw Noonan fall to a walk, and he adjusted himself to the same gait, for he could guess that Noonan was close to his destination. At that point they were half a mile deep in the woods.

All noise ceased before him. Devon had to glide forward with the greatest caution. He began to fear that he had started on this trail in vain, when he found himself on the edge of a clearing, with a pale glow of moonshine slanting across it to the trees of the farther side, and three men, like three unshapely stumps, standing silent in the well of deep shadow beneath the lowest ray of moonlight.

"Hello, boys!" Noonan gasped suddenly.

Devon froze himself against the rough bark of a tree trunk.

The other two laughed softly, with a snarl in their voices.

"How are you, Jerry?" asked one of them.

"Why, I'm all right."

The two laughed again, in the same unpleasant manner.

"He's all right, he says," one of them murmured.

"Sure. He says that he's all right. D'you think you're all right, Noonan, or do you just guess it?"

"What's up?" croaked Noonan.

And Devon saw him back against a broad stump and thrust both hands into his clothes. It was plain that he was badly frightened; it was equally plain that he intended to defend himself.

"He wants to know what's up!" one of the two remarked in the same ghastly, taunting manner.

"Sure, he wants to know what's up," said the other.

And they laughed again.

"Is this a frame?" Noonan demanded.

"He says is this a frame?" repeated one.

"Sure, he'd like to know. You tell him, Sammy, I'm kinda tired."

"Aw, so am I."

"What's this about?" asked Noonan. "If it's a game, I'm out of it!"

"He's out of it, he says," persisted the first of the other two speakers.

"Maybe he is," said the other.

And again they laughed in cold mockery.

Noonan drew a breath loudly, a gasping breath of a very nervous man.

145

"If there's gunna be any trouble," said he, "I'm gunna start my share of it right now!"

"All right, Noonan. There's your share right handy to be had!"

"My God!" breathed Noonan.

And Devon saw that a third form had slipped noiselessly around the stump which guarded Noonan's back, and now was pressing a gun against the heart of Jerry.

"You poor sap," said the latest comer. "You poor chunk of ivory! As if you ever had a chance! As if you ever had any chance at all agin us!"

And Devon recognized the voice of Pete Grierson, of pleasant memory!

"You're gunna start your share of trouble right now," said one of the first two. "Go ahead, Jerry. Now's your chance, because it looks as though trouble was right there beside you! Give him a minute, Pete, will you? Maybe he'll have something funny to say."

"What's it all about?" Noonan asked in a desperate voice.

"Why, it's all about a walk in the dark," said the other. "That's all. A walk in the dark, and about four good fellows and old friends that met each other. And whatcha think about that for a pretty story, Jerry old boy?"

"You gota good idea, I guess," said Noonan.

"You gota idea that you're gunna bump me off, eh?"

"You think that I doublecrossed you. That's what you got in your heads."

"And ain't it a fool idea — that a good guy like you, Jerry, would ever doublecross anybody? Not you! Honest old Jerry Noonan, the people's friend, he's for bigger pay and shorter hours for the workin' man. That's what he is."

"Sure. That's the kind of a guy that he is."

They laughed in the snarling, cool mockery that Devon had heard before, and he began to collect himself with a wild resolution. Noonan could be not allowed to go down in slaughterhouse fashion like this!

"You got me, and you can take me," Noonan protested bitterly, "but it's God's truth that I never opened my trap to him."

"To who?"

"Aw, hell, come out in the open, even if you gotta murder me the next minute!" said Noonan. "I mean Devon. That's who I mean. I mean him that you wanta cut his throat so bad. That's what I mean. Is that straight enough for you?"

"Look how he talks, so eloquent," said one of the sneerers. "Why, he oughta be in politics, Jerry Noonan had! He'd get a lot of votes!"

147

"Maybe he'll be in politics before long."

"He'll be there. He'll be where there's more politics than any place else in the world. He'll be in hell. That's where he'll be, in the corner where they stack up the double-crossing coyotes!"

The voice terminated in a sort of a whine of fury, which burst through all self-control.

"You lie!" said Noonan, gasping with protest. "I never said a word to him."

"What!"

"I never said a word. Why — I didn't have time!"

"Listen to Governor Noonan. 'I didn't have time,' says Governor Noonan to the press. 'I didn't have time to betray my friends, but I'm gonna do it tomorrow as soon as it's light! Gentlemen, I have nothin' more to say today.' Why you white-livered sneak, you. I gotta mind to bash in your face with the heel of this gun, and I'm gunna do it — you swine, you!"

"Go ahead," Noonan snarled. "You got me pretty. But I'm gunna say to you that I never said nothin' to him. I was gunna spill the whole works. But I didn't. I pulled up and didn't say a word, because it was just then that I got the high sign."

"Listen to him. You hear? He admits it!"

"That guy saved me," said Noonan.

"Oh, damn you!" yelled one of the others, his cry breaking out in wildest hatred. "I could cut your heart out and eat it like an apple, I could!"

"I never seen a better play. What was I to him? I was nuthin'. He tied up the Runt for me, when the little bastard was right behind me there in the crowd — my God, he would of got me —"

"I wish he had!"

"After that I sort of had to tell Devon somethin'. It was the only way that I had of payin' him back."

"Governor Noonan, he talks about payin' back. He's gunna pay his new friends out of the pockets of his old ones, and that's the way he'll keep everybody happy. That's Governor Noonan's big idea! You was gunna double-cross us, you — you — why, you fool!"

"Yes," said Noonan slowly. "I was a fool. I should of known that I couldn't get away with nothin'! I was a fool all right."

The other, who seemed the leading spirit in the party, walked straight up to Noonan and tapped him on the breast.

"Noonan, can you go straight with us if I give you another try?"

"Me? God, yes!"

"Then go back there and knife Devon."

There was a long pause. Devon felt the irregular, flying foot of his pulse, kicking against his temple.

Then Noonan answered.

"Go ahead and polish me off. I'm damned if I'll murder that one. He's too straight. I ain't gonna lift a hand at him. That's final!"

Devon brought his gun into his hand. Grierson was his target, for if he could dispose of that one, perhaps Noonan could break away. However, there was a moment's pause, and during it something made Devon hold his fire.

Suddenly the chief of the trio said very quietly: "That's pretty good, Jerry. Nobody but a skunk would take a fall out of Devon after what he's done for you. We came out here to bag you, Jerry, but I've changed my mind. I dunno. But I think that you might go straight with us after this."

"Straight?" said Noonan with a great sigh. "You couldn't rule a line no straighter than I'm gunna go after this! I've had my lesson, and it'll stick to the ribs, I can tell you!"

"Suppose that we all start back, then?"

"Where? To the hangout?"

"No. Back to town."

"Where's the chief?"

"Where he oughta be, I suppose. Come along."

They passed Devon not three steps away,

but he was securely lost in the shadows, and knew it. The wood was so dark that he hardly could make out the silhouettes of the men as they moved, and he was far from recognizing a single feature.

Recognize them he felt that he must. He already had learned much; and if one blast of light could fall upon these faces, he might be able to crowd the hands of Sheriff Lew Naxon with valuable prisoners; and his own life might be secured.

Softly, softly, then, he went after them. They took a different direction from that which Noonan had used in entering the wood, but they were easily followed for a few minutes by the sound of their steps, and by the muttering of their voices. He was afraid to come too close. Such fellows would think nothing whatever of brushing him out of their way if they knew he was trailing them. And perhaps it was overcaution and lingering on his part that made him, suddenly, aware that he heard nothing — neither voice nor step — for a minute or two. At that he pressed on more boldly, more swiftly, but coming to a broad glade, spotted only by a few small stumps, he found that the group was not before him.

Greatly troubled, he paused here, and listened to right and left, uncertain in which direction he should go through the woods. But all was ghostly still, and the small stream which moved through the center of the glade flashed and twisted among the big stones without making an audible sound.

No, after a moment, he was aware that this was wrong. Something relaxed in his mind; he was able to listen; and when he listened again he could hear distinctly the soft music of the water as it slipped over the polished slides of rock and curled gently around the jutting boulders.

And in the broad-faced pool at the lower end of the stream, nearest to him, he saw now the white face of the moon, making the whole heavens fall into that little body of water. The moon passed into a network of high cloud mists, and instantly the pool was charged with white fire.

With a disappointed shrug of his shoulders, he admitted that he had lost the trail, and he was about to try for it at random, toward the right, when he saw a slender figure of a girl run out from the woods opposite him and go swiftly down to the stream. She gathered her long skirts in one hand, and with the other arm outstretched, to keep a balance, she skipped lightly across the water from rock to rock.

On the farther shore, she glanced back, and then went hastily up the slope toward Devon.

A gust of wind — perhaps the same which had tossed the cloud mist in a wave away from the moon's brightness — now curled the wide brim of her hat, and Devon beheld the childish loveliness of Prue Maynard!

It had a strange effect upon him, for among the black solemnity of these pines, to see this girl was almost like seeing a child in pinafore frolicking over a great battlefield.

The flurry of wind passed. Looking at the thin, fluttering shadows as they departed, she laughed a little, rather breathlessly, while she put her hair in order. Then she went on, singing softly to herself.

Devon tried with all his might to fit her into a niche, but she would not go! She was like a picture out of place — a soul slipped into a wrong century or another nation, like a false card passed into a deck!

Where was she bound?

Walt swore that he would follow her with more success than he had followed the men with Jerry Noonan, and as she passed his tree he glided behind her. Too closely, now! Or else there was an extra sense in this strange creature that told her of danger for she paused, rigidly alert, and then sprang aside, behind a tree.

Devon sprang after her, and nearly leaped headforemost into his death, for she did not run, but came around the tree trunk at him with a low cry that was to live forever in the blood and in the soul of Devon, a quicksilver thread of terror at the fierceness in that voice of hers.

She had a small, old-fashioned derringer, with double barrels, one beneath the other, and he distinctly heard the click as the hammer fell. The cap failed her or the bullet would have torn into Devon's breast; then the chopping edge of his hand knocked her wrist down, and flung the gun from her fingers.

He took her by both arms at the elbows and tried to speak, but there were no words that fitted into the need of his mind. The darkness of the wood made her a shadow. He would have been glad to tell himself that this was merely a grisly phantom that he had encountered, but the warmth of her arms was beneath his touch.

And now he could hear her breathe, regularly, steadily, unshaken by fear; out of the darkness, too, he became aware of a hyacinthine fragrance.

Then something like a panic came over Devon, for his breathing grew quick and hoarse, and he thought he could hear the rushing of blood in his brain. He led her hastily back to the bright verge of the moonlight, and behold, she was looking up to him with the

155

same childish smile he had seen at the house of Mrs. Purley.

"*What* a fright you gave me!" said that sweetest of all voices. "Just for a moment I thought it was a wild animal —"

He released her arms, and she finished her words with an appropriate gesture — a quick clasping of her hands, while her eyes widened at him more and more. She even came a little closer to him, as children will do when they wish to make obtuse elders understand, and Devon receded a bit, for he felt a danger which he could not describe.

"You're a night-blooming flower, Prudence," said he.

"What do you mean, Mr. Devon?"

"I've seen you blossoming by day, but it seems that you do at night, also. The moon is warmth enough for you when you go out hunting — for your brother, Prudence? For young Willie Maynard? Do you expect to find him here among the trees?"

"Are you mocking me?" said she.

"Beautiful Prudence, of course I'm not. I take you as seriously as guns — or poison, say."

At this she made a sudden gesture, and the moon gleamed on her hand, as soft as a child's and more delicately made.

"Oh, well," said she, "I'm glad that the

cap failed to work."

"I must believe that, of course," Walt responded. "I don't think you'd like to do a murder, Prudence. You'd rather leave that to your friends, and draw people into the net for them, as you did with me, this afternoon."

"You're a ghost, then?" Prudence Maynard inquired.

"I should be, except that the old man was with me."

"Tell me what happened."

"You don't know?"

"I don't know, of course."

"What did you think I'd find when I went out to locate poor Willie Maynard?"

"A rope that would slip you out of the saddle and bump you on the ground," she said calmly.

"They thought that bullets were safer and surer than ropes," Devon explained.

"Did they lie to me?" said Prudence. She yawned a little, and covered her lips with one hand. "Poor fellow! It must have been a shock to you!"

"We'd better start back," said Devon.

"Where are we to go?"

"To wherever you were going through the woods, my dear."

"Or else?"

157

"Or else I'll take you back to Sheriff Naxon. He'd be rather glad to have you in his jail."

"I suppose he would," said Prudence. "But I won't go to either place."

"Ah?"

"Oh, no! I'll stay here, I imagine."

She raised her head as though in thought, and the moonlight flowed silver bright upon her face. Then her lips puckered, and out of them poured a thin, sweet rill of whistling that seemed, although it was so near, to come from far away, blown down the wind.

Devon, amazed, stared at her. Then the realization jumped in his mind and he stepped close to her in a rage.

She merely smiled up at him.

"You'd better go away as fast as you can," murmured she. "They'll be here in a moment."

"I'll go, and you with me," said Devon fiercely.

"Dear Mr. Devon," laughed the girl. "As if I didn't know the kindness of your heart! And you couldn't carry me very far. I'm not so light, you know!"

A twig cracked sharply among the trees. Bitterly he knew that he had failed, and that his hands were empty in spite of his find.

"Perhaps we'll find one another again," said he, stepping back.

"Go, please!" said Prudence Maynard. She clasped her hands as though in pleasure, and laughed at the disappearing silhouette of Devon beneath the trees.

XXI. A BEARER OF ILL TIDINGS

Turning around a great pine trunk, Devon stumbled on a root, and when he got to his feet, scrambling and cursing beneath his breath, he peered out and saw that she was no longer in the clearing; and off to the side he heard the thin, trailing whistle once more.

But the gambler did not follow, for suddenly he realized that he was totally helpless here in the woods. If he found the conspirators, even, he could do nothing. To trail them he was incapable, as already he had discovered. It would be luck enough if he could escape from the forest back to the town in safety.

And yet he did not hurry away, but for an instant he leaned against the big, rough trunk, gritting his teeth in fury, for it maddened him to think with what a silky ease she had taken advantage of his chivalry. If, indeed, they met another time, he would have learned his lesson, he told himself, and he would treat her as he would treat a man — at the point of a gun if necessary!

Then Devon went out through the woods, and heard not so much as a whisper on the way.

Naxon's "bull calf" was fairly silent now, for the night was very late; most of the houses were asleep with black faces of darkness; only toward the upper end of the town, where the Palace and most of the other gaming houses were located, a few yellow streaks of lamplight made bars across the light.

Devon went back to Mrs. Purley's house, entered through the almost deserted bar, and was stopped by a quietly drawling voice from a corner of the room.

There sat old Jim, placidly nursing a long-stemmed pipe. He rose to meet Devon and smiled upon him.

"What's happened, Jim?" the gambler asked hastily.

"I thought I'd be comin' in," said Jim.

"Tired of staying out there alone without Harry, eh?"

"Harry? Matter of fact," said Jim confidentially, "the peace out there around that cabin was somethin' wonderful after Harry left. There was a time, once, when I was a kid, when I lived in a valley where a river run a rantin' and a chantin' day and night, and I never knowed how much of that noise was lodged in my ear until I got shut of the valley for good and all. Seemed like I could rest for the first time in months when I got outside. And it's the same way with Harry!"

"But nothin's wrong, Jim?"

Jim looked toward a corner with his long-distance squint.

"There wasn't real call for me to come to town," he said, "exceptin' that my mule, he needs a new set of shoes. The rocks, they wear out iron somethin' terrible!"

"No doubt they do. I'll try to get you a room here for the night."

"They're full up, Walt," said Jim.

"Then you'll sleep in my room."

"I don't aim to sleep much."

"Why not?"

"I had a nap this afternoon. That'll hold me. And, besides, the best time for settin' and thinkin' is when you set up at night with nothin' between you and the dark of the wall but your mind."

"And why should you sit up all night to think, Jim?"

"The best light to read most trails," said Jim, "is the sun. But they's others that works out better in the dark. Like the trail of them that seem to have it in for you, Walt!"

Devon was quiet for a moment.

Then he asked: "You found stable room for the mule, Jim?"

"Why, he don't need stable room," Jim scoffed.

"Are you going to stand him out?"

"That ol' mule," said Jim, "will stand out till his bones wear away. He's no more use to me."

"What?"

"No sir," said Jim. "He died on the way in, Walt."

"That's hard luck. I'll get you another one, though. I'll get you a better one, Jim."

"They ain't made no better," Jim eulogized. "There never was no surer foot on a trail; and them long ears of his could take a picture of danger when it was still a mile away! He'd give one snort — like this! That meant danger, and I used to peel off my blankets and grab my rifle, and he never was wrong. Yes, sir, he was a useful critter, old Barney was!"

"How old was he, Jim?" asked Devon, sensing something strange in this rambling account.

"He was about seventeen. He had a good many years ahead of him, but so long as he had to die, I guess that he was as well pleased to drop the way he done!"

"Heart trouble?"

"By a manner of speakin', yes. It was heart trouble."

"Do mules have it often?"

"In these here parts, mules and hosses both have it, considerable. It ain't so widespread, but it kills a good many of 'em."

"But what causes it, Jim? What is it?"

"Winchester bullets," said Jim.

Devon stared.

"It was a good, clean shot," Jim elaborated, "and it finished old Barney quick. He just coughed and dropped. That cough told me to get out of the saddle, and so I was clean away when he rolled down the cliff."

"Jim, who did it?"

"Them that are after us, Walt. Them are the ones that did it. I hung around in the rocks, but I didn't see hide nor hair of nobody."

"The curs!" Devon exclaimed. "The infernal curs! They've taken to waylaying *you*, Jim?"

"Best way to part a chain is to saw away at the weakest link," Jim said philosophically. "I ain't surprised. I sort of suspected it."

"You did?"

"I did."

"I thank God," said Devon heartily, "that it happened on the trail, when you had rocks to hide in, and not at the ranch, where they could have mobbed you far from any shelter!"

"Yes, Walt," said Jim. "The ranch is tolerable bare."

"Except for the house. I suppose the old log walls would nearly turn a bullet?"

"They used to be strong old walls," nodded Jim.

"But perhaps they're partially rotted away now," Devon responded. "Shouldn't we repair them?"

"They ain't nothin' left to repair," said Jim. "It was fire that rotted 'em away, Walt."

"Great God! Fire? Did the old stove break down, or what?"

"I dunno," Jim answered. "I was comin' in from the range, wonderin' where the cows had gone to —"

Devon stared.

"The cattle gone?"

"Clean as a whistle, except one old red cow that was too lame to foller the rest."

"Rustlers!" Devon ejaculated.

"I take it they was rustlers around," said Jim, in the same quiet manner.

"By the eternal God!" said Devon. "This is too much!"

"I was comin' in from havin' a look for 'em, and I seen smoke ahead of me, and comin' over the hill I seen that the house was half rotted away in the flames, and the rest of it goin' fast."

"They've cleaned off the ranch, then!" exclaimed Devon.

"It appears like they have," said old Jim. "I was settin' the saddle, watchin', when a bullet come and sung at my ear, and when Barney started off he sort of stumbled. That reminded me that his shoes was pretty near gone, and he'd be havin' tender feet if I didn't get him shod right pronto. So I come along toward West London. That man Wright, up the street, he's a boss hoss-shoer, Walt, and he does a mighty neat job with mules, too."

"You came on in, and they overtook you, Jim?" Walt inquired.

"They was comin' hard behind me, and right and left of me, too, they was tryin' to find short cuts to head me off. But through the rocks, old Barney give them a run! He never had much speed, but through the rough he always made every stroke count for two! But when we got onto the rim of the valley, maybe we kind of stood up ag'in the moon, and they dropped him under me, and he rolled down the cliff. Seems like they thought that I'd gone with him, because they didn't bother to search around for me none. I waited for 'em, but after a while I remembered that I was pretty nigh out of chewin' tobacco, so I come along in to get some plug. But the stores was all closed!"

He shook his head, adding:

"They're gettin' too plumb civilized in these

166

here West London stores, Walt!"

Devon rubbed his knuckles hard across his forehead.

"They've swept the ranch bare, dropped your mule, tried to murder you!"

"Why, it seems like they have. You better turn in, Walt, because you're young, and youngsters can't stand doin' without sleep, it seems like!"

"Jim, could you recognize a single man of the lot?"

"They was wearin' masks, Walt, until it got late in the evenin'. They was all masked, but it seemed to me like I could see some of the hosses pretty good. To them that are used to lookin', hosses are as easy recognized as the faces of men, Walt."

"To you, or to Harry. And thank God for that! Oh, Jim, when we corner some of these fellows, they're going to swing for what they've done!"

"Yes, sir," agreed Jim, "because when you come right down to it, the killin' of Barney was sort of a murder. But I got my gun oiled up, and by sun, or moon, or starlight, I dunno that I'd miss 'em very far, Walt. Have a chew?"

He had finished his pipe and extended the remnant of his cut of tobacco, which Devon refused.

"Poor old Harry," said Jim, "dog-gone me if it don't make him turn his head away when I bite off a chew, him thinkin' of the way he's gotta champ and tear to make any head-way!"

And instantly his white, strong teeth were buried in a corner of the plug.

XXII. A BRUTAL CRIME

They went up to the room where Harry was sleeping, and he awoke painlessly and swiftly, as all old men do. Then he sat on the edge of his bed and nursed his feet while he listened to the story.

This story was even more compressed for the benefit of Harry. Said Jim:

"They've run off the cows and burned down the shack. The place is bare."

Harry listened to this and blinked his eyes at his old friend. Then he commented to Devon:

"You take most gents that got any education and they don't mind talkin'. But you take this here reptile, and he's gunna spend words like they was dollars. What in hell does it cost you to let us see what you've seen, Jim?"

Thus upbraided, Jim faithfully told what had occurred. And presently he forgot Devon, and was expounding the whole affair to his old companion in arms. In this manner Devon learned how everything had happened, down to the very marks on the ground, and how

Jim had followed the trail of the cattle to a narrow ravine that broke away north through the mountains.

"And there you left off?" sneered Harry. "Just was enough to see which way they was driftin'? Or maybe you thought they couldn't make a bend in their trail?"

Said Jim: "There was eight men started that drive, by the count of their hoofs. There was two when the cows got into the pass."

"How could you tell that?" Devon interjected.

"Anybody that wasn't born blind could of told; and the blind could of told by fumblin' the ground. There I seen a clean set of prints in the soft ground of the cañon, stamped in where the end of the cows' trailin' showed. Six was gone. Where? I turned back to see, and I come on plenty enough to show me! They had turned back and got the house!"

Old Harry, continuing to nurse his feet, listened on to the end before he expressed an opinion.

Then he said: "This here looks better and better to me."

"Sure. It would," Jim retorted. "Havin' a house burned down and Walt's cows all run off of the place, it would make you feel pretty chipper — I can see that, all right! But jus' step down and explain what you mean."

"You can't organize a heavy rain that'll all slide off in one direction," said Harry. "Whoever it is that wants to sink us, has found the game pretty hard for him. He couldn't buy Walt off. He couldn't drop him with a private murderer. He couldn't lead him into hell fire with a pretty girl — none prettier ever stepped!"

"So he begins to get miserable and lose his sleep. He says to himself that he'll get so much strength together that he'll blot out poor old Walt. He'll soak him up the way a sponge soaks up a lot of water! And there he goes! He rakes together a lot of thugs and he turns them loose, and the first thing that he makes clean is the ranch.

"Well, that's somethin' on his side of the books, but he's made two wrong steps. First, he swiped those cows, and they're worth too much for him to run very far. He'll have the brands switched and start to drift 'em back into West London. He'll want to turn that high-priced beef into butcher's meat, and when he does that, he's askin' for more trouble. Shall I tell you why? Sure I shall. Jim, it don't take schoolin' to follow my drift."

"By the jumpin' jiminy," said the other. "And then you mean that you and me can watch the butcher meat, and the hides?"

"Why," Harry explained, "that works out

pretty fine, don't it? Jim and me, we know the pattern of some of them hides as well as we know the pattern of our own faces! And when we start to tracin' up the cows, we're gonna find the disease that caused 'em to die!"

He chuckled with a savage delight as he raised this prospect in his mind. Then he broke off to say:

"Jim, did they get that old mustard-colored son-of-a-gun along with the rest?"

"They sure did get him, Harry."

"They must of been greasers, then," said Harry. "Because no white man could of raised a run out of his old hide. But the stealin' of those cows ain't gunna be the only thing that'll hang these here rapscallions. They's somethin' more, old sons! Him that wants to soak up Walt and his ranch has organized so much trouble that, as I was sayin' a while back, it can't all slip down one side of the hill. Watch, now, and you'll see that hell has busted loose all around West London. And the same trails that lead out from the hell-makers is gunna lead down to the places where they started it headed for our ranch, boys. All the roots of trouble around here are gunna lead up to one fine big shady tree! You savvy me, Jim?"

"Sure," Jim agreed. "I can foller *that* drift. But I dunno that we'll all be wearing hair when the good time comes!"

"Go away and don't bother me none," said Harry. "I gotta sleep some more on this. They's gunna be plenty of day tomorrow!"

They turned in for the night, Jim contentedly on a narrow half of Harry's bed, and Devon to his own room, where he slept heavily until the morning was bright, and a hand beat at his door.

It was Jim, saying:

"Turn on out, Walt. Harry has gone ahead to the sheriff's new jail to listen to what's said down there. Maybe you and me had better go, too! It's turnin' out fine the way Harry said it would. The Auburn stage was held up this mornin' and blood and hell fire was spilled all over the countryside!"

Devon dressed at once, and with Jim he went down to the jail. The admiration of Jim for his companion burst out as they proceeded.

"There's a brain in old Harry," said he. "Dog-gone me if there ain't a brain! Now, you look at him, and you'll see what he'll come at. He knew that these crooks was gettin' too many to stay in one pot. They had to boil over, and they're gunna show their hand!"

When they got to the jail, half the town seemed there before them, gathered in muttering groups, but it was learned that more than a hundred men had ridden out with various groups in order to comb the countryside.

For this crime had been peculiarly brutal.

When the stage drew out of West London, in the first gray of morning light, with seven passengers aboard, and more than two hundred pounds of gold, it had been waylaid not two miles from the town.

The robbers acted with unnecessary savagery. The six horses were shot to death in the first flurry of bullets. In the same outburst of murder the guard was literally shot to bits and rolled dead from the box. The driver, badly hurt, fell on his face in the road, and lay stunned, half stifled with dust.

The passengers, badly frightened by the murderous brutality of this attack, leaped from the stage, not stopping to carry any of their possessions with them, and bolted like scared rabbits into the brush on the farther side of the road. In an instant of confusion and death, it was over, and the masked men, jumping up from the rocks which had concealed them, gutted the stage.

Then, as a crowning act of stupid violence, they set fire to it, and burned it to a crisp of ashes studded with black iron-work.

So great was the savagery of these fellows that they actually had turned the driver upon his face when one of them thought he saw the man move. The driver lay still, though actually his consciousness had come back to him; and the robber had kicked him brutally in the face to draw some sign of life. He managed to show no sign of life, however, so they left him and went on.

After they had disappeared, some of the passengers, running back through the woods, gave the alarm in West London, and the sheriff rushed out to the scene. He went on to follow the trails of the fugitives as well as he could; and the badly hurt driver was taken back to the town.

He was lodged in the jail, simply because the sheriff had fixed up an extra room in the new building as a sort of hospital. Several men and a doctor were tending to him, and every word that dropped from his lips, as he lay between life and death, was scrupulously recorded by those beside the bed and passed on to the crowd which waited outside.

West London was a rough town, but the brutality of this affair was too much even for its strong stomach. It wanted blood to pay for blood, and the whole place waited with a feverish anxiety to learn what news the sheriff's party or any other searchers had picked up. Hardly a hammer struck drill head on this day in Timbal Gulch.

But there obviously would be plenty of time to wait, for the sheriff and the rest were not apt to return for hours.

Harry came out from the core of the crowd and reported to his friends all that he had learned from the jail.

The important item to Devon lay in the last words which Harry had noted — that before the attack began, a long, shrill whistle, like the call of a bird of unknown species, had blown down the wind to the ears of the passengers.

The three went back up the street and ate breakfast at a restaurant run by a pair of Chinese. As they swallowed ham and eggs, Devon told them his reason for thinking that Harry was entirely right, and that the same men who had been hired to attack him were the ones guilty of the stage robbery.

He went beyond the sound of the whistle, and gave them his narrative of the following of Jerry Noonan, and the appearance of Prudence Maynard in the forest.

It was considered a tale of the highest importance by both of the two old men; and straightway they proposed, in almost the same breath, that Devon should lead them back into the forest, if he could, to where he had met the girl.

It was perfectly obvious that she was attached, in some manner, to this bloodthirsty crew, and it was equally obvious that she had been bound for their rendezvous in the woods when Devon intercepted her.

That proposal came with something of a shock to Devon. He had told himself that there was nothing he wanted so much as to follow that treacherous and dangerous girl to the end of her trail, but now that there seemed some faint possibility of accomplishing his desire, he shrank from the execution of it.

However, it would have been hard for him to put his objection into words. And ten short minutes found the trio on the outskirts of West London, the trappers with their rifles; Devon with a revolver only.

XXIII. THE CABIN IN THE CLEARING

Old Jim found the trail readily, on the farther side of the little creek which ran through the clearing. After that it could be traced up the slope to the point where Devon had encountered Prue Maynard. Jim, having found the trail, interpreted it.

"Here he muzzles her and takes her back into the moon. Here they stand around and talk. Here he changes his mind and backs up —"

"That's when he heard the whistle," suggested Harry.

"Here she slides off sidewise, runnin'. Runs pretty well, Harry. Look at the space of these here steps, and think that she's wearin' long skirts at that! Heel marks pretty near go out, too. Which means she's got all her weight on her toes, same as she had ought to have! Foller along, Harry. I'm gunna need help through this pine needle patch!"

Carefully, often on hands and knees, they worked ahead, sometimes brushing away the needles and looking at the faintest impressions upon the more moist ground beneath; and so they went on among the trees.

They paused only once, when Harry straightened to say:

"This girl, she puts an ache in my back. She walks like she was made of feathers. If it hadn't been for that rain a while back, we'd never find no token of her here, Jimmy. Eh?"

"No more than a bird leaves in the air," said Jim.

They resumed the work of the trail, Devon following behind them.

Half a dozen times all trace of the trail was lost, and then the two old men moved in circles, like dogs, and with their eyes so close to the ground that it almost seemed that they were following by scent. But, in every case, though sometimes after a half hour of work, they recovered their sign and went securely ahead.

Devon, following them, wondered at the slowness and the fumbling uncertainty of their work. They seemed to have no superior instinct, but mere industry. Yet even when they had established the trail, the signs that had been like guiding words to them were still invisible to him!

She had not gone straight forward, but twice had turned to the right sharply, and twice again she had doubled straight back upon her trail for a short distance, and then gone ahead to the left.

On the second of these occasions, more than a half hour went into deciphering the trail puzzle which she had built up, and they finally managed to do this by walking across a fallen tree that crossed a good-sized creek. In the soft mole beyond they found the print of her slender shoe again, and went forward; Harry and Jim, after a long look of admiration cast at that natural bridge which she had used.

But presently they came to a region from which all of the virgin forest had been cleared away by fire, and there remained no more than burly stumps, and a dense secondary growth which had sprung up in the cleared spaces. Sometimes these saplings were barely sprouting, and sometimes they were thirty feet high, but they made an almost impenetrable thicket.

There Jim and Harry held a brief consultation, but they agreed that if the trail had pointed straight on as far as this, it must mean that the girl had found her way through the thicket.

They could not find her entering point, however. Once inside the grove it was so dusky that they could decipher no sign upon the ground. For that reason they had to push blindly ahead. Half a dozen times they were turned back, when the trees became to all intents and purposes a solid wall; but at length Jim found a way worming through in a narrow gap which did not close until, after a thickness of trees which they found very hard to estimate, they came out into a clearing where they found before them a small log cabin, without windows, and with the door standing wide open.

It was a singularly clumsy building, the walls irregularly put up, and the door hanging loosely from leather hinges. At the bottom, moss had grown up from the ground upon the lower logs, and the whole of the place looked in a partial state of decay.

The clearing itself was so small that it seemed in a perpetual twilight, owing to the darkness of the woods about it, even though these were only second growth.

Behind the cabin were some small corrals, in which the visitors could see a mangy-looking mustang and a woebegone cow.

In front of this shack the owner was busily at work making new stretchers for hides, and a number of the hides, on other stretchers, leaned against the wall of the cabin nearby.

As for the man himself, he looked as down at the heel as his dwelling. And in fact where buildings are home-made it is generally true that the inhabitants resemble their houses.

This was a loosely made fat fellow, with a low forehead, crossed by parallel folds of fat which gave him, continually, a whimsical expression. His hanging jowls were patched with pink, under the shadow of a four-day beard, and his eyes were dim and watery, as though from too much use of moonshine whisky. He waved a fat hand at them, and looked up slowly from his work.

Thereupon, the better to observe them, but without rising, he began to pack cut plug into his corncob pipe and stare at the strangers.

"Well, sir," he said, "dog-gone me if you didn't get through the wood."

"Dog-gone me if we didn't," agreed Jim. "H'wareye?"

"Fair to middlin'. And you?"

"Fair. Kind of heated from getting through that hedge of trees."

"And what might of made you want to come through 'em so bad, unless you wanted to call on me?"

"Why, for that matter," said Jim, "the truth is that I says to myself them trees never would grow that thick unless there was water on the far side of them, and dog-gone me if I wasn't right!"

And he pointed to the round mouth of a spring, cobbled around the edge with irregular stones, the water overflowing and running off without a course to be lost among the trees.

"You been in the woods before or you wouldn't of guessed that," said the owner with an agreeable nod. "Set down and rest your feet."

"Don't mind if we do."

The fat man heaved himself with a deep groan from the stump on which he was sitting, and disappeared into the house, hitching at the single cord which served him as suspenders.

He came again, bearing a glass jug which might hold a gallon and a half, and in the other hand he bore a cup, from which the tin handle had been broken.

"Have a piece of this," he invited.

"Thanks," said Jim. "But I ain't drinkin' paleface, not in these days. I seen the time when me and Harry, there, could get around that sort of poison, but we wore our stomachs out on it while there was still Injuns in the country, and we've had to cut it out. The first thing that gives way in an old man is his knees, and the second is his teeth" — here he looked pointedly at Harry — "and the third is his stomach. By which maybe you could tell our ages, partner!"

"You're Jim and Harry, are you?" asked the dweller in the woods.

"That's our names."

"Why, I've heard tell of you."

"Aye," said Harry, "our names has got as big a circulation as a magazine, but we don't get paid for it. How's things around about these diggin's, stranger?"

"They've picked up a mite for me," the cabin dweller admitted. "Since West London woke up, all of a sudden, I make a piece of money here and there."

"Workin' in the mines?"

"I ain't got the back for the handlin' of a single jack," said the fat man with a sigh that was half a groan. "I ain't never been too strong in the center of my back, as you might say. Slipped on a slickery barn floor, carryin' a pail of milk, when I was a kid, and I ain't ever felt strong since."

"How you make money out of the mines, then?"

"Sellin'. Raisin' of pigs has always been my main holt. And I had a right smart chance of pigs here, a while back, but I've sold 'em all off; even the old sow, down there in West London."

He tapped the jug.

Old Jim nodded, glancing around at the shack.

"You know, this isn't a bad job," he remarked, pretending to examine its method of construction. "Looks like one man done it himself. You can tell by the way he made this here doorway."

As he spoke, Jim deliberately walked inside, without waiting for an invitation, still pretending to examine the rough workmanship. Its owner made an ineffectual attempt to block the way, then lurched after the old trapper.

"Hold on! What you say?"

"I said there wasn't more than one at the makin' of this here cabin."

"Why, you're right," said the other, passing on hastily through the doorway behind Jim. "Pap, he run this up all by himself. And a mighty good, steady job he made of it!"

Harry prepared to follow into the cabin, and as he did so he winked and nodded significantly at Devon. The latter had seen nothing especially worthy of note, but now he prepared to watch with a keener eye. Certainly, in the minds of Jim and Harry, something was amiss here!

XXIV. THE STOLEN HORSES

"There y'are! There y'are!" old Jim was saying inside the cabin as he pointed to the walls. "One man did the place all right. He must of been a man, your pap!"

"Oh, he *was* a man!" said the other, grinning in sudden admiration. "I seen the day when he was sixty, and me as big as I am now, that he knocked me clean through the door and over the choppin' block. There ain't anything else in here worth seein', I'm afraid."

It was a most foul and dark and noisome interior, as a matter of fact, and Devon would have been glad to leave it at once, but Harry, by this time, had pushed open the rear door. He looked out onto the first corral, where stood a considerable stack of hay, and beyond this was another thicket of woods, with a well-stamped trail leading into its heart.

"You got enough hay to carry you through the winter, all right," Harry remarked. "Hey, where's this gent?"

"He just now picked up a bucket and went out at the front door."

"Hold on," said Harry. "I don't like that!"

And he shambled rapidly to the front door and looked out.

"He's gone!" the old man added grimly. "By jumpin' jiminy, when I seen the looks of that trail, yonder, I guessed that maybe he wouldn't stand around very long, but I didn't suspect he'd move this quick!"

Far off among the trees, quavering through the air, they heard the whistled call, like the cry of a bird, that Devon knew so well. And he exclaimed: "It's their signal, Jim!"

"I hear it mighty well!"

"They'll come in answer to that. We'd better get out of this, then!"

"Maybe we had better move," said Harry; "but first I'll just have a peek at that trail into the woods yonder!"

He and Devon went off hurriedly toward the trail; Jim remained behind, turning up odd corners of the pigsty of a house. As for the trail, it was as short as it was well defined, and after one or two twists it ended at a roughly built shed in which they found a dozen horses stabled. And such horses as these never could have been brought here for an innocent purpose.

"Look at the legs of 'em," said Harry. "Why, I'd lay to it that they're flyers, every one of 'em! They're the ponies to move. Can't you see 'em stretchin' across the hills, Walt? Look at that sorrel-topped devil with the bad eye. There's the pony for me! Look around you, Walt, and pick out what you please!"

"Take a horse, do you mean?"

"Aye, I mean that. And we'll select a couple for old Jim, too!"

He was fumbling behind an oilcloth stretched across a corner, this impromptu cabinet being filled with weapons.

"You're not serious, Harry," Devon protested. "We can't turn ourselves into horse thieves no matter who's against us in this affair!"

"Can't we?" said Harry, laughing through his teeth. "Let me tell you somethin', Walt. We'll keep those hosses until somebody comes along and explains how they happened to have this here!"

He picked up a Winchester, fingering the stock.

"I filed these two notches, Walt!" said he. "I filed 'em twenty year back, and them that took this gun burned your house for you, Walt. You can lay to that. Holler to Jim. Maybe we gotta hurry; but we'll snake out some of these hosses first!"

They worked hastily after that, tying the horses' halters together and taking them out in strings of fours, the first one saddled. They ventured on no more, though there were saddles for all hanging from pegs on the wall sufficient to have covered every one of the twelve backs.

But as they worked, drawing up the cinches on their chosen mounts, they heard through the woods the long and wavering sound of the signal again; and after that they knew that their minute remaining must be a short one.

Old Jim, running out from the shack, could not help lingering over the stack of arms and picking out a rifle here and there to drop into a gunny sack which he had in readiness to receive them. Then they went out in a procession and found no trouble in getting to the exit from the dense grove. It was an angling path that cut out among the trees, and Harry was soon jogging his horse along it. There was some snorting and kicking, but for the most part the animals followed with a good deal of docility.

They were quickly out into the more open woods, and here Jim forced his way into the lead, saying as he went past Devon:

"It's time to ride hard, Walt!"

He called the same to Harry, who responded:

"You can't ride faster than a rifle bullet, Jim!"

"You can't make twelve hosses go soft, no matter how slow," replied Jim, and he dragged his string of animals into a gallop.

They poured along through the woods, raising at once a clatter and a crashing that made the heart of Devon beat against his teeth, and so they swung into a sort of natural alley — a long, straight gap with the big trees crowded closely together on either hand and a bed of slippery pine needles under foot.

Here Jim worked up at once to a smart speed, and the great brown trunks flew past in a throng. Devon's mount, a beautiful and strongly made brown mare, began to feel that this was a race, and stretched forward in pursuit; Walt had to sit back with a hard pull to keep her in place, for the way was much too narrow to permit her to pass, with the crowding string of three other galloping horses beside her.

However, he felt fairly content, for he could see that it would not be long before they were entirely out of the woods at this rate, and because, also, the pine needles muffled the beating of the hoofs. There was little more than the whisking of the wind about his ears when they came to an easy bend of this natural road, and as old Jim disappeared around it, the brain of Devon was fairly stunned by the roar of guns!

He came around the bend into a maelstrom of kicking horseflesh. Old Jim was down; Harry, throwing away the lead rope, was attempting to ride in to the rescue of his friend, and Jim was gradually drawing himself up from the ground.

The whole space of the alley around the bend was filled with swirling, flashing, snorting horses, and from the shelter of the trees repeating rifles poured in a murderous fire so close that the flame from the muzzles fairly scorched the flanks of the horses.

Devon threw loose his own lead rope, which allowed his three led animals to wheel and rush back. Then he pressed forward toward Jim. Luck had placed their enemy all on one side of the alley, and the wide pool of horseflesh formed a sufficient barrier between them and the guns for the moment.

He got to Jim. There was a slash of blood across the face of the old man, but he seemed unhurt, and putting his foot on Devon's, he stood up beside the latter. Harry, shouting curses, was fairly behind them, and they burst at once into a full gallop. The good brown mare was amply strong enough to carry that double burden, and all in an instant they had rounded the corner.

The rifles still boomed thunderously loud through the woods, and Devon could hear the waste balls splitting through twigs and leaves; he could hear one strong voice take command at their rear, also, and shout orders, though there was too much noise for him to distinguish the words.

Presently, however, a rifleman opened directly behind them, and the bullet pushed Devon's hat gently forward over his face.

It was the last stroke.

They passed on into a tangle of trees, and in a scant minute they were in the open, heading toward the town. Old Harry pulled up beside them, his face white with concern.

"Oh, Jim, you ol' fool, did you get yourself snagged?"

"Nary a scratch," said that veteran with the utmost calmness. "I'm fit to fiddle, and I aim to make some of them skunks sing the tune for us! Go on, Harry. You want them to spill out of the trees and swarm all over us?"

They rode on into the town. Harry, fairly shaking with anger, was for raising a mob and going back to do summary execution on the men of the forest, but Jim wisely concluded that it would be best to put the matter in the capable hands of the sheriff.

Devon agreed with him. A blind mob might run into many bullets, but it would not be apt to do much harm.

So they pressed ahead, and cutting into the

main street of West London, they were stopped by a tall and slender man with a narrow-trimmed beard and neatly cropped mustache, who raised his hat to them and held up one hand.

"Gentlemen," said he, "may I ask where you are going with those horses? Particularly that gray gelding?"

And he waved to the animal which Harry was riding.

"Back up!" said Harry. "You can talk to the sheriff!"

"I can't back up, my friends," persisted the other, "until I know how you happen to be riding horseflesh that belongs to me. And yet I don't want to call you a horse thief!"

He had blocked the road at a point where it was narrowed by the passing of a long string of mules drawing a heavy wagon. And at his last word half a dozen men gathered instantly about them.

"If you own this hoss," said Harry, "you'll have worse than hoss stealin' to answer for! Back up and let me through!"

A lounging cow-puncher explained to the other:

"This here is old Harry, the trapper. You can't call him a hoss thief, stranger."

At this the stranger stepped instantly aside.

"If he's known in West London," said he,

"I don't wish to make any trouble. But I claim that horse, and I'll prove my claim. Is there an officer of the law near here?"

"Hold on, here's the sheriff now!"

Naxon came slowly through the gathering crowd, and resting a hand against the shoulder of the gray, he heard the stranger's polite exposition of the case. It was quickly settled by the exhibition of a bill of sale, and Harry, in the meantime, was exclaiming:

"Let him take the hoss, if it's his. And then I'll charge him with havin' a hand with the low hounds and murderers, Lew, that are ganged up yonder in the woods!"

"This horse was stolen from a shed behind my shack, five nights ago," asserted the other. "I can prove that as well."

"Give him his hoss," said Harry, "and get together a dozen good men, Lew. We've run down the trail of them that burned the Devon house and rustled his cows!"

XXV. A TRAP FOR LUCKY JACK

Forty men rode out from West London with Lew Naxon in the lead, and Harry and Jim to show the way. There was little showing to be done, however, for smoke guided them. They found the place where the horses had been stopped, and no fewer than four carcasses were discovered heaped over with brush which was now flaming.

The fire had burned the dead animals beyond all possibility of recognition. The few patches of hide which remained unsinged were sufficient to establish the color of the slaughtered beasts, but that was all, and it became perfectly patent that these men of the forest had done their best to keep their horses from becoming clews which might lead to their identification.

That threw a redoubled importance upon the brown mare which Devon had taken, even if the gray had been stolen recently from a respectable citizen of the town. But from the brown something important might be learned.

They left the dead horses and went on toward another high-lifted column of smoke.

It turned out to be the thing which Devon had feared. The cabin, the corral, and the horse shed of the forest dweller were wrapped in shooting flames. Even as they came up a side of the cabin gave way, and the burning logs rolled far off, threatening to spread the fire to the adjacent trees.

Enough of the posse dismounted to roll them back to a less dangerous position, and others, including the sheriff and Jim and Harry, scouted through the trees for sign. They found none of importance, the brief trails dissolving soon among the thick pine needles. Sheriff Lew Naxon did not prolong the search, merely saying:

"There ain't any use to follow a hawk if you ain't got wings, and we don't know about these gents. Maybe some of them are right here now, helpin'!"

With this discouraging thought the entire party returned to West London, after which the sheriff jogged off in the direction of the Devon ranch, obviously bent on finding what clews he could there.

All of West London, turbulent as it was, paused for a day to exclaim over the double outrage of the sacking and burning of Devon's ranch and the attack in the woods. It was so obvious that he was the victim of a strong conspiracy of the lawless that the most obtuse could see it; immediately he became a celebrity in West London.

What it meant to be a celebrity in such a town he could soon see. One of the barbers invited his patronage, quite willing to work free of charge if the great man would sit in his chair once a day. The Levingston boarding house was glad to offer him its best room if he would come there to live, confident that the rest of the house would be filled with the curious.

And the Free Mason saloon was willing to offer him all the free drinks he wished and a permanent choice table in their card room if he would spend a portion of his time at that emporium of pleasure. For wherever he went it was certain that the curious would follow with staring eyes to see a man about to die.

That his life could be saved by anything except immediate flight did not occur to the most optimistic. And when it appeared clear that Devon would not run for his life, the whole town rubbed its hands with a ghoulish pleasure. It was not that West London was more bloody minded than other Western towns, but it loved excitement, and could not have enough at the expense of the other fellow.

This change of atmosphere was the last thing

which Devon wanted, even if it put money in his pocket. For there was never any trouble, now, in filling a table with a prosperous poker game. Every one was glad and eager to sit in at a game with a dead man, for there was nothing that the West loved better, in those days of blood and iron, than to rub elbows with the famous men of guns.

There was not a notch on the handles of Devon's Colts, but that made only a slight difference. It became known that he had mastered Grierson, and that he had at least come safely through several attempts upon his life. For that reason he was a gunfighter.

Immediately the curious found other reasons for admiring him. He was young, clean bred, handsome, and above all, he played a straight game of poker when honest men sat at the table with him. That placed him off in a class by himself, for most Western gamblers were gold-diggers.

Three men took four thousand dollars from him in a single evening over the green felt; he won it back the next morning, but the loss was remembered where the winnings were forgotten, for it was known that the tricks of the trade were at his fingertips, and the three winners had simply been the honest possessors of a streak of luck.

When people commiserated with him because he had been so methodically victimized by his secret enemies, Devon assumed a cheerful air and declared that everything was in the cards; when they asked him what he was going to do about it, he declared that the case was in the hands of the sheriff.

But, as a matter of fact, old Harry and Jim were constantly at work, trying to unravel the mystery.

Then appeared a new complication.

On the front of the post office there was a large board on which notices were posted. Sometimes they were official descriptions of outlaws with a price upon their heads. Sometimes they were offers of reward for the return of lost or stolen property. Again, these placards offered objects for sale, from diamond pins to guns. West London lacked a newspaper, and this was its nearest substitute.

Upon this billboard there was seen one morning a broad sheet of white paper on which was boldly written:

Dear Devon:
What's your price for the brown mare? I could use her.
Ever yours,
Lucky Jack.

West London gathered to read and to laugh.

The bold ways of Lucky Jack had made him almost beloved. He was a continual sensation. And Devon, hearing of the sign, wrote on the same sheet beneath Jack's signature:

There is no price on the brown mare until I find out who owns her.
Best wishes from,
WALTER DEVON.

That night the paper was changed, and the following morning the outlaw, or one of his friends, had pinned up another notice.

DEAR DEVON:
Five hundred should be a fair price and leave something over to heal your conscience. As for the other fellow, dead men never ride.
Yours,
LUCKY JACK.

To this Devon responded simply:

The mare is not for sale.

And Lucky Jack replied duly:

I take what I need, and I need the best horse in West London.

At this the town sat up with a gasp of interest. As though Devon had not troubles enough, this new one, of the first magnitude, had been heaped upon his head. It was now a duel for the possession of the mare, and no one doubted that the outlaw would make an attempt upon her in the near future. What precaution would her owner take to keep her safely in the little horse shed behind Mrs. Purley's boarding house?

The precaution of Devon was of the simplest nature. It was not hard. In the shops which supplied the mines with their equipment for setting off blasting charges, a pair of dry batteries and a length of fine copper wire insulated with rubber, and with a small globe as well, he was prepared.

The brown mare, as a tribute to her quality, was installed in the only box of the Purley stable, and in the course of an hour or more, Devon ran his wire from the latch of the stall door to his bedroom. After that, when the latch was moved, a single flash appeared in the bulb which was at the head of his bed. He was a light sleeper, and therefore he was confident of the result.

Two days passed. It was noted that he had established no guard over the mare, and certainly did not keep ward upon her himself. West London made up its mind that he

201

was letting her slip.

"And why not?" said Mrs. Purley, who had opinions on all subjects. "Would a sensible, self-respectin' guy like Devon mix himself up with gunfightin' trash of the order of this here Lucky Jack?"

And the very next night it happened.

Devon wakened with the knowledge that something had just flashed in his eyes, and in the thin coil of the bulb he could see the red faintly dying. He stepped from his bed into slippers of thin leather that made no weight on his feet, and left him as active as a cat. Then he slid through his window, Colt in hand, dropped to the ground, and was rounding the house on the run ten seconds after the warning flash.

When he came to the rear of the place he paused at the last corner, and peering cautiously around, he saw a mounted man, almost lost in shadow against the wall of the horse shed from which he was riding out. Another horse, riderless, stood near. Devon could guess that Lucky Jack was a fast worker indeed, and had changed his own horse for the brown mare even in this short flight of seconds.

"Evening, Lucky," said Devon, and stepping into the open he fired straight at the head of the other.

He knew he had missed. The brown mare

was spun toward him and driven at him through the moonlight like a flash. Stretched along her neck lay Lucky Jack with revolver extended. Again the gun coughed from the hand of Devon, and again he realized that he had failed.

Then the buzz of a hornet flicked past his ear. Lucky Jack, his long hair blowing, was towering above him as the hammer of Devon's gun clicked on a dead cap. He had no time to spin the cylinder and shoot again, but he threw back his arm and flung the heavy weapon as Jack's Colt spat a crimson flame in his very face.

Scorched and blinded by the burning powder, his ears half deafened by the report, Devon staggered for a moment in a black mist. His foot caught and he stumbled upon a soft body.

Then, as his senses returned, he saw a man lying face up, with outstretched arms, and the red mark where the revolver had struck between his eyes.

Still, for a moment, he could not understand, and only gradually could he come to know that this was famous Lucky Jack!

XXVI. JACK CONTEMPLATES HANGING

There was in West London a universal rule of good sense in one respect, at the least: when guns sounded in the streets the inhabitants remained indoors. Nothing could have shown greater wisdom, for even in the hands of comparative experts a pair of Colts can cover an amazing amount of ground in all directions except toward the target; and bullets are no respecters of innocence.

Therefore not a man came forth in spite of all the roaring of guns behind Mrs. Purley's boarding house, but out rushed that lady in person, armed with a weapon which she trusted more than a gun, and this was a walking stick with a knotty end.

Her ample form was gathered into the capacious drapery of a Mother Hubbard. Her hair straggled wildly over her shoulders. And she looked like a goddess of war as she burst open the rear door of her house.

"You murderin' devil," said Mrs. Purley as she came; "have you done for poor Devon? I'll knock your brains out!"

Devon looked up; the hand and the club were arrested. She stood aghast, looking down at her boarder and his victim.

"My Gawd!" Mrs. Purley exclaimed. "It's Lucky Jack — at last! Have you — have you killed him, man?"

"I — don't know," Devon gasped. "We'd better — take him inside — he hasn't moved!"

"And he may have some of his gun-fightin' friends around," said she. "Take his head, while I hoist his heels. What a pair of spurs he's wearin', eh? He could hang onto the flanks of a streak of lightning with a pair like this!"

She lifted the knees of the fallen man, and they carried him through the rear door of the house just as windows began to be slammed up and curious heads were appearing in the moonlight. In the deserted kitchen they laid Lucky Jack upon the floor.

"Bah!" said Mrs. Purley after a single glance. "He ain't hurt. Not enough to let sense into him, anyway! There, he's comin' around. He's a fatal beauty for you, Devon, ain't he? You'd almost take him really to be the brother of that lyin' kid that called herself Prudence Maynard. Keep him safe here. I'll have the sheriff here in two jumps!"

"Hold on a moment," said Devon. "Don't go for him yet — there's time for that!"

Lucky Jack suddenly groaned and stiffened. Devon, dexterously "fanning" him, took forth a pair of Colts — one from a spring holster beneath the pit of his arm and another inside his belt. A capable knife also was found, but the guns were most interesting. Two notches had been filed neatly into one handle, and three into the other!

Lucky Jack, with a gasp, thrust himself up to a sitting posture by a single movement of his arms, and Mrs. Purley, in alarm, heaved up her club.

"Sit where you be," she commanded. "Sit where you be, you hell-cat, you. Look at him, Devon. He could jump off his hands as easy as another guy could jump off his feet!"

In fact, Devon felt that he never before had seen a man who was a more perfect incarnation of activity than this youngster. He could not have been more than twenty-two or -three, and he was made with a slender and catlike perfection. His blond hair, worn long after the old frontier fashion of the mountain men, fell back from his head, brushing his shoulders, and Devon looked down into a face in which he could not see a single trace of debauchery or professional crime.

No doubt there was too much boldness in the eyes which stared unrelentingly back at him and his commanding gun; but the features were perfectly made, the eyes big and bright; the whole face intelligent and awakened by the power of the mind.

After his first movement he did not stir, but remained as though waiting for permission, but a restless glance to either side suggested that he might be estimating his chances of escape by some bold and sudden move.

Devon, watching him earnestly, realized that death had no terror for Lucky Jack. It was an old familiar, with whom he had often rubbed elbows.

"Suppose you sit in the chair by the window," said Devon.

"Tie him up before you let him budge," cautioned Mrs. Purley.

"We'll put him in the chair," Devon insisted, and the other accordingly rose and sat down by the window.

A drop of blood trickled down from his cut forehead, making a crimson streak across his face, but he appeared to pay no attention to his wound. He was smiling and nodding a little to Devon.

"I shouldn't have played with you while your luck was in so strong," Lucky Jack drawled. "But I wanted to buck the game while the stakes were big!"

"I understand," said Devon. "And you nearly won."

"I? Not at all," replied the youth calmly. "In the first place, your Colt missed fire. In the second, you slammed me in the face and knocked me kiting, fair and square. You can be witness that I confess to a fair beating, Mrs. Purley!"

She frowned and drew a little closer to him.

"You know me, Jack?"

"Oh, I know you, of course. Every one knows you, and that you don't short-change the boys, drunk or sober."

"You young devil!" said Mrs. Purley. "Is that why you never raided my place?"

"Oh, never that in a thousand years!" Lucky Jack remonstrated. "No need of it in an open-handed town like West London, where so many tills are left open. It's a charitable town, is West London!"

"Charity my hat," said Mrs. Purley. "The kind of charity they got here'll twist your neck for you, young Lucky Jack! Your luck is run out, it looks like!"

He nodded at her, smiling again. Without the slightest change of color, with a sort of impersonal interest, he fingered his brown throat.

"I suppose it *has* run out," he sighed. "Mrs. Purley, you haven't a cup of coffee in that big pot on the stove, have you?"

"Listen to him!" said she, with a grin of

pleasure and admiration. "Askin' for a hand-out at a time like this! Maybe you'll ask your way out of the place you're gunna go to, young feller!"

"If you'll give me luck, Mrs. Purley."

"Aw, I'll give you luck, well enough."

She brimmed a tin cup with black coffee and placed it on the table at the elbow of the prisoner.

"Mind you," Devon warned, "if you try to use that hot coffee for anything but drinking, a bullet travels faster than that!"

"Hello!" said Lucky Jack. "You're a mind reader, Devon! But at least I can drink it."

He raised his cup, nodded to them, and drank. Then he sat at ease, and asked permission to roll a smoke. It was granted. Presently he was breathing forth smoke.

"Jack," said Devon, "who put this idea into your mind?"

"About stealing the mare? Why, no one. I wanted her, that was all."

"Wanted her this badly?"

"I would have bought her. When you turned me down, I thought of the other thing. You've been stealing my limelight, Devon. I've been the main excitement around here long enough to want to keep the center of the stage, but you were stealing my place. I suppose that was my chief idea."

"Listen to him!" said Mrs. Purley, fairly biting her lip to keep from smiling. "Bashful and timid and scared, ain't he? The poor little darlin' is lined with brass."

"You don't think I'm some one's hired man?" suggested Lucky Jack, with a frown.

"It only seems a little odd," said Devon, "that when my hands already are full, you should be added on the other side of the scales."

Lucky Jack shrugged his shoulders.

"Coincidence!" said he. "It's a queer thing. Queer enough to hang people, as a matter of fact. I'm sorry to keep you standing, Mrs. Purley."

"I'll walk, then," said she. "I'll have Naxon here in five minutes, Devon. Watch the cat, or he'll scratch your eyes out in a second!"

She went out. Lucky Jack leaned back in his chair and smiled.

"You can mark this day in red," he suggested.

"I suppose I can," answered Devon.

"You're actually downhearted, man!" said the other. "Cheer up. This will get you into the newspapers, and throw a chill into the other side as well. They won't be too free with you after this. I flatter myself about that, Devon! Now that you've handled me —"

He paused, his teeth clicked, and a light of

fairly devilish malice for an instant glinted into his eyes. It was plain that he had greatly overtaxed his powers of acting for the moment.

Shame and fury flared in his eyes; then he mastered himself again.

Devon, all this while, watched with a sort of melancholy interest and pleasure combined. Again and again he could not help visualizing hard, hempen rope bite into the throat of the outlaw.

"As a matter of fact," said Devon, "I'm thinking of some one else."

"Who else?"

"A girl, Lucky."

"No girl will have a broken heart when I dance on air," said the cold-blooded youngster with a shrug of his shoulders. "I've been too busy to waste my time on booze or the ladies."

Devon nodded. He was beginning to see this fellow more and more clearly, and everything that he saw fitted into a strange but consistent pattern. There was neither shame nor fear in Lucky Jack. He lacked brutality; but he also lacked consideration for others. By his talk he had been raised to the age when he could learn proper speech in the right sort of household. But if he were not tempted by liquor or by women, danger was the lure for him. He was a hunter, and his hunting was for men.

"I was not thinking of a sweetheart of

211

yours," said Devon. "I was thinking of your sister."

He had intended to qualify that word by saying "the girl who called herself your sister," but it had come out unaccompanied.

The effect upon young Lucky Jack was startling. He clutched both sides of his chair. Every whit of careless insouciance was knocked out of his eyes, and he stared at Devon as though a cannon had yawned before him.

XXVII. THE GET-AWAY

"My sister!" breathed Lucky Jack at last. "My sister?"

Devon hastily followed the track which he had stumbled upon.

"Prudence."

Jack stiffened in his chair.

"By God!" said he. "I think you really know her!"

"So does half of West London."

"Half of —"

"Prudence Maynard, looking for her brother."

Lucky Jack grew white.

"She wouldn't give that name!" said he.

"Because it's the right one?" guessed Devon.

"Right? Of course not," denied Jack, but his voice was very feeble. And his glance wandered helplessly.

Some hint of what the truth might be jumped into the mind of Devon. It was barely possible that Lucky Jack was ignorant of the girl's coming.

"Would she have known your business, Jack?"

"Business?" said the outlaw with a groan. "How could she have known that?"

"She came here honestly, then, to find you?"

Jack raised his hands and let them fall heavily.

"God knows why she came — unless it was to make trouble — she's always been an expert at that. But not for me! Not for me!"

He dropped his head in his hands and stared first at the floor and then at Devon. It was like watching a new man, so utterly was he altered from his former indifference.

"What name did she give me?"

"Maynard."

"It can't be Prue!" groaned Lucky Jack.

"With your picture, Jack."

"Then she's lost her wits completely! I wish — I wish to God that your gun hadn't missed fire, Devon!"

The gambler nodded.

"I understand," said he. "You thought that you were completely out of her reach?"

"Thought? I was sure! Two thousand miles of airline — isn't that enough?" Then he added: "Not with her to find the trail! But what deviltry is in her mind? What does she mean?"

"Maynard —" began Devon.

The other winced, then set his jaw to endure.

"Shall I drop that name?"

"Yes. If you will."

"As far as I'm concerned," said Devon, "I've no wish to hurt your pride. But how does it happen that you haven't heard about her? Half the town, at least, knows how she came to town and tried to lead me into a trap in the woods."

"Lead you?"

"Aye. To find her brother — Maynard! His picture shown to me. And Slugger Lewis glad to show me the way. He's a friend of yours, I take it?"

"The Slugger? He's a dog, but useful enough. Yes, I know the Slugger."

"He was to lead us out to find you. But, of course, you know these things. You laid the trap for us that so nearly bagged Harry and me."

"I laid it? I'm hearing about it for the first time. It's news, sure!"

"I want to believe you, Jack."

"Believe me? I don't lie, man! I'll swear it to you. Trap? I've never trapped a man in my life. I haven't had to. I've met them face to face, gun to gun, however you want to put it!"

Devon hesitated. There was a flaring honesty in this statement that he could not doubt. West London told many a tale about Lucky Jack, but none that made him out a sneak.

"Very well, then," said Devon. "She was working for some one else. The others — the gang that wants my head, Jack."

"She'd never do it," declared Jack, with the same surety as before.

Devon smiled.

"I dreamed that I was sent out into the woods? I dreamed the bullets, too, perhaps?"

Lucky Jack made another gesture of despair.

"It wasn't Prue. It was some one else, wearing her name."

"Looking a shade like you Jack."

The outlaw gritted his teeth.

"Not unless she's gone mad — she couldn't do such things! Prue? She's wild as the wind, but she's as straight as a string."

Said Devon earnestly: "I'd like to believe that."

"Believe it, then. I know her as well as my own mind. I know her better. She'd swim a river for the sake of excitement. But she'd never do a wrong turn. She couldn't. It's not in her, I tell you!"

Devon shook his head with a smile.

"You think I'm talking shadows?" said Lucky Jack. "I know you're straight with me,

Devon, and I give you my word that I'm straight with you. I'm half mad with what you tell me about Prue. To come here — to use that name — to show my picture, when at least she must have guessed — God knows what could have come into her mind!"

"Suppose," said Devon, "she was trying to force you back to your people?"

Lucky Jack exclaimed with mingled anger and understanding: "That's the sort of an idea that would pop into her head. Oh, the little devil! She wanted to badger me out into the open, where she could get her hands on me!"

"Could she make you go, then?" asked Devon curiously.

"She," said her brother, "could make the devil put on slippers and dance; she could pull the whiskers of a lion; she could turn a boy into a man or a man into a boy!"

"I believe she could," said Devon, smiling a little.

The youngster looked sharply at him.

"You've been exposed to the disease, I see," said he. "It's a seven years' fever, Devon and it never can be cured in a shorter time."

"She gave me bullets for a cure."

"There again I don't recognize her. I can't make the Prue that I know fit into your picture of her, Devon! Oh, as keen as a whip, and as stinging, sometimes, but never a coward, and never a sneak — good gad, no!"

"I may see her again," said Devon, "and then, perhaps, she'll explain."

To this Jack did not answer, but looking past Devon, his eyes suddenly narrowed, and that was enough to make his captor whirl — that and the faintest of noises, like the creak of a floor board under foot.

And he saw in the frame of the door which opened from the kitchen into the hall the faint shadow of a man with a glimmer of steel in his hand.

He leaped sidewise, snapping out his Colt, and the other fired with a curse that announced the futility of his aim even as he pulled the trigger.

The door crashed behind Devon; in a glance he saw that Lucky Jack was gone — lucky in this adventure, also! And the beating of hoofs began as Devon sprang wildly through the rear door of the house.

Far off, disappearing around the farthest corner of the barn in the moon haze, he saw the rider fleeing like a bolt from a bow, and now completely dissolved. But it was not the brown mare he had taken. No matter how Lucky Jack prized her, he had left the mare behind him, and Devon could wonder at this deliverance.

He did not pause.

There was that murderous lurker in the middle of Mrs. Purley's house. He ran around to the front of the place to intercept his retreat, if he could, and he arrived there just as a shape fled across the street and paused at the mouth of an alley to look back, gun in hand.

All the heart slipped from Devon. Whatever he attempted turned to the thinnest mist of failure in this accursed place! And he was not mad enough to pursue an armed man through the tangle of West London's byways.

He went back to the brown mare, put her in the stable, and returned to the house in a grim humor to meet Mrs. Purley and the sheriff just arriving.

"Is he gone?" cried Mrs. Purley. "When I heard the shot I told myself that poor Devon was a goner, and that wild cat had clawed his way loose! Oh, I never seen the like of him. There's a slick boy for you, Naxon. God help him. I hope he learns how to buck up and go straight. He's got a pretty way of talkin', Devon, ain't he?"

"He's gone," Devon admitted. "He talked prettily enough to keep me facing him, while some one slipped down the hall to take a crack at me from behind. I owe you for that window pane, Mrs. Purley!"

"Aye, you do," said she; "but make it a

lump sum, Devon, will you, and put in the price of a coffin, too. I'm gunna have the buryin' of you before the year's wearin' long pants! If I was you, Devon, I'd hop out and take a change of air. Looks like it's far West for you, or kind of high and hard on your eyes!"

"Lucky Jack's gone," sighed the sheriff. "Now, there's one that I'd of been glad to send up to hang."

"Why glad?" asked Devon.

"Because he's one that's been raised to know better. I got enough trouble with them that have hell fire in their blood, without addin' on outlaws like Lucky Jack, that are always playin' at man killin' as though it was a game. But he's slipped through my fingers again. So long. I'm goin' home to sleep!"

He departed at once.

"And that's the end of our Lucky Jack to-night!" sighed Mrs. Purley.

It was not quite the end, however, for on the bulletin board at the post office the next morning the town of West London was able to read:

DEAR FRIENDS:
   I called on Devon, and nearly stayed for life. He keeps the brown mare, and I keep a sore head. But there's more than

220

one hand in a pack. Better luck another time.

My compliments to you all, and especially to charming Mrs. Purley and her coffee!

Your obedient servant,
LUCKY JACK.

XXVIII. JIM GATHERS EVIDENCE

Old Jim stepped into the butcher shop and looked over the line of hanging carcasses, while the butcher, in person, a pencil over his ear and a cleaver in his hand, nodded at him.

It was the slack time of the day. The drowsy afternoon buzzed and hummed outside, and the noise of a pair of hammers at work nearby was like the clacking of busy, gossiping tongues, insisting upon utter nonsense.

There was another sound, from which West London never was freed, day or night, and that was the work at the mines; but this was usually a dreamy confusion, all floating up hollow and faint from the deeps of the gulch, except that now and then a single stroke of sound, luckily reflected from the rock walls, rang and echoed boldly — the crack of hammer on drill head sounding like the report of a rifle, or a foreman's shout turned into a yell of rage or pain.

But all of this confusion of utterance was brushed back, for the moment, and West London slept. There were few drinkers in the saloons. There were no loungers in the streets. West London at three in the afternoon was like most places at three in the morning. And it was for this reason that the butcher had a chance to pay attention to his casual visitor.

"What'll you have, old-timer?" asked the owner of the shop. "I can show you some cuts today. Now, there's a cow that'll turn out a T-bone for you, or a full-size porterhouse, if you want that much!"

"I don't want to buy any meat," said Jim. "I'm just lookin' 'em over. They seem familiar!"

The butcher was young. He had red hair, and his eyebrows were no more than a pale streak thumbed upon his flushed and puffy face. Like all of his complexion and type, he was filled with self-confidence, and now he slapped his red-stained left hand upon the chopping block and laughed.

"Yeh," he said, "I can imagine that! The sight of a lot of fresh meat like this must be better'n roses to one of you gents that has spent all your time on the range! Livin' on canned tomatoes and stale bacon ain't so good after a while."

"Well," said Jim crudely, "it's kind of a pleasure to see six cows that ain't gunna give no cowboy no more trouble — see 'em all hangin' in a row with their heads off. There ain't much brains in a cow, I'd say."

"There ain't," agreed the butcher. "For lack of brains a cow would outrank anything in the world, I guess. But you say you've seen this stuff before. You ever been in the business? Or you been down to some of the big towns, maybe?"

"No, no," said Jim. "Big towns is worse'n poison to me. What with their wranglin' and their noise."

"Listen!" the butcher responded. "West London ain't silent, either."

"Aye," said Jim; "but it's the noise of nacher, or the noise of men fightin' nacher and takin' her riches out of her heart. But in the cities you got the noise of iron grindin' on iron, and that's a thing that wears the soul of a man mighty thin, I'd tell you!"

This was a stage beyond the mind of the butcher to comprehend; therefore his glance wandered, and he yawned.

"You was sayin' that you seen somethin' like this? You didn't say where?"

"It was in the old days," said Jim. "I've seen the prairie stained with it. I've seen the red on the grass. I've seen the red on the faces and the bodies of the Injuns. I've been red myself, and I've sort of wallered in it."

The butcher ran the pink tip of his tongue

across his lips, and his eyes glistened.

"That would be slaughterin'. I suppose they used to knock 'em over by the hundreds?"

"You'd 'a' seen 'em scattered like flies."

The butcher rested his chin upon his hand, and nodded at Jim, who was now examining the carcasses again.

"You sorta like that beef, do you?"

"Well, I dunno," said Jim. "I'd say that she was raised in some kind of a poorhouse."

The butcher laughed again and ended in a grunt.

"That ain't more'n a two-year-old cow," he explained. "But look at the way she's turned out. There ain't a couple of pounds of fat in the whole of her. I betcha there ain't enough marrow in her bones to make a decent dog snap at 'em!"

"I don't suppose there is," said Jim. "You know meat, all right, my son."

"Maybe I don't!" declared the butcher, wrinkling his pale brows in pride. "Maybe I don't know it, just! I tell you what. That's a cow off of the starvation ranges around here!"

"Well, well," said Jim, "ain't you kind of hard on our country round about here?"

"Am I?" sneered the butcher. "You think it's pretty good for cows, do you?"

"That's what I've always heard people tell."

225

"Well, lemme tell you somethin'. You go to Iowa and look at the fat on corn-fed beef. That'll show you somethin'! That'll show you meat that a man can set his teeth in. Why, melt in your mouth, what I mean to say. Jus' nacherally melt in your mouth!"

He laid a hand upon his stomach and sighed.

"You gotta have corn for a cow, or else you gotta have a lot of fresh feed for her," the butcher explained, looking into the mild, wide eyes of Jim. "You take a look at this here. There ain't no fat on it. There ain't nothin' worth seein'."

"I would of said that this here young cow come up from the grasslands down the river," Jim volunteered.

"You would of said that, would you?" the butcher inquired grimly. "Well, and what would of made you say that?"

"Why, I dunno. I just would of opinioned that, as you might say."

"You might say, but you'd say wrong," the butcher replied fiercely. "Some of you old-timers would be more at home among buffalo than among cows. I tell you, this here cow ain't off of green grass!"

"It ain't?"

"No, it ain't."

"Well, maybe that's a matter of opinion, after all," said Jim with a mild stubbornness.

"Opinion?" flamed the youth. "Why, opinion be hanged! You think you know, do you?"

Old Jim prodded gently at a long seam on the ribs of the carcass, looking as though it had been made by a barbed wire cut.

"There ain't hide nor hair of her, nor horn to tell by," said Jim in the same gentle persistence. "There ain't hoof nor brand to spot her by, nor any earmark. How would anybody be able to swear to her, then?"

The butcher nodded. He was so angry that he did not speak for an instant; small souls always are enraged by small offenses.

"Why, darn my heart," said he, "ain't it a fact that I bought the cow that walked inside of that hide?"

"Ah, did you?" said Jim. "And wasn't it one of them red Durhams from down the river way?"

"Red Durham?" shouted the butcher. "Why, that poor, lean, brindle roan didn't have a drop of good blood in her. She ain't fit for nothin' but sausage, though she'll go down the throats of the drunks in this here town like nothin' at all."

"Brindle roan?" murmured Jim. "You pretty sure of that?"

"Why in tarnation shouldn't I be?" roared the butcher. "Didn't I buy her off of young

227

Sam Green not more'n a couple of days ago?"

"Did you?"

The butcher was silent in his consuming wrath.

"Well, maybe I better be goin'," said Jim.

"Maybe you had," said the butcher meaningly.

And so terminated that friendly conversation, while old Jim sauntered out into the sun, blinked at its brightness for a moment, and then turned down the street, whistling tunelessly. However, when he had turned the corner he lengthened his step and made straight for the sheriff's house. Him he found laboring in his garden, digging up potatoes from a small vegetable patch. He raised a miserable and sweating face in answer to Jim's hail.

"You know a gent by name of Sam Green?" asked Jim.

"Sure. I seen him down the street not more'n an hour ago. Why?"

"Nothin' much," said Jim, "except that I'd like to have him arrested for hoss stealin' and cow rustlin', and for arson besides!"

228

XXIX. JUST A FRIENDLY STROLL

There is nothing that the West loves half so much as a leisurely approach to an important task, so that the accomplishment may be tested and tasted, so to speak, beforehand. Now the sheriff and Jim laid their heads together with old Harry and with Devon.

When they had framed their plan, Devon looked to the polish of his boots, brushed his coat and hat with care, and then walked down the street, swinging a light walking stick — in his left hand!

That was no affectation, because, as every one in West London understood, there might be vital need at any moment for the use of that right hand on the handle of something much heavier than a walking stick.

He had heard that Sam Green was in the First Chance saloon, and to the First Chance he made his way. Literally it made its fortune on the red-hotness of the thirst which tormented men coming up from the desert on this trail. They could not wait, and it was told of many a man that the First Chance was also the Last Chance for him, for once at the bar he could not leave.

Otherwise there was nothing about this down-at-the-heels saloon to keep its patrons long.

Devon pushed open the swinging door with his walking stick, and saw, with a swiftness and precision of eye which only a gambler could use, that of the half dozen men scattered down the length of the bar, not one had a familiar face to him.

At the farthest end, however, with his heel on the bar rail, and his back comfortably resting against the wall, was Sammy Green, as he had been described by the sheriff. He was a youth in his early twenties, with extremely broad shoulders to make up for his lack of height, and his face was given a boyish look by many freckles.

Devon entered, took his place at the end of the bar nearest to the door, and waved his hand to the others. He noted with pleasure that every man in the place knew his name; and if he had paid for that celebrity by the danger of his life several times, still it was eminently worth while to have a friendly atmosphere in West London. There was even a possibility that the crowd might make some movement against the next would-be assassin.

Above all, the adventure with Lucky Jack

had captivated the imagination of the good citizens of West London.

"Ain't seen you in here before, Mr. Devon, have I?" asked the bartender.

"No. Never been to this end of the town before."

"Aye. Where the flies are the thickest, there you'll find the suckers risin'," the bartender said sourly. "Out here we got quiet and the smell of the pines, which is worth somethin' for them that got a nose in their head. Have one on the house. This here is Lefty Jack Marvin, and there's Bud Lampson and Chuck Parry, and Big Hal Murphy, and Chris Long, and —"

Devon, shaking hands with the rest, nodded at Sam Green.

"You're Sammy Green, I take it?"

"Sure I am," said Sam, delighted by such recognition from a celebrity. "Didn't know that you knew me, Mr. Devon."

"I've heard of you," Devon replied, smiling. He had been primed by the sheriff for this conversation. "I've heard of your days in Tombstone."

"Oh, I was in the long grass down there for a while," said Sammy, with a sigh of satisfied reminiscence. "It come to me in both hands, for a spell. But it didn't last forever."

"You shook out a good deal of seed, I believe," Devon inquired.

"I did. But it didn't grow. They kept the bar floors too clean down there in Tombstone," said Sammy Green. "But I had my party, and I was willing to pay for it. You can't eat your money! Who told you about me and Tombstone?"

"Several," said Devon, noncommittal. "They remember you in that part of the world."

"Well, I painted my name big enough, and the paint wasn't fake gilding, either. Have one on me, Mr. Devon."

"I'm out to stretch my legs," Walt evaded. "Will you walk back to town with me?"

The glance of Sammy Green wandered for an instant in thought, and his glance rested firmly on the face of Devon. Then he nodded shortly, unwillingly, like a man unable to refuse temptation.

"I'll come along. I wouldn't mind a stroll myself," said he.

"Hey," grinned the bartender in pretended dismay, "you put in one and you take out two Mr. Devon!"

Thus Devon wandered out from the saloon with his man, and walked downtown in the rose of the evening light. Timbal Gulch was quiet, except for one single jack, battering hurriedly in the distance as though to make up for lost time. The town was coming to life again, and people were beginning to stroll out from their houses, black silhouettes in this glare of light. And, like bees, the forms swarmed at the doors of the saloons.

"Mining up here as at Tombstone?" asked Devon.

The other glanced sidewise at him, a suspicious glare.

"Nope," he answered. "Not exactly. I'm off the old lay for a while, unless I can strike something. But they've tapped every rock in Timbal Gulch, like a dentist taps every tooth in your head."

"There's not much else to do, is there?" asked Devon.

"Why, there's always a way to pick up coin, here and there," Sammy Green answered more cheerfully, as they entered the heart of the town. "Over there at the Palace I worked as bouncer for a while."

"That's a quiet place," said Devon, looking up at the formidable front of the big gaming house.

"Sure," said the other. "Les Burchard has got everybody in his pocket. They're sort of afraid to speak out loud in that dump."

"He's straight," suggested Devon.

"Is he? Aw, I suppose so. I dunno why everybody is so sure of that, though. He ain't got a diploma for squareness yet, that I know about! The way these gents talk, you'd think Burchard was a tin god. Why? Because he just happened to strike it up here. That's the only reason."

"He's made a town," said Devon.

"Him? I dunno. It ain't so much at that. You look at Tombstone —"

"Give West London time."

"You like it, eh?"

"Why, it's not a bad little place," said Devon. "There are plenty of games here, and the stakes are reasonable. That's my business, you know."

"Sure," Sammy Green agreed. "Everybody has gotta follow his own line. Some fish with nets, and some with flies. But the thing that fills the old basket is what I'm after."

"The sport is something," suggested Devon.

"So they say. Sure, when you're a kid. But when you grow up you gotta take things more serious."

"No doubt that's correct."

"I done my share of chance takin' when I was a kid," said this experienced youth, "but I'm tired of that line now. I want something sure. Have a drink in here?"

"Let's go on a way. There's a good solid building, now."

"Sure. You know what it is?"

"I don't recognize the back of it."

"Don't you? It's the jail!"

Sammy Green laughed loudly at this hit, and Devon smiled in turn.

"That's the sheriff's work, I suppose?" said he.

"Sure. He busted himself to get it built. Made speeches in the saloons and everything. You heard about Lucky Jack?"

"No."

"He swiped fifteen hundred dollars off of the Last Chance bar, and he gives fifteen hundred dollars the next day to the sheriff for the purpose of making his jail bigger and stronger. 'Because,' says Lucky Jack, 'maybe I'll come and spend the night in your jail, some time, if it's comfortable enough to keep out the rain.' "

"Did the sheriff keep the money?"

"Sure he did. He don't care where he gets the coin, as long as he gets a chance to soak it into his jail. You know what he's got in there for making the bars of?"

"Good steel, I suppose."

"Good steel? I'll tell a man. Tool proof is what he's got!"

Sammy Green wrinkled his nose in strange distress.

"Why not step in and take a look at it?"

suggested Devon as they turned the corner of the building.

"Inside the jail?" asked Sammy, with another of his quick, probing glances.

"Why not?" Devon countered blandly.

"And why so? I've seen the inside of a jail once or twice. It don't make me comfortable. What about you?"

"I'm curious," said Devon. "And besides, you might learn something that would be of use later on."

"Useful for what, Devon?"

"Useful when you have to get out, you know."

"I have to get out?"

"Oh, yes," said Devon. "Because I suppose you'll go inside with me now?"

Sammy Green whirled on his heel, doubtful, but with fear in his eyes.

"What you mean by that?"

He found the lean face of Devon coldly set.

"I haven't walked you all the way from the First Chance to this place for nothing, Sammy," said the gambler. "Now walk up the steps and go through the front door."

Sammy Green gasped. His right hand made a quickly jerking movement, but he saw that one of Devon's hands was buried in his coat pocket, and he had wit enough to guess at once what that meant. Something like a finger pointed toward him through the folds of the cloth.

"By God, I almost think you're doublecrossing me!" gasped Sammy Green. "Me!"

"You have too many friends in this town," said Devon, "for an open arrest to be made easy. I didn't want to be shot in the back by one of your friends, the rustlers, and so I thought we'd take a friendly stroll together down to the jail. No one would think anything about that, Sammy — seeing us walk together into the jail."

Sammy stared.

Then he turned and walked slowly up the stairs, with Devon half a step behind him. But just before he reached the big door of the jail, Green tipped his head, and through the air ran a long, trilling whistle. It was interrupted in the midst by the long arm of Devon, which thrust his captive before him into the interior of the jail, and into the waiting arms of the sheriff.

XXX. DEAD MEN TELL NO TALES

The interior of the jail was one big room, except for the sheriff's office, which was set off in one corner, and the kitchen, which occupied another. Otherwise the interior was checked off in regular little squares by cages made of strong steel bars — the tool-proof steel which had made such a profound impression upon the soul of Sammy Green.

Through the cells went two narrow corridors, one traveling across the body of the room to connect with two side doors, and the other penetrating the building from front to rear, where there were also doors. Where these passages intersected there was a little open space, a square in which the guard could sit with a shotgun across his knees, and there were several stools for his convenience.

Upon these Devon and Sam Green and the sheriff sat down. Old Jim and Harry were there, as a matter of course, but they preferred to stand at the front and the rear doors with their long rifles. "Because," said Harry, "you never can tell when the wind might blow one of 'em open and scatter your ideas like leaves, eh?"

The sheriff readily agreed to this arrangement, and sent the guard into his office to watch the windows there, for it was plain that the signal which the prisoner had raised, interrupted though it had been by the long arm of Devon, might have been heard by those for whose ears it was meant, and in that case a desperate effort might be made to liberate Green.

"And what about a cross draft from them two side doors?" asked old Jim before he went to his post at the rear of the jail.

"I reckon there ain't any need to worry about that," said the sheriff; "fact is that the gents that laid out this jail, they didn't like all of my ideas. One door was what I wanted. Because who wouldn't rather stand guard over a solid wall than where doors are punched in. But you'd think that the boys thought this here might be used for a theater some day, they was so dead set on punchin' a lot of holes in the wall. When I sashayed into here and seen the four doors, I just took the only two keys of the side ones and I dropped 'em into a hot forge fire, and I blowed the bellows myself until the iron of them keys jus' nacherally run like water. And they ain't any other keys to fit 'em. Not in the world, I take it!"

So the rear and front doors were guarded, and the three sat down for their conference. There were no other prisoners. Though a regular crop was planted in the building every evening, the local justice of the peace had a formidably quick way of disposing of disturbers of the peace at his morning sessions. In the afternoons he was to be seen again at his familiar seat near the roulette wheel in the Palace.

Sam Green was highly offended by his arrest.

"This here is what anybody in the world would call a frame," said he. "I'll tell you what, Naxon. You've won a lot of respect around here, and everybody likes the way that you've handled things, but here you send out a gent that ain't a sworn deputy or nothing, and you let him make an arrest. No, it ain't any arrest. It's a dog-gone trick to snag me and to get me down here!"

He grew hot, so hot that he had to loosen his collar.

The sheriff listened to this outbreak attentively.

"You gotta lot of right on your side," said he. "Fact is, I worry a lot about doin' things rough and irregular like this. But this here is a rough and irregular town."

"Ain't you the sheriff?" asked Green, his

temper rising still higher. "Are you gunna turn loose all of your pets onto the boys in this here town? I tell you, Naxon, they won't stand it, and they'll let you know that, pretty pronto."

"Aye. I'm afeared they will. Now, what would be likely to happen, Sammy, if I was to of walked into that First Chance, yonder, and asked you to go along with me?"

"Why, I'd of gone along with you. I got nothing to fear from the law!"

"Aye, aye! If you're a plumb innocent young feller it would of been all right," said Naxon gently. "And maybe you are. I sure hope you are. But if we're right in suspectin' you of somethin' else, then I sure think it would of been dangerous for me. And I got a family to think of, son. I only take chances when I got to. Suppose that you went along with me, maybe some of your friends would of gone along with me, too! Y'understand?"

"You mean that they would of jumped you?"

"I'm just supposin' they might of. It's better to think twice before you drop, you know."

"It's a dam' outrage!" Sammy Green blurted out. "And as for the sneakin' way in which *you* put this over on me —"

He finished his sentence by turning to glare balefully at Devon.

It was growing very dusk in the jail; and the lamp which the guard had brought was refused by Naxon.

"Because," said he, "there ain't any doubt that some folks in this here town might be willin' to look in with something more than eyes!"

"I wanta know what's the case agin me?" Green asked aggressively.

"And I'll tell you, me son. We ain't got much of a case. But we want to talk a mite, for the sake of helpin' justice along."

"Bah!" said Green. "You think you can make a fool out of me? Well, you'll see!" Then he barked: "What you suspect, anyway? What you accuse me of?"

And nothing occurred to the sheriff better than the formula of old Jim.

"Nothin' but attemptin' murder, and hoss stealin', and cow rustlin', and arson, too."

Green sat straighter. With all his heart Devon wished that he could see the face of the man, for he would have sworn that there was guilt on it. However, the dusk was now too deep to be penetrated.

A little silence followed, and then the manacles clinked softly as the prisoner stirred.

"It's all a dirty lie!"

"Why, I hope it is," said the sheriff. "I sure hope it is. Then everything will go along all right."

"Murdering who?" barked Sammy Green.

"Mr. Devon, here. You tried to shoot him in the woods."

"Me?" asked Green, with a long, rising whine of what might have been either injured innocence or else fear. "Me? It's a lie!"

"I hope it is," said the sheriff in his usual mild way. "It ain't any pleasure to me to have a man hung!"

"Hung?" asked Green hollowly.

"That's what they generally do with 'em in this here town."

"Even supposing I was guilty — which I ain't — a man ain't hung for trying a murder that don't come off."

"No. Twenty or thirty years would be enough for that."

"Twenty or thirty years!"

"Yeah, I suppose so. Unless the judge got real mean and mad and gave you the limit. But maybe there wouldn't be no chance for the judge. Maybe the gents in this here town would take the thing up into their own hands."

"Whatcha mean?"

"You've seen lynching parties, son."

"Lynching! By God, you'd turn me over to them?"

"Me?" protested the sheriff in the most innocent of voices. "Why, I never would do that, willingly. But supposin' they was to bust the door open on me and come in. I couldn't very well stand up agin the whole town, could I?"

"My God!" whispered Green. "This here is all framed. There ain't an ounce of proof."

"And besides attemptin' the murder," said the sheriff, "there's the idea of runnin' off of Devon's cows and hosses, and then burnin' of his house."

"I didn't have nothing to do with it!"

"Sure, I hope you didn't. But I'll tell you what. The boys in West London have got thinkin' a lot of our partner Devon, here. They seem to sort of like his style. He don't sneak down back alleys. He keeps his head up. He walks in the middle of the street, and he sure don't get a yaller streak worked up in him. They couldn't run him out of this here town."

"What's all that got to do with me?"

"Why, you see how it is, Sammy? Suppose that you was to be actually accused of all of these here things, and the boys was to make up their minds about you —"

"They got no evidence!" cried Green. "Not a dam' bit of evidence agin me. I'm innocent, Sheriff! I tell you I'm innocent, and —"

"You cur!" cried the sheriff, in a voice that struck a thrill of terror even into the heart of Devon. "You've sold Devon's beef to the town butcher. Can you lie out of that? You've sold a roan cow with a horn-marked side to her! Is that evidence? Enough to hang you, you lyin' hound! But I'm gunna give you a chance to save your yaller, sneakin' hide by turning State's evidence on the rest of the gang. We want the heads, not the feet of this outfit."

This terrible denunciation made Green wilt visibly, even in the darkness.

And then he whispered:

"My God! My God! I feel kinda sick!"

The sheriff said not a word. Devon burst into a heavy sweat. The jail was utterly dark now, except that one western window was blushing faintly.

Then the whispered words went on:

"If I say a word they'll kill me — they'll tear me to pieces!"

"We're here to help you," said the sheriff with a sudden change in his voice. "Stand agin the law and I'll run you down with dogs; stand on my side and I'll do anything to keep you safe. You got your neck in a noose. You want to take that noose off?"

"God — God —" Sammy Green whispered in the darkness. And then he groaned: "I gotta live — I can't die — I done too much to die now — Oh, God, I gotta tell you."

"And then we're with you, steady and true," said the sheriff. "I want right out the name of the head of this here murderin' bunch!"

"Him?" said Sam Green. "Well, I might as well begin by telling that. You suspect anybody?"

"We ain't answerin' questions. We're askin' 'em," said the sheriff.

"All right," said the other, "it's —"

And then he jumped to his feet with a gasp.

"They're here!" screamed Green.

As Devon jerked his head around he saw a long flood of light blown down the corridor from the southern side door, and behind that light a rifle spoke.

Sammy Green fell forward on his face.

XXXI. THE DISAPPEARING HERD

They reached the open door in a rush, but there they found no more than a curious crowd swarming out toward them from the nearest saloons. Some one had seen two men at the door of the jail; but where they had gone he could not say; no doubt he did not care to tell. At any rate, in the dusk, he had made out no features.

Tucker Vincent came out of the mob, with Charlie Way behind him. Tall and handsome was Charlie, while Tucker Vincent was small and withered and dark. Vincent always wore gloves with long gauntlets of stiff box leather, but the hand and finger parts of those gloves were of kid, unbelievably thin. Men said he wore through a pair in a week, but the softness of that costly leather enabled him to draw a fast and accurate gun. He offered his services and those of Way.

"There ain't anything to do," said the sheriff. "Once more it's just a question of waitin'. There ain't any eyes here in West London, because nobody wants to see."

Way and Vincent entered the jail and looked at the body.

"The man who fired that shot was an expert," asserted Vincent. "He knew he'd find dead center, there between the eyes. One bullet, and off with him. That's marksmanship, Naxon — by lantern light!"

The others agreed in silence. They gave poor Sammy Green into the hands of the jail guard to prepare him for burial, but first they searched him, and found only one item of interest. In a buckskin wallet, stowed within a tight twist of paper, they found a liberal pinch of brightly shining stuff —

"Like brass filin's," said old Harry.

"Like gold dust!" the sheriff corrected.

It was locked into the desk of the sheriff in his private office.

"There you are," said Jim. "There's a pinch of the stuff they live for. How d'you know where this here Sammy Green got it? Maybe he dug it in the Klondike. He was up there! Maybe pulled it out of a hole in the desert. Maybe he grubbed it out of rock right here in Timbal Gulch —"

"He didn't mine here," the sheriff replied tersely. "Maybe he stuck somebody up, and this pinch is the last of his haul. Now, partners, there ain't a thing we can do except get onto the trail of Sammy Green's cows and see what they'll tell us."

"Aye, if cows'll talk," said Harry.

"I'll make 'em talk," Naxon predicted quietly. "There ain't a Canada or Spanish or Texas steer on this here range that I won't make talk in my own lingo, because I'm gunna work out this trail, old sons, even if it was as bare of sign as the palm of my hand."

"You're kind of worked up," old Jim counseled. "Keep your dander down, Lew. It won't serve you to get riled."

"If I was a father," said the sheriff, "and a son was shot out of my arms, I wouldn't feel no worse. Mind you, friends, I been workin' a long time, and I've had the crowd boilin' around me like steam around an egg, but they never took a man out of my hands since I was the law, not till to-night. And they're gunna pay for it deep and red!"

He was such a casual man, as a rule, that this outburst of trembling passion meant all the more. The others said nothing while their horses were got.

"Who knew Sam Green the best?"

"The bartender at the First Chance," said Harry.

"We'll go there."

They rode through the darkness, through the yellow bars of lamplight, until they came to the First Chance, and there they entered, one behind the other.

"Hey!" called the bartender. "Is it true that Sam Green was got just now?"

The sheriff nodded.

"What would of made them snipe a harmless guy like Sammy?" asked the other, half angry.

"For the sake of the cows that he's holdin' up in the mountains," said the sheriff. "If I knew where I could find 'em, I'd ride for 'em now. Sammy has a mother tucked away somewhere, and it's a shame if she don't get his money."

The bartender squinted his eyes and nodded.

Then he said thoughtfully:

"I dunno who said so — was it Sammy or somebody else? — but seems to me like I'd heard that he had a bunch off behind the dead lake, on grass there. I ain't sure, though."

"Thanks," said the sheriff. "I'll take that direction."

And he led his men into the dark.

"Well?" said Harry, as they mounted.

"Well?" answered the sheriff. "Is he straight, that bartender?"

"The crookedest snake can dig a straight hole," said old Jim, "and then he'll live in it. But they's more permanent bends in that barman than in any snake ever I talked to in my life."

"I never would trust him," said Devon. "He was too cheerful about that shooting. I saw him laughing and talking with Green not so long ago."

"I think with the pair of you," Naxon agreed. "He's crooked, and he's given us a crooked steer. The dead lake is straight down there to the south, and I think that we'll take the opposite line, boys."

"Aye," said Harry. "Them that have to lie quick, without no forethought, they just nacherally go by opposites. I've noticed that with Injuns, when they get pressed. They ain't handy with their tongues, no matter how willin' to lie they may be."

"There's the opposite of the dead lake," said old Jim. "And there's the way to get to it. Chimney Cañon is right north, across on the far side of the Timbal, ain't it?"

"Who'd quarter cows up the Chimney?" growled Harry.

"You ain't got no imagination," said Jim.

"Imagination wouldn't feed a crow, and there ain't no grass nor imagination neither up the Chimney Cañon," declared Harry.

"You take them that're always usin' their eyes on print," said Jim, "and it sure is a mighty sad thing to see the way that they can't use their eyes on nothin' else."

"Why, dog-gone my hide," said Harry, "I

didn't find in no newspaper that Chimney Cañon was as bare as my head. But I seen with my own eyes when there wasn't enough grass to fill your hat!"

"When you see that?"

"Last fall."

"Aye, that was after the sheep was drove through it."

"There wasn't no special sign of sheep."

"The big rains had come and washed it off."

"Listen to that there!" cried Harry. "Doggone me if he ain't like a woman, makin' up his ideas as he goes along."

"Foller me to the Chimney," said Jim stubbornly, "and if I don't find the cows there I'll eat my hat."

"You'll have to, you old goat!" Harry retorted. "You ever been up to the Chimney in your life?"

"Aye — once," said Jim.

"When was that?"

"In the winter," said Jim.

"Hey! Was there snow?"

"Yes."

"Deep?"

"Nigh up to the belly of my hoss."

"Then whaddya know about grass up the Chimney?"

"The Chimney's opposite dead lake," old Jim explained, "and it's a likely ravine to hold cows in. Lew, you'd better start on. Harry has got started to talkin', and he'll never let up till the mornin' comes!"

The sheriff laughed, but when he led them down the side of Timbal Gulch, he was pointing them straight at Chimney Cañon. It appeared as a black, narrow slit in the face of a tall cliff, whitewashed by the moon, and, indeed, the mouth of the gulley was so narrow that they barely could ride two abreast.

"We'd be pie for one or two yeggs up that valley," admitted the sheriff. "If it was daylight I'd send one of you to climb to the top and look into the valley that way."

"Aye," said Jim; "but it's easy to die by night. You don't see so much of the world that the last look will make you homesick when you get to the far side of the shadows, as they say. Come along, Sheriff. I can pretty near hear a heifer bawlin' in there right now!"

The others laughed, but they rode on into the thick blackness of the gorge, though above their heads they could see the far-off brightness of moonlighted clouds.

They turned an elbow corner of the gorge.

"Ha!" said Jim. "Say, d'you hear somethin' now, Harry, you that know so much? You that read the newspapers? You find any articles in 'em about cows up the Chimney Cañon?"

Harry did not respond. Out of the distance, plainly, they heard the clacking of hoofs; and then a distant thunder came booming down the ravine as one of the cows bellowed.

"Why," Jim continued, "I pretty nigh onto recognize the voice of that old spotted fool of a cow. Her that nigh had me down last winter. Come along, boys, and we'll get 'em if we can!"

"Ride hard," said the sheriff. "They're headin' the other way!"

So hard they rode through the darkness, until they heard a rumbling above them, and then down the steep wall of the cañon plunged a mass of rock which, gathering fresh accumulations from the debris of the slope, now roared and plunged, and threw up its tail of dust into the down-reaching hands of the moon.

A hundred tons of massive rock roared down into the floor of the cañon. And their horses shunted back and then waiting, cowering, while the huge mass seemed to boil for an instant, the recoil making monster boulders leap back into the air.

The rage of the sheriff was wonderful to see as he tried to force his pony up the towering mass of the obstruction. Then he scrambled up on foot and raised his hand for silence.

Far off, very distinctly, they could hear the bellowing and the trampling of cattle, receding. All of this noise gradually turned a corner — perhaps an elbow, or through the mouth of a branch ravine — and then it was gone.

Said old Jim deliberately:

"They ain't any use. We can't get those hosses over that much rock. And follerin' on foot wouldn't make us catch up with the tail of that there cyclone. We gotta find a new game to pass the night away. Sheriff, what'll it be?"

XXXII. THE MYSTERIOUS RIDER

They searched the sides of the ravine with care, in the vague hope that they might find some way of getting to a path that would surmount the rock heap, but there was no trace of such a lucky thing. The sheriff actually groaned aloud, for, as he said, they would have had their hands crammed with proofs, beyond doubt, if they could have located that herd.

Even now it was drawing rapidly away from them; if they tried to ride back down the Chimney and come around from the other side, there was not a chance in a thousand that they would hit upon the right trail in that network of ravines. Or even if they did, the herd would have a hopelessly long start, and was probably being split up and sent this way and that even now.

It was Harry who suggested that they might ride back by the Devon ranch, since it was not far out of their direct line to West London, for, as Harry pointed out, the enemy had come there before, and might come again by night.

There was no objection to this scheme, both

Jim and the sheriff being too downhearted over the failure of their night ride to dispute any suggestion. So they pushed on down the narrow throat of the Chimney and out again into the leprous white of the moon.

On the verge of the cliff the sheriff's veteran pony suddenly began to pitch. Bodily he soared against the moon and came down with a snap and a jar, his iron shod hoofs shattering the rocks on which he landed, until old Jim shot the noose of his ever present lariat over the head of the pony and dragged him back to quiet and a safer position.

The sheriff accepted this exhibition with pretended anger; in reality he seemed to have been soothed by combatting the mustang instead of the mental troubles of the trail.

"The old devil is feelin' better, now that he's limbered himself up," said Lew Naxon. "Dog-gone my hide, Harry, I'd like to make you a present of this here hoss, except that I like him too well. This here's the one thousandth time that he's promised to heave me over the edge of a rock into Kingdom Come. The next time maybe he'll live up to his word. Look at him now — plumb happy, damn his old hide!"

For the pony now jogged along with contentedly pricking ears. Over the virtues and the vices of the mustang the three veterans conversed seriously as they went up the trail, and Devon fell a little behind. Watching them, he could not but feel that he had in them the keenest eyes and the sharpest wits on the range, and if man could help him to a solution of his mystery, these were the ones to accomplish the trick in safety.

They descended from the height onto the open hills of his ranch, and from a distance they could see the black smudge which had once been the old shack.

"We'll go and take a look at the place where the hoss of Charlie Way camped that night," suggested Harry.

"Leave the print on the trail alone," said Jim. "We ain't gunna hatch by moonlight any ideas that didn't pick through the shell when the sun was shinin'."

"If you fumble your gun at the first holt," Harry replied, "are you gunna let it go without tryin' again? They's many a man been shot in the dark, besides; sayin' nothin' of a good moonlight like this here!"

"There ain't no fool like an old fool," muttered Jim. "He's ashamed of returnin' to West London without nothin' to show for it. But we gotta go, or he'll talk you brain weary in no time."

So they turned, the sheriff remaining silent in this family dispute, and jogged slowly over the naked hills until Naxon, in the lead, suddenly swung his arm above his head and backed his horse. The others halted, and the sheriff came back to them.

"There was somethin' in Harry's idea, right enough," said he. "They's a man over yonder by the edge of the tank, on his knees, lookin' like he was prayin'."

"Spread out, then," said Devon, "and we'll bag him."

Straightway they divided, the sheriff taking a detour to the right and Devon to the left, while the two old men went straight on over the hill. Their yell, as they reached the summit, made Devon drive the brown mare forward with his spurs.

As Walt topped the rise he saw Harry and Jim flogging toward the hollow — far to the right the sheriff's rifle clanged and through the hollow itself, streaking for dear life, went a fugitive rider!

Devon shot the mare down like a hawk from above, stooping at a smaller prey. For before him was a slender rider and as slim-legged horse flashing through the moonlight.

For all his spurring and the downward slope, the mare could not gain a step to the floor of the hollow, and Devon jerked out his Colt for a flying shot. But then he noticed that the brown was gathering headway. She

259

was a big animal, and required unlimbering; now she fairly flew. Presently she held the other even, then slowly she gained.

The whole face of the ranch was as open as a hand, except for what shelter the contours of the hills themselves could give, but the fugitive was pressing for woods which scattered to the west of the hills.

Beyond the woods, as the trees thickened, the ground broke into a tangle of gulleys, leading up to deep cañons. There was no doubt that the rider would be almost safe if he could reach this broken country, and though the mare gained, Devon looked narrowly ahead to judge the race.

It was hard to tell whether he should win or lose. He glanced back and saw the three veterans far outdistanced, falling deeper and deeper to the rear, so he lightened himself in the saddle and threw his weight still farther forward, bending along the reaching neck of his horse to cut the wind with less resistance.

Her blood was good, for nothing responds to the pressure of a race like the thoroughbred strain, and every moment she extended herself more fully.

Now her stride was telling. With every bound the fugitive came back, jerked by an invisible thread to the rear, and the man who fled seemed to sense the flying danger behind him. He whirled in the saddle, his gun flashed, spoke, and the bullet sang above the head of Devon.

That maneuver cost the flying rider two lengths, at least. He turned again, and this time Devon steadied himself to put in a finishing shot. He was deterred when the other fired wildly and even the sound of the bullet did not reach Devon.

The first scattering trees loomed before them, and they swept in among them with the tail of the fleeing horse not a yard from the mare's nose.

Now was the time, surely, for the fugitive to try his gun, and Devon waited, ready with a sure aim in case the stranger turned. However, the other was now giving all his mind to the flight; and as he reached a large tree he dodged his nimble horse around it — to run straight into the arms of Devon!

For the latter had guessed at the maneuver, and swung to the left to meet it. He could shoot down the man as the little horse dodged and swung back. But the chance was so sure that it was little better then murder. Instead, he dropped his revolver and reaching out with his right arm, he gripped the other around the body.

Walt felt a shock and a strain that threatened to tear his arm from its shoulder socket, but

261

the body of the fugitive then swept away in his grip, a lithe, light body, strangely soft and yielding for the frame of a rider of the range.

And now, as he mastered the hands of the other, and the brown mare lumbered to a halt, Devon found that both wrists of the stranger fitted neatly, helplessly into his left hand, while his right arm crushed the breath from a slim body.

And then the wind tipped up the broad brim of the hat, and the moon shone down on the face of Prudence Maynard!

He almost let her fall in the dizzy shock of that recognition. She was stammering:

"Let me go before they come! Let me go! Let me go! You don't understand —"

He let her go, indeed. His hands were suddenly nerveless and helpless to hold her, and she leaped to the head of her own horse.

It was much too late. Like three lean, hungry greyhounds, Devon's friends were sweeping into the wood. The sheriff drove straight in behind her. Old Harry stopped his mount with a jerk, and dropped the muzzle of a rifle against her breast as the shout of Devon reached him and made him hold his grim hand.

"Hey!" cried Harry. "What's this? What kind of a fish are we catchin' this night? Look a here, Lew, will you? Crowd around, Jim, and have a sight of this!"

They crowded around, indeed. The moon beat full against her face, and the girl, suddenly limp and weak, leaned back against the shoulder of her panting horse and, with one hand twined in its mane, seemed to support herself.   Her eyes were lowered to the ground; her breast heaved; and Devon saw that tears were streaming down her face.

"Now, now," said Jim. "You ain't hanged yet. You ain't murdered, neither. If we've give you a fright, we're sorry. Harry, help her on to her hoss, will you? But the next time, ma'am, maybe you'll not rig yourself up in boy's clothes, or use a gun in the face of a gent like Walter Devon! Hey, Walt, you come and talk to her. She's pretty sick, she's so scared, and she can't understand what I'm sayin'."

Devon dismounted and drew nearer. Looking down in her face he wondered, with a bitter pleasure, if God ever before had made a thing so lovely, or so evil. But even then, much as he knew of her, it was within his heart to let her go. Reason had to come to his aid. He had been near to death on account of her.

"Naxon," he said, "maybe I'd better introduce you to her."

"Why, son, d'you know her?" asked the surprised sheriff.

She roused suddenly from her trance of sorrow and fear, and throwing out her hands to Devon, she breathed:

"Will you give me one chance more? If he takes me to the jail I'll kill myself! I'll kill myself!"

"Steady, Walt," said Jim tenderly. "Great guns, don't you see she's scared to death?"

"She has reason to be," answered Devon. "She'll not kill herself, Jim. Harry, this is the girl who sent us out into the woods to look for Lucky Jack. Don't you remember her now? It's Prudence Maynard. There's no man on the range needs hanging half so badly!"

XXXIII. PRUE IS CROSS-EXAMINED

The ways of Devon had taken him many a time into parts of the world where criminal women have their share in wrongdoings and are freely punished for it, and he had been so long from the West that he had forgotten the peculiar virtue which is tacitly ascribed to all the weaker sex on the frontier. But now he saw his three companions stand as still and as frozen with horror as the pine trees around them.

And old Jim was the first to break that silence by saying gently: "Walt, you wouldn't say a thing that you wasn't sure of?"

"It's the woman who claims Lucky Jack as her brother," said Devon, "and he's admitted that she's his sister."

"There's worse men than Lucky Jack," suggested the sheriff in troubled haste.

"Of course," said Devon. "I like him very well. For his sake I'd like to be as easy as possible on this girl. But what can we do, Naxon? Are we to let her run loose?"

"Ah, Walt," old Harry interjected, "there

ain't a lot of harm that one small heifer can do to a whole range! I beg your pardon, ma'am!"

She turned a truly beautiful smile on Harry.

"You know that I can't have done wrong!" said she. "Just as a father knows that of his daughter. And I *haven't*. Don't you see" — she turned to Devon — "that all three of these men believe in me? And they are older than you!"

"Of course they're older," said Devon, "and a hundred times wiser on the frontier. But I doubt if they've ever had much to do with women of your class."

"Hold on, Walt!" whispered Sheriff Naxon, as one alarmed. "Don't go to talkin' about such things as that!"

Devon shrugged his shoulders. Then he challenged the girl:

"You know what stands against you. If there's an explanation, I'm the last man to want to put you behind the bars."

"Ah, it's not true," said the girl. "You hate me! I don't know what I've done that you should! But you hate me!"

"Suppose we get down to facts," suggested the sheriff. "It seems as though you've sent Walt out into trouble, once. He holds that agin you, ma'am."

"But how could I know?" asked the girl.

"I came here hoping to find my brother. I couldn't know what sort of man he'd become. And I didn't ask Mr. Devon to go for me. I told Mrs. Purley who I wanted to find, and she asked Mr. Devon to go, and then Harry went with him."

Her voice, as she touched the name of the old man, paused and softened a trifle, and Harry, with a start, could not control a smile.

"And we rode out into the face of guns!" said Devon.

"Yes, yes!" cried the girl excitedly. "After you started, I heard in the boarding house that that man who went to guide you, Lewis — I heard he was a wicked fellow. Then I started after you, but you had gone too far away. I ran on to the edge of the woods — I was afraid to go into them. They looked so great and dark and cold and lonely — I — I — besides, could I have caught up with you to warn you?"

Devon growled beneath his breath, but old Harry and the rest seemed thoroughly convinced. They nodded at her.

"That isn't all," Walt responded. "How can she explain the time I met her in the great, dark, cold, lonely woods at night?"

"Aye," said the sheriff, very gently. "How would you explain that, ma'am?"

"I'd heard that I was suspected of making

trouble in West London. I was frightened to death. I — I ran off into the woods, do you see? And there, in the midst of them, I saw Mr. Devon —"

"Frightened you quite terribly, of course?" Devon interrupted with sarcasm tinging his voice.

"Why should it frighten me?" asked she. "I knew that you were a gentleman, Mr. Devon."

"And the signal which you had learned to whistle?"

"What signal?"

"You've forgotten that?"

He tilted back his head a little, and made the whistle rise and blow down the wind; he had heard it so often that the thing was perfectly in his mind and could be translated easily enough into sound.

"Ah, I remember now," said she reminiscently.

"I'm glad you do," Devon responded grimly.

"As I was stumbling through the woods that evening," she said, bating her breath a little as the memory returned to her, "I met a man suddenly —"

"What did he look like?" asked Devon sharply.

"He was very fat, and wore only a string

for suspenders — and he was a big man," said she.

"Ha!" said Jim. "I'd like to meet up with that same one again! And what about him, ma'am?"

"Well, I was frightened, coming upon him suddenly, and I stopped, and he asked me where I was going. I told him I was simply out for a walk —"

"Is that likely?" asked Devon as sharply as before.

"I didn't know what else to say," the girl replied. She caught her breath and clasped her slender hands, so that they flashed beneath the moon. "It was a terrible time. I could hardly breathe! Anyhow, he grunted and walked off, but before he went into the woods he stopped and called after me. It nearly made my heart stop when he called to me that second time. I had to lean against a tree, but I faced around at him again!"

"Well might you fear a great greasy pig like him!" said Harry with a muttered oath.

"He seemed to be kind, though," the girl continued. "And he told me that I was foolish to walk there in the woods unless I knew them very well, because it was easy to get lost in them. Then he told me that there were people living in them, and if I got lost I could whistle in a certain way, and probably men would

come and find me. So he taught that whistle —"

"And when you met me?" Devon persisted.

"You frightened me. You were so dreadfully
fierce and accusing, Mr. Devon! You frightened me terribly. All at once I remembered
the whistle — and I tried it — and suddenly
you ran away! I don't know why to this day!"

"Why, ain't that all mighty likely?" said
Jim.

"Do you believe this rot?" Devon asked an-
grily. "A girl is wandering in the woods. She
meets the fat pig, and he is such an incom-
parable half-wit as to betray to a stranger the
secret signal of a gang of criminals. And then
she stumbles upon me and gives the signal.
Don't you see that none of this stuff will hang
together for a moment?"

"Seems pretty logical to me," Jim murmured.

"Would you mind tellin' us where you been
livin' all this time, ma'am?" the sheriff interrupted. "If you don't mind?"

"I don't mind at all," the girl replied. "I'm
living with Mr. and Mrs. Gregory Wilson."

"I know Greg," said the sheriff. "As decent
a gent as they is on the whole range! His wife's
mighty fine, too. They couldn't be a better
place for a young girl to put up. How about
that, Devon?"

"I'm not her judge," said Devon. "I suppose she met Gregory Wilson in the woods, too?"

"I was trying to get away," Prue responded in a low, hurried voice, "and I met Mr. Wilson suddenly among the hills. He didn't frighten me like the fat man did."

"And he took you home and put you up, eh?"

"Yes," the girl replied.

"What for?"

"Because I was footsore and hungry, and tired." She hesitated, then added: "And because I cried a little, I'm afraid!"

"Then explain to me," demanded Devon, "why it is that we find you here, dressed as a man, on my place in the middle of the night!"

"I wore out my own clothes pretty badly," said Prue, "and the clothes of Mr. Wilson's boy fitted me quite nicely. Mr. Wilson let me have a horse to ride, too."

"That gives you the horse and clothes," Walt persisted. "It doesn't bring you here — by night! How do you account for that?"

"I couldn't sleep," she said. "I began to think. I began to wonder if ever I could meet my poor brother, and how I ever could persuade him to reform and go home with me — and — finally I thought I'd better go for a ride. I slipped out. It was beautiful moonlight, and I followed my nose, as you might say, until I was very thirsty from facing the wind. I saw a sheet of water and got down to have a drink, but I touched the scum and saw it was filthy — and then —"

"And then we come roundin' over the hills!" the sheriff interrupted. "And we scare you out of a year of life."

"Ah, but that's over," said Prue, trembling. "Thank Heaven, it's over, and the dreadful chase!"

She looked with an uncertain smile at Devon.

"In which you tried to blow my head off with your pistol?" he asked dryly.

"I only fired in the air. I tried to frighten you away. I should have known I couldn't do that, though! You're not afraid of anything!"

And again she tried a smile at him, but Devon was like iron. He remembered vividly the whistling of the first bullet.

"Harry," said Devon, "this is the thinnest lot of nonsense I've ever heard in my life. She knows that she can't make me believe it, unless I'm hypnotized. A walk in the woods, eh? A moonlight night? Nonsense!"

All stood silent.

"And — what are you going to do with me, Sheriff?" asked the girl. "I haven't done anything."

"Why," said the sheriff, "you're as free as

can be for all of me! You can go where you please, ma'am."

"Ah, thank you!"

"Wait a moment, Naxon. You'll arrest her and take her along. And when you get her to West London, I'll swear out the warrant. I want her in the jail, and I want her there for conspiracy to murder!"

XXXIV. THE YELLOW PERIL

How many leagues Devon dropped in the estimation of his companions, at that moment, he would have hesitated to estimate, but he knew that he was by no means the man that he had been before, in their eyes. They stared at him in silence.

"Murder!" whispered the girl. "Oh, no! Not murder!"

"Get on your horse, if you please," said Devon, "and remember that if the others are a trifle sentimental and weak-headed about you, my dear girl, I've passed completely through that stage and come out on the other side! Let me hold your foot and give you a hand up."

So he passed her up to her saddle, and Prudence sat in it with hanging head, and with both hands clutching hard upon the pommel, as though she were faint and about to fall.

The sheriff muttered: "This looks kind of hard to me, Devon. Besides, I dunno that I gota right to arrest her before they is any warrant sworn out!"

"If you let her go," Devon said grimly, "I'll tie her into her saddle, and then lead her horse to West London at the end of a rope. I mean that, Sheriff!"

At this the sheriff surrendered with a faint groan of embarrassment.

"They's gunna be a lot of talk about this," he warned. "The roundin' up of an innocent girl, I mean — a young girl like this here, for all the murderin' and the stealin' that has been goin' on around West London! There's gunna be considerable of a laugh about that, I'm thinkin'."

"I'll accept my share of the laughter," Devon assured him. "And in the meantime I'll guarantee that you'll find Miss Maynard is big enough to raise the devil. Why, Sheriff, if you look at her again you'll see that she's too pretty to be good!"

"Have it your own way," the sheriff grunted in anger. "I've tried to show you sense, young man!"

And they all mounted and rode on, the three elders in front and Devon doggedly in the rear. Walt went beside the girl, with a brief warning that she was not to attempt to whistle or make a signal of any kind. Then he called to the three veterans that no matter how innocent they thought the prisoner might be, it would be wise to keep their eyes open for dangers along the road.

So they rode slowly out from the trees into the westering light of the moon. Old Jim called back:

"You dropped a handkerchief or something along yonder by the brush, didn't you, ma'am?"

"I? Oh, no!" said she.

"Seemed like I seen somethin' fall, over there," the old man persisted.

"It — it couldn't have been a thing, Jim. You see, I have my handkerchief!"

She raised it in her hand and fluttered it at him.

However, the idea was lodged in the mind of Jim.

"It must of been somethin' else," said he. "Seemed like I seen it perfect, archin' across and lodgin' along the brush, somewheres. Seemed like it was yonder, near that stump of a willow. Didn't you see somethin', Harry?"

But, swinging down from his horse at the edge of the brush, Jim began to probe the foliage with his gloved hand.

"If it were anything, it wasn't of the slightest importance," insisted the girl.

"Here it is!" Jim cried with an air of triumph, and raised a fluttering bit of white cloth into the air.

"What a clever, quick eye you have, Jim!"

the girl said cheerfully. "But it's nothing. Just an old rag of a handkerchief, now that I come to think of it, so you can throw it away again, in spite of all your trouble, thank you!"

Jim, however, was of a most deliberate nature. Like most dignified and simple souls, thoughts came to him one by one, and now he stretched the handkerchief in the moonlight.

"Dog-gone my hind sights, ma'am," said he, "there ain't nary a hole in it, after all! You shore must be mistaken!"

"Perhaps I am, perhaps I am!" Prudence responded in a flurry of rather angry impatience. "But let me have it, then."

She stretched out her hand for the handkerchief, when a sudden thought made Devon pull his horse about, snatch the handkerchief himself and stare at it earnestly.

The handkerchief was filled and crossed with wrinkles; obviously it had been knotted around some small object. Walt spread the damp cloth flatter, and now the moon revealed definitely glittering dust!

He shook his head at the questions of the sheriff and Jim's protests. Turning from the moon, so that a black shadow fell upon the cloth, he lighted a match and examined the handkerchief again. There was no doubt that small yellow particles glittered on it.

Carefully he retied the handkerchief and passed it into his pocket. Then he said:

"We'll go back to the edge of that tank where we saw her first this evening. There's something there worth finding out, partners."

"What?" asked the sheriff.

"The reason that Tucker Vincent — if he's one of them — and all the rest, want to get the ranch. The reason she was there tonight. What reason do you think, Harry? What would make people hungry for land, Jim?"

"I dunno," said Jim. "I'm beginnin' to guess, but it ain't at all likely!"

"Gold!" said Devon. "Go back there with me, and I'll wager that we can wash it out on the edge of the tank!"

XXXV. A TOUCH OF CHIVALRY

Gold! No word in any language has such meaning, but nowhere more than in the West, where men have seen raw wealth dug out of the ground. Tender regard for Prudence Maynard suddenly disappeared. She would have been left to drift quietly to the rear had it not been for the sheriff, who forced her to stay with them.

And at a full gallop the riders stormed back across the hills to the edge of the tank.

The slant moonlight showed the surface clearly, the thick scum around the edges, the boggy holes left by cattle and horses after wading out to drink.

"And this is where the young lady says she got down on her knees to drink!" said Devon. "Why, a blind man would have known the water was foul by the smell of the margin here; and then for any one other than blind, there's the sight of the scum. Did she have to get down on her knees to find out the water was filthy?"

Old Jim and Harry did not attempt a response. They hardly seemed to hear what was spoken, but they waded out into the edge of the mud where the water met the ground. Devon tore off his shirt, and with bare hands they scooped up the mud, taking that which lay next to the hard ground beneath.

Presently the shirt was half filled, after which they ladled in water from a canteen, and washed the mud slowly away.

They were grimed to the shoulders. They looked more like wallowing pigs than men.

Muddy water dripped over their trousers. Their feet came out of the mud bottom with a loud sound of sucking and bubbling water. But they did not seem ridiculous or ugly, either to themselves or to those who stood by and watched.

The great bulk of the mud was now washed out of the shirt which Harry and Jim worked back and forth like a primitive cradle, while Devon poured in the water. Now there was hardly a double handful of blackness remaining.

"If it's mud, all the rest," said old Harry, "then I never seen stuff so heavy before! Wash out, Walt. For God's sake, hurry up and wash out. I can feel somethin'!"

"I got the taste of it in my teeth!" said Jim hoarsely. "Walt, will you hurry up?"

And Devon hurried with trembling hands.

The mud turned to water, but still a substance remained, a definite weight upon the surface of the shirt. And as the stained water grew purer, suddenly old Harry caught away the cloth from Jim, folded it, and wrung it thoroughly.

They went back to the dry ground. Then, dropping upon their knees, they unfolded the shirt bit by bit. They did not look into the faces of one another, but with set teeth they watched the progress.

At last the shirt lay flat open, and in the center of it, where the mud streaks made a pattern, they saw the glimmer of metal, a heap of shining grains!

Then, at last, they raised their heads and looked at one another in silence, and all drew in their breath as though they were drinking.

Above and behind them they heard the voice of the sheriff:

"They've found it, by God!"

Beside the sheriff stood Prudence Maynard, who might easily have slipped away on her horse, unnoticed, so deep was the fascination under which every one lay. But she had remained where she was, staring, lips parted.

Old Jim, carefully gathering the dust into the palm of his hand, held it in the shadow of his shoulders, while both Devon and Harry lighted matches. Seen by this light, the yellow heap glowed as though it were an actual flame that Jim was holding in his hands.

The old man closed his hand over it with a sudden violence and his whole body shuddered.

"Lemme tell you," he said. "They's fifty pound of mud been washed out of that shirt, Washed plumb careless. But they's fifty dollars' worth of gold here'n my hand. Y'understand? Harry, you hear me? They's fifty dollars' worth here — *in my hand!*"

He threw back his lean, wrinkled head and laughed. The wind blew back his long, thin, white hair like a flying mist across his shoulders. It seemed to impart a forward movement to the veteran, and Devon's brain whirled.

It seemed that more than gold had been sifted from the filthy mud of that tank. In his excited mind Devon saw cities rising, the gleam of lights on paved streets, the proudly nodding heads of fine horses, and he heard the whirring of wheels, the clanking of hoofs, the thin music of violins, and the laughter of women. There was a fragrance about him, too, like the fragrance of a thousand gardens, distilled in subtle perfumes.

Then Walt caught his breath and he was back beside an ill-smelling tank, his knees aching, his body cold with the wet and the wind, while beside him were two tattered and battered old veterans of the frontier.

He arose to his feet.

"You're convinced, Sheriff, I suppose?"

The sheriff looked moodily, dreamily at him.

"Convinced of what, Devon? Of the gold? My God, yes! If the tramplin' of the cattle ain't worked that gold down to bed rock, why, they's a million lyin' here in the surface of the draw. I dunno — I dunno —" he mused. "What would of brung it here, Devon? Would it of been the washin' down of the stream from the hills? I mean in the old days — it'd make your head ache to think how old, since the draw was a runnin' river, off of the mother lode, back yonder! That was when this here must of been dropped, an' the ground all salted with it!"

Devon looked at him earnestly. The gambler knew that he was a good man and a man of iron, yet now his head jerked as he talked. It reminded Devon of the manner in which the muzzle of a Colt jerks up and down when it is being fired.

"I don't mean that. I mean — you're convinced now that she was lying to us?"

The sheriff pushed the hat far back on his head. He turned toward the girl; by degrees he appeared to be forcing his mind back to the consideration of her.

"Maybe — maybe —" he muttered. "I dunno."

"Look again," said Devon. "Here's her handkerchief. Is that proof enough, Naxon?"

"Yes, yes," he agreed, recovering at last from the dream. "There ain't a mite of doubt about it. She'll have to go back and sleep in the jail tonight. Why, Devon, it'll be sure the first time that a woman has been inside a jail of mine. But she ain't Western. She's out of the East, where I dunno the human breed so well!"

"Do you hear?" said Devon to the girl.

She looked him steadily in the eye and did not answer.

He went on:

"We understand that you know the inside of what's going on. You can give us the names of the men behind this business. I mean the curs who have been trying their hand at murder, after they couldn't buy this gold for a song? Give us their names, and I know the sheriff will ask no more from you."

Prudence Maynard still was silent, looking from one face to another, swiftly, but always back to Devon in the end.

He frowned.

"Otherwise," said he, "I don't think you've followed the thing out to the end. A man with the jailbird stamp on him is bad enough. A woman is a thousand times worse. You surely know that, and once you've been in the fire, decent people will be through with you. This is your chance to keep your name clean. We don't want a heap of evidence from you. We want names, that's all. Is that right, Sheriff?"

"Aye, aye," said the sheriff hastily. "I'd be best pleased to have no woman on my hands. The judge would be best pleased, too, and so would all the men of West London, I reckon! Talk out, and you'll go free, for all of me!"

She twined one hand in the mane of her horse, and still she looked steadily at Devon, but did not speak.

Then old Jim said quietly:

"You see how it is, Sheriff? She ain't a gunna talk. She ain't the yaller dog breed, like Sammy Green was! She's gunna keep still, and never give away on her pals."

Prue glanced at old Jim after this speech, but then her eyes, as always, drew back upon Devon. It was a glance neither scornful nor hard with defiance, but a haunted look as though she could not shift her eyes elsewhere.

Devon abruptly turned and began to pace up and down.

"We'd better get on back, Sheriff, eh?" he asked at last.

"I reckon we'd better," Lew Naxon agreed.

"I'll give you a hand up," Devon said to the girl.

He stood close to her, and she, with her head fallen back against the shoulder of the mare, looked up to his face.

"When you're mounted," said he, "fall back. There's no man here who will bother you, I think, except me, And I can't do it. I know what you are. Ten men could never do the harm you'll manage in your life, but I can't harden myself to trouble you. Get on your horse, fall back, and then spur across the hills. Tell your friends that their game is almost up, though they've still a chance if they can manage a few murders quickly. Quickly, quickly, my dear! And we'll be watching for them the best we can. But murder's like a rat; it can get into the strongest house in the world!"

Walt lifted her up to the saddle; then he mounted in turn, and they started forward. The sheriff and the two old trappers were in the van, as usual, and they kept close together, never turning their heads, while the party rode back.

Finally, from the top of the ridge, they could see the distant lights of West London.

Then Devon rode up to the others. As he did so old Harry turned quickly in the saddle and peered back across the hills. After that he reached out his big hand and laid it on the shoulder of the younger man.

"All the time I knowed, Walt," he said softly. "They was too much man in you to do such a thing!"

The sheriff shrugged his shoulders. And he said not a word as they dipped down into Timbal Gulch.

XXXVI. A RENDEZVOUS

Up the trail on the nearer side of Timbal Gulch they were discussing their next steps. The strong advice of the sheriff was to take a pair of experts out from West London and stake out the whole course of the draw as soon as possible, washing here and there to determine whether the gold deposit was widespread, and digging into places to make out the thickness of the gold-bearing ground.

After that they could determine on what a scale they wished to commence. The probability was that it was a surface deposit which could soon be looted, no matter how enormously rich it might be. And the more quickly this work was completed, the more certainly they would have removed the temptation which their enemies were under to use murder or any other foul means for the possession of the place.

The sheriff himself would supply the two trustworthy experts, he said.

The riders had come to this conclusion, therefore, when they reached the upper lip of the gulch on the side of West London. Here Devon turned in the saddle. Far down the valley he saw the glimmer of a light, hardly brighter than the light of a star, rising and winking through the horizon mist.

An instant later, with an exclamation, he reined in his horse and turned it to face the light, for he had detected a rhythmic pulsing which spelled the letters of the Morse code rapidly:

"Found gold. Everything depends on next throw. Meet here tomorrow night at ten."

And the blinking ended.

Devon, turning his horse again, strained his eyes toward the town and over the hills, to see if any answer were made by a visible signal from any direction. Then he stared back at the place from which the first signal had come; but there was nothing except the glimmer of house lights.

Even these, for the moment, seemed to his excited imagination to be repeating messages, but he soon saw that this was only the work of his own mind.

He had spoken aloud as he spelled out the message, and the meaning was plain enough to the others.

"It was a light, winkin'?" asked the sheriff.

"That was it. Did you see it, Naxon?"

"I seen nothin' but the rabble of lights down

yonder in the valley."

"It was one of those!"

"Where?"

"I don't know, exactly. It seemed far away."

"Can't you spot the place, Walt?" Jim asked anxiously. "Dog-gone it if everythin' don't mostly depend on spottin' the right place!"

"I can't remember, exactly. When I turned back to watch for an answer, I rubbed the exact spot out of my memory. But it seemed far off — and down the valley!"

"Far off? That depends on the size of the light used, mostly," old Harry suggested.

"It would," Devon agreed. "Wait a while. They'll surely talk again."

"They won't!" said Jim with conviction. "Chances like that don't come twice in a row. It's as if you was to hear a voice in a crowd talkin', sayin' he was a murderer, but you don't spot the face. What good is hearin' the voice, then, except to upset you?"

"It's somethin'," declared the sheriff. "We know that somewhere down the valley 'they' are gunna meet tomorrow night at ten. 'They' means the murderin' gang, or a part of 'em. Listen, Devon, your room at Mrs. Purley's house looks straight down the cañon, here. Suppose you go there and watch to see what happens. I'll stay here and try if I can spot anythin'. Jim and Harry had better go to bed."

They arranged to act upon that plan.

Walt went straight to the Purley house and to his room, where he sat before his window and stared long down the lower cañon, where Timbal Gulch spread out into a half arable valley.

For a half hour he stared, concentrating so hard that his head nearly swam; but he could make out nothing, and he was settling himself for a long vigil when suddenly a voice said from the darkness behind him:

"Sit steady, Devon. Don't turn this way. Keep looking down the valley and you'll come to no harm!"

He set his teeth, tried to curb the hammering of his heart, resolved to whirl, dropping for the floor at the same time, but then he realized that the moon shone brightly across the window, even though it did not enter the room. It made a perfect background, against which he must loom as a large target, outlined in black. Better shooting no one could ask than that.

Therefore he remained quiet, breathing hard, and the sweat starting on his face.

Said the voice behind him:

"Do you recognize me, Devon?"

"No."

"I'm Lucky Jack to the people of West London."

"You have me in the palm of your hand, Jack," Devon admitted calmly.

"Of course I have," said the outlaw. "But I'm not going to close the fingers unless you make me. Devon, I've not come to harm you. I want information, not trouble, from you."

Devon nodded. "Say what you want, then."

"You can more than half guess, beforehand. I want to know about Prudence. You told me something the last time I talked to you. I thought I could find her, after that, but I was wrong. She's with no one I can locate!"

Devon paused to consider.

"Jack," he said at last, "I've no malice against you — none in the world. But I can give you good advice on this. Forget that you ever had a sister."

Said Jack: "I know that you mean the best by that, Devon. But she's new to you. You don't understand her."

"No, I don't," Walt returned. "But after she's tried the hands of others for my life, and then tried her own, I began to guess a good deal."

"Her own?"

"Yes, her own!"

He could hear Jack sigh in the darkness behind him.

"Devon," said he, "I've known her all my

life, of course. Prue is wilder than any boy. But I've never known an unfair thing about her. She can use her wits so as to make a fool of a man, but there's no crookedness in her."

"There was a bullet not a foot from my head this same night," Devon said quietly.

"Great God!" exclaimed Lucky Jack. "You saw her again tonight?"

"Yes. She tried to rob me and the two old trappers. As she's been working to rob us before."

Jack exclaimed impatiently.

"You're her brother, Jack," Devon added.

"There was never a soul in the world," Jack declared, "so straight from the shoulder and with a more open hand. Devon, I know you wouldn't lie to me, and you're trying to tell the exact truth as you saw it, but I know you can't be right. You can't change nature. Not in one short life, like hers!"

"Jack," said Devon, "there's a big pull in blood."

"And what of that? Her pedigree is as long and as fine as that of any lady in the land!"

"Perhaps it is. There's the same pedigree in you, Jack. And you haven't built up a peaceful reputation around West London, I take it?"

"Ah, no," Lucky Jack said hotly. "But have you found one man who says that I ever fired a bullet from behind, Devon?"

"No, no. Not that."

"Or that I've ever tried to rob people by sneak thieveries?"

"Not that. But you've raised the devil so often that you can't expect me to be surprised if your sister does the same thing — in a different way."

"Devon," said the voice of the other, actually trembling with earnestness, "there's a thousand miles of difference between a fair fight and a murder. You know that!"

"Yes, I know it."

"If what you tell me is true — well, then I wish I'd never been born. I left her the wildest girl in the world, but the straightest, and the bravest, and the truest. If I find her what you say that she is — Devon, give me some trace of trail of her. Something to follow, in the name of God!"

Devon was greatly moved. It was no easy thing for him to talk of Prudence, if that were indeed her name, and already that night his heart had been wrung as never before. At last he sighed.

"I saw her on my ranch," said he. "I saw her there tonight."

"Tonight?"

"Yes."

"What in the name of Heaven could she

be doing there on the hills?"

"I can't tell you that. I saw her there. That's all that I know."

"Did you see in what direction she rode off?"

"I didn't, and I didn't want to. Because it was my job, with the others, to bring her in to jail!"

There was another muffled exclamation, and finally Devon said:

"You can't show yourself by day around West London?"

"Can a wasp show himself in a bee's nest?" asked Jack.

"Then, if you'll meet me in the lower part of the gulch at dusk, Jack —"

"Well?"

"I'll ride with you to the house where she *says* she was!"

"Do you mean it?"

"I do."

"Devon, turn and shake on that."

Walt turned and joined hands with Lucky Jack.

XXXVII. A DANGEROUS YOUNG MAN

In the gray of the dawn Jim and Harry departed with the two experts which the sheriff had provided, and Naxon himself accompanied them, "to see the look of the land and what the old ranch is raisin' besides grass in these here days," he explained.

All the morning Devon waited; in the afternoon early he saw the sheriff on a foaming pony and went down to meet him at the door.

The man of the law was pale and grave with excitement. His fingers blundered as he strove to fill his pipe, and the words rattled from his lips.

It was richer than they had guessed in their fondest dreams, he said. The whole draw was not filmed through with the golden deposit, but there were spots and holes filled with wealth.

Undoubtedly, according to the experts, their guess had been right. The draw was simply the bed of an old river which, in ancient days, had ground its way into the heart of the mountain strata. It had reached rocks rich with gold, and, sawing through them, it had drifted the yellow deposit down its bed, scattering it in the pebbles, and rubbing the pebbles themselves to dust in the course of the ages, until the whole bed was streaked with riches.

Of course it was impossible to estimate what the exact return would be. But both of the experts vowed that a dozen fortunes could be harvested here.

So far, West London had learned nothing of the discovery, but the news could not be contained for long. And if, as the sheriff said, the eyes of men were to fall upon such a sight as this, the town would go mad with excitement, and every one would turn out to prospect the river bed above and below the distance that it ran across the ranch. That must be prevented.

Then, covertly, under the flap of his coat, the sheriff unfolded a bandanna, and exposed for a single instant a sight of glittering nuggets.

"Got out of one wash hole in the draw!" he told Devon with glittering eyes. There would be many another rich little pocket such as this. And what would not be developed when enough water was brought onto the land for the proper exploitation of the mines?

To this Devon listened calmly enough.

He had remained at the hotel that day by special request, because if a random bullet should find his life, then all the matter of possession of the ranch might be thrown into confusion, and a flood of lawless claim jumpers could gut the ranch lands in a comparatively short time.

He should remain there still, the sheriff insisted. Old Jim and Harry were keeping an eye upon the ranch and the work that went on there. He, the sheriff, would recruit a dozen good men — he felt that he could put his hand upon safe fellows — and dispatch them to the ranch to further the labor at once.

And so the sheriff was gone, leaving Devon to take up the long watch.

But his thoughts were already reaping the harvest, and a dozen times he had to shake himself out of a dream.

For he knew that the work was not yet done. If they had fathomed the purpose of his enemies, they had not yet disarmed them; they did not even know the head or heads of that enemy power. Suspicion had brushed upon Tucker Vincent and Les Burchard, but that was not enough. They must have far more than suspicion before the hand of the law could be laid upon their shoulders!

So Devon kept himself firmly in hand and refused to let his fancies fly out too far toward all the joys which great fortune would bring!

Then he found that the sun was at last hanging low in the West, and he remembered his promise to Lucky Jack.

No matter, then, for his promise to Harry and Jim to remain quietly indoors. He would be safe enough, he felt, under the shelter of the dark, and somewhere in the lower sweep of the gulch, Lucky Jack himself would be waiting for him.

He had not the slightest intention of disappointing the outlaw. But, first of all, he went downstairs and discovered from the bartender the location of the house of Gregory Wilson, in that part of the cañon where the floor was broken into a far wider sweep.

Gregory Wilson, well known as hunter and trapper, ran a few cows upon his ragged hills, and even picked up a little money carting fish to West London; but he never had been tempted by the mines. That was his reputation, as well as a name for sterling honesty. Of this, Devon had made sure.

So Walt saddled the brown mare, and headed at once through the rose of the evening down the cañon. He was armed to the teeth. He carried a repeating Winchester in the long holster that angled down under his right knee; a pair of heavy saddle holsters contained a brace of Colts. And he carried his favorite weapon in a spring clip beneath the pit of his left arm.

He was prepared to meet trouble, but hardly expected to find it, for his enemies by this time must know what was happening out there on the barren hills of the Devon ranch, and they would be in an agony of expectancy, tearing their hair to discover some means of stopping the work or of appropriating the proceeds. For that reason they were apt to keep a less vigilant watch over him.

At last Walt dipped his mare over the edge of the gulch, descending by a zigzagging trail that worked from side to side until it had entered into the deeper shadow of the cañon.

All was still there, now, except for the random voices of a few late workers, trudging up the trails, and these seemed to sound far away, and there was a sort of warmth of peace in the air.

So Devon came down to the lower level, and rode along by the brawling of the creek whose patient waters had torn this mighty trench through the mountains! He kept ardently alert, looking to either side at every bush, at every rock that could shelter so much as half a man!

Again and again he turned his head sharply and stared down the trail to the rear, but always there was emptiness behind him.

The darkness was almost complete when he heard a sharp whistle out of a nest of rocks. He had a pair of guns in his hands instantly, and a secure knee grip upon the mare, when he heard his name called cheerfully, and recognized the voice of Lucky Jack.

The outlaw came up to him with a wave of the hand and a call of greeting through the dusk.

"I was beginning to be afraid I couldn't spot you, it was so late," said Lucky Jack. "Which way do we bear from here, Devon?"

"Straight ahead, Jack."

"To a house?"

"Yes, to a place down the cañon."

"Which one?"

"The house of Gregory Wilson."

"I know that fellow!"

"Well?"

"Fairly well," said Lucky Jack. "I ran into him when I was talking to the people of an outbound stage, one time. I mean to say, I was sticking them up, Devon! And I trimmed this fellow Wilson for a couple of hundred dollars. He didn't look very prosperous, and I asked him if he could stand it. What do you think he said?"

"I can't guess, unless he said it would break him."

"Not at all. He simply said he'd lost more

money than that before! But afterward I found out he's a poverty-stricken chap. I couldn't stand for that, so I dropped around and gave him the money at his house."

"That was a mighty decent thing, Jack. As a matter of fact," Walt pointed out, "you're leading a foolish life out here, and you know it. It isn't the money — it's the game that keeps you at it!"

"Devon," said the other, "did you ever get rich at your *own* game?"

"No," Devon replied slowly; "but one of these days, in a rich poker layout —"

"I understand. You take money away from other fellows at the point of your wits. I take it away at the point of a gun. There's not so much difference."

"No," said Devon readily, "there's not. I wasn't preaching to you, however."

"I know you weren't. But what about Wilson?"

"Your sister said she was living at his place."

"Ah, the devil!" cried the outlaw. "While I was looking for her all around West London itself!"

"That's her story," said Devon.

"You doubt it?"

"I doubt everything. I have to, Jack."

"Not Prue. There'll be a time, perhaps, when you'll know her a great deal better.

You'll agree with me then when I say she can't be wrong, Devon!"

Devon shook his head in the darkness.

"Ah, well," said he, "can you tell me if Gregory Wilson will tell the truth when you ask him a question?"

"Of course he will! Look here, Devon, how could he refuse to tell me the truth, since I played white with him?"

"I should think he would," said Walt. "I simply wanted to make sure, because then we can get through this business with one question: you can ask him if your sister is there, and what will end it when he answers, eh?"

"Of course it will end it!"

"That should be the house over there, I take it?"

"Yes, the one with the lighted upper window over the rocks. Wilson built in style — a two-story cabin!"

And Lucky Jack laughed.

"I'll have Prue in another five minutes," said he. "She's come out here to get me, and it'll be a lark for me to get her instead. Devon, I'm going to be eternally grateful to you for this!"

But Devon answered not a word. At that moment he was telling himself that he dared not trust a soul in the world, and particularly that dangerous young man who rode beside him.

XXXVIII. JUDAS ISCARIOT

When they tapped at the cabin door it was opened by a tall man of middle age with powerful shoulders, who was holding a lantern up close to his kindly face, the better to see his visitors.

It occurred to Devon that never before had he seen an act of such bold indifference in a country as wild and dangerous as that section of the West. For the light which he used to throw upon his visitors was an ample glow in his own face, and would make him a perfect target.

It was a simple and effective tribute to a man's perfectly quiet conscience, yet it seemed to Devon to be touched with foolhardiness as well. It was folly to take chances in a country overrun by half savage natives, who in their cups would think no more of murder than of sniping at a grouse.

"Hey? And hello, Jack!" said the other, as he recognized Lucky. "Step down off'n your hoss. Is this here a new partner?"

Wilson held out his hand to Devon with

a grip as firm as the pressure of rock. In that revealing touch Devon recognized the man's power.

They were conducted into a quite large living room or parlor, with a few books on a shelf over the fireplace at the farther end, and skins on the floor, and horns and other hunting trophies scattered about upon the walls. The chairs were homemade, but they were fashioned with skill and for comfort.

Immediately the big man waved his guests to seats.

"We'll eat in a little while, I guess," said he. "My wife is up the valley. They's a poor gent layin' in a shack with the fever, and she fetched him up a snack. It'll take her a while to tidy things around a bit for him, too, and that's why she's late home. Reach yourself that pot of tobacco, Jack, and help yourself. It ain't lately I've seen you, son!"

"I have to travel in jumps, Wilson," Lucky Jack responded. "You may guess how it is. A good many pairs of eyes are looking for me, and no sooner found than gone, you know!"

The big man nodded and smiled.

"Not in this house, son."

"It's the getting here," said Jack; "but now that I'm here, I can relax a little."

"Aye, of course. I dunno that you've inter-

305

duced me to your friend, Jack; but maybe interductions ain't necessary?"

"You've heard of him, and I'm surprised you haven't seen him. This is Devon, the fellow who made a fool of me when I tried to run away with his mare — you've heard of that?"

"Ah — ah —" said the hunter. He smiled broadly at Devon. "You shook hands after you fought, eh?"

"We did," Lucky Jack answered. "He shoots straight, Wilson — like you! That's one reason I was glad to bring him down here this evening."

"And another reason to see me, I hope?"

"That was another reason. And there's a third reason, too!"

He sat stiffly erect in his chair and his eyes blazed.

"Smoke out your pipe, son," said the hunter. "It's the Injun way before they talk bad business, and I aim to think you ain't got a pleasant idea just now!"

"It's a short question," said Lucky Jack, "and I'll ask it in the beginning. I can't wait. Wilson, have you had a girl living with you in this house lately?"

Gregory Wilson looked fixedly at him, with neither surprise nor anger, but as one in thought.

"You understand, Wilson. I don't mean any scandal," Jack explained. "She's my sister. It is important for me to know!"

"Why, no, man," said the hunter. "You know the way I live —"

Jack flung himself irritably back into his chair.

"She's not here, Wilson?"

Slowly the other shook his head.

Lucky Jack closed his eyes and strained back his head with a groan. Devon said not a word; from his heart he pitied the young outlaw; from his heart he despised the lies of the girl.

Then Jack sat up again, catching at a feeble hope.

"Wilson, if she hasn't been here, will you tell me if you've ever met or seen a girl of that description?"

"You ain't described her yet, Jack."

"Blue and gold, and the loveliest thing you ever saw."

Again, slowly, the ponderous head of the hunter was moved in negation.

"I've seen nobody like that, Jack. I've seen a few of the girls up in West London, but they ain't that kind!"

Lucky Jack threw out his hands and then struck them on the rude, whittled arms of his chair.

"Devon, you were right!" he said bitterly.

307

Silence followed. Lucky Jack started up with violence.

"I'll move on. I know all I wanted to find out. I know too much!"

But the big fellow stopped him at the door, as Devon rose in turn.

"They's something workin' in your mind, Jack," said he. "But don't you let it be that way. If you go a rampin' and a rampagin' out into the dark, like this, you'll get yourself into a lot of misery, son! Jus' calm yourself down and don't give this here trouble, whatever it is, another thought, until you got a good meal into yourself, and had a smoke afterward. Then things'll seem the way they are. Just now you're half poisoned; every gent is poisoned when he's sad. Set down over here. I ain't gunna let you budge!"

Lucky Jack, as though unable to resist the impulsion of those might hands, was taken to a chair and there he slumped down, his face in his hands, and sat without moving.

The big host went gently about the room, lighted a lantern that gave only a dim and dull glow, and then took his place by the hearth, where a small fire was burning.

A horse neighed shrill and loud in the distance; two more took up the chorus.

"What's that?" Jack asked uneasily.

"Gents driftin' up the gulch toward the

camp," was the reassuring reply.

"Ah, yes," said Lucky Jack. "Thank God, there's this one house where I don't have to be on guard. Wilson, every hour that I've spent in this place has been gold to me. It's been a perfect rest; but after tonight I never can think of the house without pain! I've been shot through the heart!"

"Aye, it's the way with them that belong to your blood," said the hunter. "A wife can do wrong. But a child or a sister — or a brother — the sins of them are your own, you take 'em into your own heart. Aye, man, but I know that!"

He sighed, and studied the fire for a moment.

"But there's the passin' of the days," Wilson continued in his deep, calm voice. "There's the passin' of the days that rubs out the corners, and covers your mind with dust, and under the dust the trail of the old time lies. It'll cover it so thick, finally, that it'll take a mighty powerful wind to lift that dust and show the bare face of the things that hurt you in other times!"

He turned more toward Lucky Jack.

"I've had my own hurts, Jack. But you see how I am. I'm a happy enough man. Because I've waited, I've let time take care of me. It's got bandages softer'n spider webs, and better for the stoppin' of blood!"

To this wisdom Lucky Jack listened with a sigh, but at length he uncovered his face. They fell into silence, and big Wilson gradually resumed the talk.

"The wife is pretty late," said he. "I've expected her a good spell before this. But when a woman gets to carryin' on at a sick bed, she's sure gotta waste time. Time don't mean nothin' to her there, when she can fuss around them that need her!"

He laughed as he spoke. His laughter was like a deep rumbling of thunder. He waved his right hand back and forth, smoothly illustrating his words with gestures, while a trail of smoke hung in the air from the bowl of the pipe which he held.

Devon watched him in the absent-minded manner which is habitual with those who suffer in the mind, and while he watched he saw the smoke hanging in the air in long strokes and short —

But his absence of mind ended abruptly, and he was staring at the gradual wavings of that hand and the pipe which it supported. It was often interrupted by a puff, but the massive hand clearly spelled in signal:

"Now — by — the — back — door!"

Walt could not believe his eyes. He sat back, blinking. He rubbed his forehead and looked again.

But this time the waving of the hand had ceased. Devon cast a hurried glance over his shoulder. There he saw the small, black square of a window, from which, to be sure, any experienced eyes could have watched this signal and have understood.

Then he turned back to Gregory Wilson. The eyes of the hunter were no longer dim and kindly. They were sharp as the eyes of a hunting cat, and they read the face of Devon with a cruel brightness, and pried into his suspicious mind!

XXXIX. MARKED CARDS

Then Gregory Wilson nodded.

"You're a bright fellow, Devon," said he. "Dog-gone me if you ain't got a quick eye and a quick head, but — come in, boys!"

The door to the rear of the room fell open, as Devon leaped to his feet, and he looked into the most convincing of all weapons; a pair of double-barreled shotguns stared forth from the doorway, one confronting him and the other turned full at Lucky Jack!

Behind those gaping funnels of destruction he saw two unpleasantly familiar faces — Slugger Lewis and Peter Grierson.

There were others behind. Out of the darkness he distinguished Jerry Noonan's ugliness, and the lean, handsome face of Charlie Way. These were not all; where faces could not be distinguished, guns gleamed in the darkness of the room beyond.

A Colt revolver had jumped instantly into the hand of Devon, but his host said:

"Don't kill Devon, boys! We may need him later. Devon, you see what's happened? There ain't a bit of use kickin' up a fuss! Lucky, I'm mighty sorry. I'll have to ask both of you gents to back up agin the wall, there, and stick your hands up over your heads!"

Lucky Jack seemed utterly stunned. Agape, he stared at the yawning guns in the doorway, and then back at Gregory Wilson, the "honest man."

"Put them up," said Wilson in a harder tone. "I dunno that y'understand what you're agin, here. Put them up — shove them up as high as your ears, boys, or we'll stop talkin' and let the guns work for us!"

That steady array of guns staring from the doorway was enough to convince more stubborn spirits than those of Devon and Lucky Jack, and they accordingly backed obediently against the wall and held up their hands. Through the doorway now slipped Grierson and Lewis. Behind them Charlie Way and Noonan entered.

"That's enough," said big Gregory Wilson. "Kick the door shut and slap some ropes on these two friends of mine, will you, boys?"

The "boys" appeared glad to oblige. And Wilson went on:

"Slugger, go outside and throw a guard up and down the valley trail, and another back in the rocks behind the house. Now that we got these two, there's apt to be a mite of trouble made. Particular from the sheriff and from them two old goats, Jim and Harry. They'll sniff the air for trouble when they miss Devon at Mrs. Purley's house!"

Wilson grinned a little as Lewis left the room in haste. Then he added:

"And Mrs. Purley might ride out on the trail herself, if she could suspect. Dog-gone me if you ain't got a way of slippin' into the kind thoughts of people, Devon! Almost slipped into mine!"

In the meantime, with slender strips of raw-hide, Devon and Lucky Jack were secured. Ropes may be frayed through and chains may be slipped, but rawhide fits to the bone, and is almost as tough as metal. The wrists of both men were lashed behind their backs, then their knees and their ankles were bound firmly together.

Gregory Wilson himself overlooked these preparations. He satisfied himself that all was right, and saw the two so securely lashed placed in chairs side by side.

"You better fit in the gag yourself, Greg," Noonan cautioned. "Either I choke a gent or else it's so loose that it works right out on the end of his tongue."

"I'll do the gaggin'," said Wilson. "I know all about that game. And there ain't a better thing in the world, boys, than just to know the right way to handle a gag. The finest talker in the world ain't half as fine as a silent tongue can be."

Lucky Jack stared with undisguised horror. From the first he had appeared too stunned mentally and physically to make the slightest effort at self-defense.

"Wilson," said Lucky at last, "of course I see what's happening, and I try to understand it, but somehow I can't. It's not natural. You're an honest man, Wilson, no matter what you may seem to be doing to Devon and to me!"

"Sure," Gregory Wilson said in his fine bass voice. "I'm honest to myself."

"Will you tell me what it's all about?" asked Jack, horror still working in his face.

"I don't mind," Wilson replied. "A gag is a mean thing to wear between your teeth, even when it's fitted by a plumb tailor-made expert like me. First I'll smoke out this here pipe and talk things over with you boys. The rest of you back up and give us room!"

He threw the last sentence carelessly over his shoulder at the three, and straightway they scattered. Still addressing them, he continued:

"If these here friends of mine take a notion to move too quick, or talk too loud, or make any strange play in any way, I want you boys to salt them down with lead. And him that

misses his mark on this kind of a night —
I'll make him wish that he was already in hell!"

This remark was uttered almost without
emotion. In fact, Wilson spoke gently, but
Devon gathered by degrees that this open-
browed man was the very prince of evil!

The captor started his pipe and began to
smoke slowly, with a relish. As he smoked
he expanded his philosophy.

"You're set back a-ways by this, Lucky,"
said he. "You take it that after you turned
back that two hundred dollars to me you had
a right to —"

"Wilson!" exclaimed Lucky Jack. "It wasn't
the money that made me feel safe here. It was
because you'd called me a friend!"

"Aye, that's true, too," said Wilson. "But
I aim to show you, son, that they ain't any
such thing as love and foolish friendship, without no self in it. Lemme tell you that a man
can get hungry for a woman, same as a dog
can get hungry for meat, and a parent can
get fond of its child, mostly because it's used
to havin' the brat about. I liked you, Lucky,
because of the two hundred that you passed
back to me. I didn't want to harm you none
in this job, but you run your head into the
fire. How could I tell that you would be such
a fool as to make yourself a friend of this fellow
Devon, just when the whole weight of us was

about to drop on him and break his neck? It's your fault, Jack. A fool ain't ever gunna succeed permanent in this here world! It's made only for the strong to win!"

Turning to Devon, he continued:

"So he thought you could show him the way to his sister? He played you for a sucker, and you come on into his game. And so the two of you landed here like a pair of salmon that land themselves high and dry tryin' to jump up the falls!" He chuckled, pleased with his comparison.

"I'm gunna tie a tin can to the tail of the law, and in a day or two I'll run West London ragged. That's what I'll do!" he continued.

"Not you in person," Devon broke in.

"No? What makes you say that?"

"You're a great deal too clever for that, Wilson. You talk in the grand manner about despising the law, but when the time comes for open air raiding, you'll sit here in your house and direct things. You're a Napoleon who leaves the dirty work to the hired thugs, who get out of it no more than the pay of common cowpunchers. Not even gratitude, because you would let them rot in jail if they were no longer useful — or murder them, as you had Sammy Green murdered, if they tried to help themselves!"

"By God, will you stop!" shouted Gregory

317

Wilson, springing to his feet.

"I've simply turned your hand face upward, Wilson, and let your own friends see the marked cards you play with. Silence is a rich thing, Wilson, especially for a dishonest dog like you!"

XL. DEVON GETS A CHANCE

The sudden turn which Devon had given to the conversation took Wilson almost as much by surprise as his own first change of front had paralyzed Lucky Jack. He heaved his bulk around in his chair and stared at his three myrmidons, to discover, if he could, how the suggestions of Devon had worked upon their minds.

With set stares they had been regarding the back of their chief, and now their hostile glances were fixed unrelentingly upon his face.

Wilson gritted his teeth. He saw that in the pride of this double capture he might have talked enough to more than undo his triumph.

Then he sprang with an oath, at Devon, struck him brutally in the face, and called him a smart rat.

"And all rats are drowned!" said Wilson. "Boys, don't listen to the squeakin' of this here dead one. He wants to annoy us if he can, but he sees his chances are slim. Pick up him and Lucky Jack and take them up after me. We're gunna reserve 'em for a little while! They may be needed — Devon specially!"

He led the way, while the others seized the helpless captives and bore them out of the room and up a steep, twisting flight of stairs.

A door was opened; they were flung down onto a hard floor; and big Wilson said:

"Here you, Lewis and Grierson. You've both had enough taste of Devon, I'd reckon. You stay here and watch the pair of them for me. And watch each other, too. I ought to gag that Devon, but he's gagged himself already with you two! And I'll need to let him talk later on. Mind you, while you're watchin' him, I'm watchin' you!"

He closed the door, and his heavy step departed.

"Oh, damn his heart!" said Slugger Lewis suddenly.

"He's got the mind of a pig!" declared Grierson. "All that he's thinkin' of is his own fat chops!"

"Aye, he said as much. What a swine he talked like, son!"

"He did! Devon showed the way to him, like a signboard pointin' down a road!"

"We could of seen it for ourselves without no pointin'!" said Lewis. "What's he ever given me except a hoss now and then, and some clothes, and ammunition, and a small piece of money now and again. Promises is what he's crammed with. That's all!"

"Promises, ain't they enough to make fools and geese fat?" asked Grierson. "Oh, damn his hide, but I see the truth about him now!"

"What'll we do with that kind of a truth? They ain't any market for it that I know of!"

"Maybe not. Lie low, Slugger. Lie low and we'll have a think. Ask Devon and Lucky Jack. They got brains!"

They sat down close to the prisoners. The dull glow of a lantern shone through the room and gave the faintest of lights. It revealed only the outlines of heads and shoulders and the shadowy hint of movements.

"Hey, you, Devon," whispered Grierson. "You're the smart one. You got pulled in by this skunk of a Wilson, but you dodged us all for a long time. Look here, Devon, what would make it worth while for us to cut from that guy Wilson and tie on with you, Devon? Can you talk turkey to us?"

Hope bloomed like a great light in the heart of Devon.

"Do you know what's happened on the ranch?" he asked.

"The gold, you mean?"

"Yes."

"Sure. You've got the stuff lined out, but

how'll you ever get it home?"

"With armed men, Grierson. You'll be one of them. And I have others. The sheriff has his shoulder behind me, too."

"The sheriff's an old fool."

"Do you think that?"

"Look what they've done to him all of this time. They've rode in circles around him. Hell, man, if he'd had his eyes opened any wider they would of bumped him off and gone ahead with their game; but what difference does it make to them? They'd just as soon have an honest fool as a crooked sheriff that they would have to buy. They'd *rather* have an old bat like Naxon around, that's only awake in the mornin' and the evenin', and never catches nothin' but a small mosquito now and then, and lets all of the fine fat bugs get by him!"

Grierson laughed.

"Shut up, Pete," said the Slugger. "Let's hear what Devon has to say."

"Put us out of the house, and I'll guarantee you twenty per cent of the total returns of that field, Slugger and Grierson!"

"What you mean by 'us'? Are you bargainin' for Lucky Jack, too?"

"I am."

"What in hell has he to do with it? It'd be hard enough to get one man outside of this hell hole, let alone two!"

"Take care of yourself, Devon," urged the outlaw. "This was my party tonight. I got you into this trouble. If you can get yourself out alive, you're a lucky man!"

Devon shook his head.

"Both or neither," said he.

"That don't make sense," Grierson snarled.

Slugger Lewis exploded a faint curse.

"You see how it is, Pete?" said he. "After what that dog of a Wilson had to say, the sneakin' hypocrite, I wish to God he could be here and listen in on this gent's talk!"

"I wished he could," Grierson agreed; "but it don't make sense, just the same. We never could smuggle the pair of them out."

"Why not through the window, there?" asked the Slugger.

"How could that work?"

"Why not? There's plenty of rope."

"They got the outside of the house watched. You heard Wilson give the orders."

"We could make a rush for it. Besides, if we lined up with these two, it would make four men fightin'. And they both shoot straight, as I happen to know, if you don't!"

"And make for the hosses?"

"That's it! How about it?"

"I dunno but what it could be done. There would be a good deal of powder burned,

323

though. And a good deal of bullets singin' of course."

"You can't get somethin' for nothin', the way that things size up in this here world, partner."

"By God," said the other, "you're nothin' but right. Take a look out of the window, will you?"

The other went to the window and stared out.

"The moon is just slopin' up through the trees," said he, "and I don't see nothin' out there very clear."

"We'll wait a while. When we can make a better lookout, then we'll try the break. Devon, what'll make us sure that you'll pay up?"

"Nothing in the world can make you sure, unless you'll trust my word," answered Devon.

The two conferred seriously together.

Then: "We'd better take the chance," said the Slugger aloud. "We seen him play square with Lucky Jack. Why shouldn't he play square with us, then? He had his life to win, that way. He's got it to win this way. Besides, what better can we do?"

They agreed at once, and in the meantime, the pale flush of the moon appeared across the small window. Grierson went to the tangle of rope heaped in a corner and was working over it, sorting out pieces of a proper length and strength when the door opened abruptly from the head of the stairs.

"Here we are, beauty," said the voice of Charlie Way. "Walk straight in. You're gunna see some friends in here."

And Way passed into the room, with another armed man behind, thrusting before him a small and slender form no larger than a boy.

He added to Grierson and the Slugger:

"Turn out of this, you two! There ain't any call for you to hang on here any more. They got other jobs for you below. Up here, maybe you'd weaken a little! Turn out, will you!"

And, at that Way flashed the light from his bull's-eye lantern across their faces.

"What's your game over there by the rope?" he asked sharply. "Maybe old Gregory is a fool, but only in places. And this day I'd say that he'd guessed something worth knowing. Turn out of here, the pair of you!"

Slowly, sullenly, they filed out of the room, with final glances of grim disgust at the prisoners. Devon, relaxing in despair after hope had been so high in him, closed his eyes.

But then he heard Lucky Jack call, his voice trembling: "Prue! Prue! By God, it *is* Prue!"

And the voice of the girl answered.

Charlie Way cut in:

"Set down here, beauty, if you want to. I'm sorry that I can't free you to hold his hand. But you can rest easy here, and talk your heart out if you want to! That's all square with me. Talk is the cheapest thing in the world, but it's a comfort to more parcels of fools than you all!"

Devon, sitting erect now, his shoulders wedged against the wall, saw Prudence Maynard, her hands bound behind her, leaning her head against the shoulder of Lucky Jack, and he heard her weeping softly, controlling the agony of her grief.

"Hush!" said Lucky Jack. "We may not have long for this chat. Let's use our time better than this."

She mastered herself at once.

"It's a damn touching thing," Charlie Way chuckled. "Ain't it, Ben?"

Ben, in whom Devon recognized the fat man of the cabin, snickered heavily.

"It's sure sad," he admitted. "This here is a kind of a reunion, I'd say."

"It's a reunion of suckers," said Charlie Way. "Listen to 'em!" he paused a second. "Keep a good watch, Ben. You got a shotgun. If you should mess up this job, Uncle Gregory would take you in hand himself. I gotta do something better than stay here."

He leaned over Devon.

326

"You!" he said. "I'm gonna free your legs and take you downstairs and give you a chance for your rotten life. But it hangs on whether you don't make a fool move on the way down. Nothing would please me more than to let light through you, you rat!"

XLI. THE UNHOLY TRIO

Pushed before the revolver muzzle of Charlie Way, Devon was escorted down the stairs, while his legs, in which the circulation had been partially stopped by the tightness of his bonds, gradually resumed their normal power. Then, halted at a door, Way fumbled for the knob and rapped.

A voice called to them to enter. The door was drawn open, and Devon walked into the same living room in which he had been before. He found there gathered Gregory Wilson and the lean, dark face of Tucker Vincent, and fat Les Burchard, who nodded and smiled at Devon.

"I told you to free him altogether," he told Charlie Way.

"And then walk him down a dark pair of stairs?" Way retorted. "Not me, Burchard. Not even with your orders behind me!"

"If he had tried to escape then we would have had him off of our consciences!" said Burchard. "The way that it is now, we gotta manage something else. Loose his hands for

328

him right pronto, Charlie."

Way obeyed, muttering something to the effect that this was not his idea of common sense, and that the result could rest on their own heads!

In another moment Devon's hands were free, and he was flexing the fingers to restore strength to the numbed muscles.

Burchard, who was patently the controlling influence in the room, hooked his thumb over his shoulder and Way departed.

"Keep a man walkin' around the house every minute," said Burchard. "And you yourself, Charlie, you keep on driftin' around on the outside from one of your sentinels to the next."

Way, with a nod, disappeared.

"There's another one let in deep!" Vincent growled, with an impatient jerk of his head. "Why should Way mean so much and have so much to do?"

"Set down, young man," Burchard said genially to Devon.

The latter nodded, but did not move. He preferred to remain standing for many reasons. He who is seated is rooted in his chair for at least fifty per cent of a second, which is quite a sufficient length of time for him to be shot to bits. Standing, he had little chance to be sure, unless he could accomplish some such miracle as snatching a weapon from one of the three, shooting the lamp out, and then making his escape through the darkness.

But these chances were slight, indeed. Yonder was the lantern, with Gregory Wilson, now grimly silent, seated beside it. He had a shotgun across his knees, and his eyes were as restlessly alert as the tossing of the flames upon his hearth.

Still, it was better to be standing than to be seated, in the opinion of Devon.

His hands were freed. His legs were unlashed. He could at least fight as he died. So he waited calmly, alertly, ready for the end, whenever it might come, and in whatever way fate chose.

But only half of his mind was there with him. Another portion was lost yonder on the heights of West London, wondering what the two old men would think and do when they found that he was not at Mrs. Purley's house; and yet again, his thoughts were with Prudence Maynard, who sat in the room above them with her brother.

In at least one thought he had been wrong — that she had acted as an agent for his enemies. Otherwise she would not be a bound prisoner! And that gave Devon, with a sudden bounding of the heart, the hope that in all

330

other of his surmises about her he had been wrong.

Let her be innocent of all except a wild spirit of mischief and of reckless adventure, and in all the world there would be nothing of her worth in the eyes of Devon.

But he brushed from his mind the thought of the old trappers, and of Prudence Maynard, and Lucky Jack, and all the rest. Here before him the question of his life and death was being settled. Burchard was talking.

"How you feelin' now, Devon?"

Walt smiled at the fat man.

"Well enough," he responded at last.

"Are you? That's a good thing," said Burchard. "You take when a man is in good shape, then his brain'll work a lot better, too! Have a plum!"

He held out some little yellow plums, their skins transparent and bursting with the rich juices within.

Devon shook his head.

"You're wrong," Burchard admonished, "because if you was to taste one of these it'd make you think all the clearer and the better; this bein' a time when you need to be tolerable straight, I'd say! How about you, Greg and Tucker?"

Wilson shook his head, while Tucker exclaimed impatiently: "Will you stop this damn fool business and get down to work, Burchard?"

"Why, it ain't fool business," said Burchard. "What makes you say that, Tucker?"

"The two old men have noses like bloodhounds. They could run down a trail in the dark by the sense of smell, I'd say. And there's the fool of a sheriff with them!"

"Aw, don't be callin' Lew Naxon a fool," said Burchard, "him and me bein' such good old friends, as you might say! Don't you be callin' him a fool, Tucker. I got a lot of respect and likin' for Naxon. He's a regular chum of mine."

"Because you can rest easy while the blockhead is runnin' the affairs of the law in this county," put in Vincent.

He was a waspish man in form and in temper, and his dark eyes glittered vengefully at Devon as he talked.

"If the sheriff is a fool, the more reason we got for takin' our time," said Les Burchard.

"But if the two old men lead him up to the mark, he's a fightin' man, Les. For God's sake, get this business over with before I explode with impatience!"

"Well, well, well, well!" murmured Burchard.

He popped a pair of the luscious yellow plums into one side of his great mouth, swallowed, and from the other side he squirted the pits at the hearth with such good aim that the seeds were instantly hissing in the flames. Meanwhile he smiled kindly upon the rest, and particularly upon Tucker Vincent.

"Don't you see that we got everythin' safe and cozy here," said Burchard, "as a baby wrapped in a shawl?"

Just as he spoke the front door was rattled with terrible violence. The window shutter slammed at the same moment. A wild howl passed over their heads.

Gregory Wilson dropped from his chair onto one knee and leveled the shotgun straight at the heart of Devon, his face set and black behind the sights.

Vincent leaped into the air like a fighting cock, and came down facing the front door and the window, with a long Colt in either hand.

But Les Burchard did not stir. Of that, Devon took most particular note. The fat man merely raised a pulpy hand and said:

"Just a little touch of rain, gents!"

They could hear it, then, muttering and puffing away to smoke upon the roof of the stout cabin and now and again, as the gust down the valley increased in force, battering at the front door and shaking it furiously.

"That rain'll take the heart even out of old

trailers like Jim and Harry, I'd say," said Burchard. "Whatcha think about it, Devon?"

It amused Devon to be appealed to at such a time as this. And reflecting, he consulted his honest opinion and answered:

"Their eyes won't be worth much in such a night, Burchard, but weather will never stop them if ever they start on my trail!"

"Ah, now," drawled Burchard, continuing to eat his plums, "that's what I call real touchin'. That's affection. You, Wilson, ain't you ashamed, the things that I've heard you say about there bein' no love in this here world of ours?"

Gregory Wilson grinned, a gleam of light and appreciation crossing his calm face as he heard the words of his master rascal and inspirer.

"But the rain is for us, Tucker, you gotta admit," said Burchard.

"Damn me if it is!" declared Vincent. "It's a walking forest behind which a thousand men could walk right up to the door of this cabin and not be known to us! How can our lookouts see anythin' when this here storm has put out the moon and blinds their eyes?"

"There never was a night when men couldn't see somethin'," said Burchard. "Look out here now!"

He went to the window and pushed the

shutter wide. Then, since the light of the lantern within the room was so exceedingly dim, they were able to look at a great square of the sky, and there the men could see piled mountains of cloud sweeping, and the cold transparency of the moon's light shining through them.

"Look at that," said Burchard. "There's light to watch by, and there's light to shoot by."

He stepped back. Another squall, in passing, darkened the window like the stride of a ghost, and slammed the shutter in his face.

"Damn rude, the wind is," Burchard remonstrated, turning unperturbed back to the others.

"Burchard, in God's name, will you spill the whole night talkin' rot?" demanded Vincent, "or will you get down to business and finish the thing off right pronto?"

"Steady, steady, old man," said the proprietor of the Palace. "The fact is, I never hurried at nothin' in my life. Partly you leave it to your wits and partly to your luck, and when the fruit is plump ripe, it'll fall from the tree, Tucker. The only thing is to be standin' underneath with your mouth open! But if you take to snatchin' of it while it's green, all you'll get will be a belly-ache, and no good."

Vincent made a gesture of disgust and exasperation with both hands.

Burchard went on:

"If I'd hurried when my wagon busted down, there never would of been a West London, old son, nor no mines in Timbal Gulch! If I'd hurried there wouldn't be three of us settin' here, waitin' to hatch the finest chicken that ever come out of an egg. A chicken with legs and feathers, and all made of gold, by jiminy!"

He laughed as he spoke, and with his fat hand he resoundingly smote his fat knee.

"All right, Tucker," he concluded. "Now it's time to begin, maybe."

He ate another pair of plums and voided the seeds with his former accuracy. Then he said:

"The question is, gents, whether it's better to buy Devon's land at a price, and get his signature onto the deed for it, or blow his head off and gut the gold lands, while thumbin' our noses at the sheriff. I'll have some votes."

XLII. UNINVITED GUESTS

Devon, hardly believing his ears, stared fixedly at Burchard.

"And what do you think we'll stand for?" Vincent cried harshly.

"It's your turn to speak up next." Burchard turned to Gregory Wilson.

"Look here, partners," said Wilson, who seemed to be the least important member of this triumvirate. "If you wanted to be sure of gettin' yourself bit, wouldn't the best way be to take a dog with good sharp teeth, an' drag him off the street and beat him, and then turn him loose?"

"That's the first sense I've heard spoken in the whole evenin'!" said Tucker Vincent.

"Well, well, well," Burchard commented. "You all are mighty hard on me! Would you throw an eye on my side of the case?"

"We have to, and you know it," Tucker Vincent admitted in his irritable manner.

"No, no," said Burchard. "I wouldn't have all of the responsibility throwed onto my shoulders. Age has made me pretty weak. My

337

knees can't much more'n hold up my own weight, friends!"

He turned to Devon: "Would you agree to make a treaty of peace with me, young Injun?"

"For my life?" said Devon.

"Well, for your life, yes!"

"To deed over the ranch to you?"

"Aye, that's the thing. And more'n that: to promise to take yourself and old Harry and Jim away from these here diggin's. And not never to come back!"

"Les," broke in Gregory Wilson, "would you be fool enough to think he'd keep that promise, even if he made it?"

Burchard raised a peremptory hand with a frown.

"Greg," he said, "I wantcha not to forget after this, that we're now doin' business with a gentleman —"

"Gambler!" Wilson corrected.

"Aye," said Burchard. "One that knows how to lose and how to win."

"Then show me your hand," Devon requested.

"Tonight, you're a dead man," said Burchard simply.

"Yes." Devon spoke willingly, since that truth was self-evident.

"Livin' is better than dyin', ain't it?"

Devon nodded.

"Then what's wrong with makin' a bargain with us? A long time ago you was offered twenty-five thousand for that ranch of yours. Well, sir, why shouldn't you take that now? It'd be money into the pockets of you and Harry and Jim — that I wish the best luck to, the pore old codgers!"

The face, the very voice of Les Burchard reeked with kindness and good will to all men!

"By God, Les," Tucker protested. "Are you gunna throw twenty-five thousand dollars away like this?"

"I'll pay out of my own pocket," said Burchard. "That's all it is to you! I'll sleep better afterward."

He went on to Devon: "Look here. You come out to settle up the old ranch. What is it worth? Ten dollars an acre? Not hardly! Nor would it never of been if Charlie Way hadn't scratched gold out of the Devon mud, over yonder by the tank! But it was him that found the stuff, not you. He brung the news to us. How was he and us to get the land away from you? We tried to buy it, fair and square, and we offered you two and a half times the market value."

Devon nodded, with the faintest of smiles.

"Now, then, can't you forget that they's gold on the place, and that you found out about it? You take twenty-five thousand. You pass on maybe five thousand apiece to Harry and Jim, seein' that you're that kind of a generous gent. Well, then, instead of bein' a dead man tonight, you're livin', and you got fifteen thousand dollars in your pockets, besides what more you've picked up in West London. You go East. Nobody sees nobody else. Everybody's happy forever after, like the end of a real good book!"

"Except the dead!"

Burchard looked him straight in the eye.

"Except the dead," he admitted.

"Will you tell me what *you* and us get out of this?" asked Gregory Wilson. "It's plain sailin' to see what *he* gets!"

"I'll tell you," said Burchard. "We got him, ain't we?"

"Most certainly we have!"

"And all that we gotta do is to cut his throat?"

"And that's easy?"

"Sure it is."

"But look at the other side. They's an old sayin' that murder will out."

"That's fool talk," said Tucker Vincent with surety.

"Sure it is," nodded the amiable Burchard. "One murder ain't so apt to out, but half a dozen sure are! Well, then, we've built up our place on murder. The dead are lyin' pretty thick along our trail, and we've got the old hounds on our heels. Suppose Devon disappears, old Harry and Jim would bust their hearts unless they find out something about him, and already they got suspicions pointing at some of us! Murder ain't so likely to make trouble, accordin' to the kind of man that you do away with. Ain't that sense?"

Tucker Vincent said nothing, but Gregory Wilson, unwillingly, nodded.

"It would leave a pile to the honor of this here Devon," said Wilson.

"And his honor sure would stand the strain," declared Burchard firmly.

That sudden hope of life took the breath from Devon. He gathered his reeling wits and said suddenly: "There are two more upstairs — Lucky Jack — and the girl you never had seen, Wilson!"

"You want them?" asked Burcbard, shaking his head.

"I'd have to have them free before I'd sign."

"You want us to chuck loose all three of you?" said Wilson. "Let you go on your own honor? There ain't that much honor in the world!"

"You see how this stands," Devon explained. "Rub me out, and the world is fairly sure to learn of it, and to hunt you down. Or at least there'll be a rumor that will blacken the names and the lives of all of you."

"We'll have the gilt to put over that kind of a smoky stain," grinned Tucker Vincent.

"We will!" Gregory Wilson agreed.

"I came here with Lucky Jack," said Devon. "I can't see my way to going off without him — and his sister."

"Lucky Jack is one that's always played with chances like this," declared Burchard. "As for the girl — damn it, I tried to shoulder her out of the way and off of the trail, and finally we put her up safe and snug here at Wilson's. But she was too smart for her own good. She had to go nosin' around. Ridin' by night was the thing she liked the best!"

"And not riding for you, then?" Devon asked eagerly.

Burchard snorted.

"My God, boy," said he, "would we fool around with women? Do we need 'em? What was that?"

The front door rattled and shook. All four men stood frozen with interest, but presently the long breathing of the wind sighed with a whistle past the top of the house, and they relaxed.

Burchard turned back to Devon.

"It was you," said he. "She wanted to pry you loose out of this. How could she do it? By keepin' you from knowin' about the gold.

She got the wind of what was agin you. She got it here in Wilson's house, and then the brave little devil stayed right on here, to learn what she could, and so to protect you! But if you found the gold on the place, nothin' could keep you from stayin' on — and therefore nothin' could keep you from dyin' young! She come out here to save her brother from livin' like a fool. Tried to shame him back into a decent life by the exposin' of his name. But while she was doin' that, she got interested in Walter Devon — and the result is that she's a dyin' woman tonight, and well she knows it!"

Devon, after a moment, was able to speak.

"Is it this sort of a girl," he asked hurriedly, "that you expect me to desert without making an effort?"

Burchard burst out in a roar.

"Damn it, boy, I'm tryin' to save your life for you — I like you — but we can't scatter three tongues loose in the world! One of 'em is sure to talk, and ten words means the hangman's rope for all of us! What're you askin'?"

Devon closed his eyes.

And the call of life in his young blood was like the roaring of a great wind — a wind filled with music and with beauty. After all, it was only one step forward, and a resolute turning of his back upon the past —

But then the blood of his ancestors, and the honor of his name, and all his manhood rushed up hotly from his heart.

"I can't take my life and give you all clean hands in such a deal as this."

"Then you're a dead man — and a fool, which is worse!" growled Burchard.

He jerked his thumb at big Gregory Wilson.

"And the sooner it's got over with, the better for all of us, includin' him."

"All right," said Wilson. "Only I guess you don't expect me to dirty up the floor of my best room!"

He rose with a harsh laugh, and took a step toward Devon, with his double-barreled shotgun tucked under his right arm.

"Now, I'm saying we've taken the only sensible way out of this," said Tucker Vincent. "Les, I was beginning to think your heart was made of mush."

"I like the kid," said Burchard with bitterness in his voice. "I like him damn well. He's upstandin'. He met us when we used everythin' we had agin him. What was with him except a pair of dodderin' old half useless men? But he met all we could do, and he beat us, and he run us pretty near to the ground, through the girl havin' wandered to Ben's place in the woods. And if fire hadn't fought

344

for us, in rubbin' out of trail, it would of gone hard with the whole of us, as you know. He's the kind of gent that I would of liked to have go on with me. I would of made a son out of him — and instead, he's gotta be snuffed like a smokin' candle."

There was a strange sigh, but it did not come from the lips of Burchard. The flames of the hearth sucked suddenly to the side. The light jumped and went almost out in the lantern.

For the door had sagged open, and against the darkness appeared lean, hard faces, and the glimmer of guns!

XLIII. THE EYES OF PRUE MAYNARD

As the wink of lightning shows a great mountain scene in a single flare, so Devon saw the face of the sheriff, in the lead, and the grim eyes of Harry and Jim beyond; then he dropped to the floor as the shotgun roared from the hands of Gregory Wilson.

The double charge flew into the wall behind the spot where Devon had been standing, and the kick of the heavy explosion drove Wilson staggering back.

The latter had not yet recovered when Devon leaped like a cat from all fours and was at his throat. Together they slammed against the wall, and as they toppled, the flash and the roar of guns filled the room.

The head of Wilson was underneath as they fell, and the might of the arms which were strained about Devon's body suddenly relaxed. Wilson, for the moment, was out of the battle.

Dragging a revolver from the belt of the hunter, Devon whirled to see the progress of the fight.

It was ended even as it began!

Tucker Vincent lay dead on the floor, shot through both head and heart; big Les Burchard stood against the wall with his hands thrust stiffly above his head. And he swayed and panted as though he had been laboring hard, though he had not even attempted resistance to this surprise attack.

"He's safe!" old Harry cried in a cracked voice. "Oh, Lew, here's the grand day for us!"

"Watch these fellows!" Devon said to Harry and Jim. "Naxon, we've another job waiting upstairs for us!"

And he whipped out of the room like a greyhound. Naxon followed.

At the head of the stairs he saw the form of Ben looming, calling out: "What the hell's happened there? House fallin' down?"

"Put up your hands, you greasy pig," ordered Devon.

Seeing the face of the grim sheriff behind Devon, the fat man, with a groan, obeyed. The sheriff took charge of him.

Devon, alone, burst into the room of the prisoners, and saw the light from without shining straight into the eyes of Prue Maynard.

Out on the trail lay Noonan with his head smashed in. The three, approaching in a volley of rain and mist, had encountered him and

347

struck him down before he could fire the gun he pointed toward them. And that pointed gun had been what showed them they had come to the right place!

Such was the fate of Burchard's careful precautions! For the sheriff and the two old men had had no clew when they rode down the valley. Only, with vague fear, they connected the disappearance of Devon with the winking light which he had seen spelling a message from somewhere in the heart of the lower valley. And they had come, fumbling blindly through the rain and the wind, disheartened.

Had the house been unguarded, they would have passed it, hardly heeding its lights. But men are not ordinarily posted, gun in hand, outside of an innocent house. So they went to the front door of Wilson's place, and through that door they heard enough to convince them that this was their place.

The lock was not a difficult one, and the storm made enough noise to cover the manipulations of the sheriff. Once the wind had almost torn the door from their grasp after the bolt was turned back, and as they waited for the favorable crisis inside the room.

If the life of Devon was to be spared, they had determined not to charge. They would not imperil him in this manner. But when the decision went against him, they had burst in at once.

With the central three dead or secured, Devon was left on guard in that room while Lucky Jack and the other three scoured the vicinity.

They heard nothing but the rapping of departing hoofs, and the only things they saw were shadowy forms that melted at once into the rain mist.

In the meantime, Burchard and Gregory Wilson, tied hand and foot, sat in the living room. Gregory said not a word, but Burchard was as full of talk and good humor as ever.

"I knew it was wrong," he said. "There you are, Greg. You and Tucker wanted blood, blood, blood! Couldn't have enough of it. Dog-gone it, we can choke in our own juice now. Devon, hand me the rest of them plums like a good boy, will you? They'll be over-ripe in the mornin'!"

Devon, watching this man curiously, finally leaned beside him.

"Burchard," he said, "there's murder against you, but there's something else for you. If you can get out of here you'll be able to rummage up a horse in the darkness. Then ride to the Palace, fill your pockets with your cash, and — get out of the country."

"Well, well, well, well," Les Burchard murmured. "Dog-gone me if this ain't like somethin' right out of a Sunday school lesson!"

Two slashes of the knife liberated him.

At the door he paused and waved a soft, fat hand at Gregory Wilson.

"This here'll show you the advantages of the right kind of bringin' up, Greg. You think about it, while you rot in hell fire. So long, Devon. If you ever run broke, look me up! I'll have a spare corner for you, and an extra bunk!"

And he was gone into the night!

XLIV. AT THE TRAIL'S END

That escape of the fat man's irked the sheriff greatly, for having been such a friend of the owner of the Palace, he had wanted to talk out the past with him. And then put him snugly in jail for the remainder of his days.

But, after all, there was no special need for the presence of Burchard. Gregory Wilson, his back against the wall, did not turn State's evidence, but simply confessed, and the long list of the hypocrite's crimes staggered the imaginations of men in that day.

He supplied enough information to send the patient sheriff on the trail of Charlie Way, and Charlie in person was brought back to stand trial.

He was not the only one. Grierson and Slugger Lewis made their due appearance. And fat Ben was hanged by the neck along with the rest.

They died like men. Only Gregory Wilson, strangely enough, gave in at the end, and had to be carried out onto the scaffold to his shameful end.

Those executions cleared the atmosphere at West London, and that cheerful town boomed and boomed.

But no place was more changed than the Devon ranch a year or two after these events. Two old men, riding slowly over the hills, regarded it with squinting eyes of amazement! For where the little shack had stood, there now stretched a red-roofed and white-walled Spanish house of ample dimensions, and big barns stretched behind it, and all the rolling fields in front were spotted with sleek-sided cattle.

The two ancient men, one bent, one slenderly erect, looked upon this scene with a smile.

They looked like two ragged vagrants of the cow range, but a nearer inspection showed that one wore golden spurs, and here a five-thousand-dollar stick pin glinted like a bit of fire, and yonder actually was a big ruby on the butt of an ancient Colt six-shooter of a primitive pattern!

Before the big mansion they paused, counted its windows, and then rode into the patio. A white clad Mexican servant ran out and coldly demanded their business.

"Son, keep clear of us!" one said.

He who was bent and seemed the feebler of the two, cupped his hands and sent a great voice booming:

"Hey, Prue! Hey, Walt!"

There was an instant of pause, while the echo sprang from wall to wall, far off. And then feet scampered, and a gay voice called in the distance:

"Walter! Walter! They've come back to us! Uncle Harry and Uncle Jim! Come, quick!"

And she, without waiting for him, ran down the great stairs to them, holding out her arms.

Max Brand ™ is the best-known pen name of Frederick Faust, creator of Dr. Kildare,™ Destry, and many other fictional characters popular with readers and viewers worldwide. Faust wrote for a variety of audiences in many genres. His enormous output, totaling approximately thirty million words or the equivalent of 530 ordinary books, covered nearly every field: crime, fantasy, historical romance, espionage, Westerns, science fiction, adventure, animal stories, love, war, and fashionable society, big business and big medicine. Eighty motion pictures have been based on his work along with many radio and television programs. For good measure he also published four volumes of poetry. Perhaps no other author has reached more people in more different ways.

Born in Seattle in 1892, orphaned early, Faust grew up in the rural San Joaquin Valley of California. At Berkeley he became a student rebel and one-man literary movement, contributing prodigiously to all campus publications. Denied a degree because of unconventional conduct, he embarked on a series of adventures culminating in New York City where, after a period of near starvation, he received simultaneous recognition as a serious poet and successful popular-prose writer. Later, he traveled widely, making his home in New York, then in Florence, and finally in Los Angeles.

Once the United States entered the Second World War, Faust abandoned his lucrative writing career and his work as a screenwriter to serve as a war correspondent with the infantry in Italy, despite his fifty-one years and a bad heart. He was killed during a night attack on a hilltop village held by the German army. New books based on magazine serials or unpublished manuscripts continue to appear. Alive and dead he has averaged a new one every four months for seventy-five years. In the U.S. alone nine publishers issue his work, plus many more in foreign countries. Yet, only recently have the full dimensions of this extraordinarily versatile and prolific writer come to be recognized and his stature as a protean literary figure in the 20th Century acknowledged. His popularity continues to grow throughout the world.

We hope you have enjoyed this Large Print book. Other Thorndike Press or Chivers Press Large Print books are available at your library or directly from the publishers. For more information about current and upcoming titles, please call or write, without obligation, to:

Thorndike Press
P.O. Box 159
Thorndike, Maine 04986
USA
Tel. (800) 223-6121 (U.S. & Canada)
In Maine call collect: (207) 948-2962

OR

Chivers Press Limited
Windsor Bridge Road
Bath BA2 3AX
England
Tel. (0225) 335336

All our Large Print titles are designed for easy reading, and all our books are made to last.